I'M THE SAME

SAME

A Novel

JAMES
UNGURAIT

UNGURAIT
HOUSE

ALSO BY JAMES UNGURAIT

Phoenix Knight The Lost Son

AUTHOR NOTE

This book was not easy to write.

I'm The Same was born from questions I couldn't answer and memories I couldn't ignore. It explores survival, not just the kind that keeps the body alive, but the kind that must contend with silence, shame, and the long echoes of grief.

Within these pages, you'll encounter difficult themes: trauma, emotional abuse, family estrangement, death, and the quiet devastation of unresolved pain. These are not just narrative devices. They are lived experiences, for many. For me.

This story is fiction, but it carries the weight of truth. It is not trauma for spectacle. It is not identity for points. Every scene was written with intention, and every word was placed with care.

If you carry wounds of your own, please take care with this book. You do not owe anyone your pain—not even a fictional reflection of it. But if you find pieces of yourself here, I hope you feel seen. Not pitied. Not explained. Seen.

Thank you for reading. Thank you for being here.

— James Ungurait

First Edition April 2024

Published in the United States by Ungurait House LLC

Hattiesburg, Mississippi

Library of Congress Control Number: 2023921441

Hardcover ISBN 978-8-218-31250-3

Paperback ISBN 979-8–999-38093-7

Ebook ISBN 979-8-999-38090-6

www.unguraithouse.com

To my Parents, who always made me feel loved.

I'M THE
SAME

I'M THE
SAME

"Your silence will not protect you."

—Audre Lorde

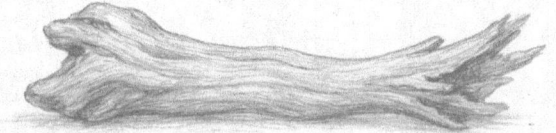

Your silence will not protect you.

—Audre Lorde

CHAPTER 1

W e lived in a constant state of survival. It sat just beneath the surface, humming like a fault line. No matter how far we ran, it always caught up. Even here, in Oregon, under a sky too gray to promise peace, I could feel it—the echo of Mississippi, the wreck, everything I lost. Yet I silenced it, so I could enjoy this moment, one where the gray sky bordered the tall, green pines that lined the cliffs.

The small beach stretched out before me was quiet, leaving me to only my thoughts. I stumbled on a place where the wind didn't pierce through me. As I sat on a long piece of driftwood which must have landed the night before, washed white, its limbs broken and shattered, I stared out at the ocean, taking in its endless horizon. The greenish-blue water foamed as it rushed ashore with the tide.

I told myself I came to escape. But even the ocean felt empty—like it knew I'd brought the wreck with me. Maybe this wasn't such a good idea. Hell, I would have to live with it now. At least for a year, I didn't know where I would go. I didn't think I could be happy anywhere. Not yet.

Oregon was never the plan. There had never been a plan. I was on this see-where-life-took-me moment now that college was done. Honestly, Oregon was one of those places I never thought I would live, yet there I was, taking in its famous coast. Strange where a writing fellowship could bring you—especially when you're still trying to figure out what you're running toward.

When I got the offer, I had been surprised, and threw all caution to the wind, much to my mother's displeasure. The result was more than a thousand-mile move away from my family and everyone I knew. I ran. Ran from the pain. Ran from all the judgment, the weight of people's thoughts that were pressed against me. So maybe I could find peace where the fir grew tall.

Everyone I talked to before moving told me how beautiful it was, at least the ones who had visited here. The coast, and the mountains—it was a place that showcased the full power of nature and how it took your breath away. They were right, of course, but no one had mentioned how cold it would be. I would need warmer clothes, otherwise, I would freeze before I could write a line.

The sun lowered in the sky as the gray darkened, making the air crisper, and that same sense of fear erupted, commanding me to leave. However, I still had one more task before I headed home, as I needed some reading materials. Inspiration, for me at least, was most likely just another way to procrastinate. In my current state of mind, I would rather read than write. It was safer and easier than writing.

Returning from the beach, I stepped into Alnwick, a small yet vibrant city. It was one of the bigger towns on the coast. A row of buildings sprawled on each side of the road. Windows filled with styled clothing, and other merchandise. Patios buzzed with low conversation and the occasional burst of laughter. The smell of grilled seafood drifted through the air as waiters weaved between tables, balancing trays. It all felt a little foreign—like life was happening in a language I hadn't learned yet. Of course, more civic and office-like buildings, which were quiet at this time of the day. The number of cultural things to do in a town of this size surprised me. It wasn't as large as the sprawling cities inland, like Eugene and Portland. There was enough, though, just enough. Never too much traffic, but you also didn't feel like you were in the middle of the boonies. Not a single stoplight kinda of town.

Turning to the main corridor, I came to a stop in front of a small storefront just as the streetlights turned on, illuminating the pavement in a warm light, even if you could still make out the landscape. Novel—that was the name of this store. I found it clever, and the branding on point. The sign was in Times New Roman font, black against the white wood siding. Upon entering, the familiar scent of paper and coffee mixed, greeting me—a smell I loved. If someone bottled that scent—paper and coffee steeped in quiet—I'd burn it every night until the silence didn't feel so loud.

I traversed further into the shop. The shopkeeper was busy helping another customer as I browsed the book selection. I found a cover that caught my eye, so I read the description, the author's bio, and then a few lines of the first chapter. I found a few to purchase as I browsed, and I was shocked to peer through an entire display of Mississippi authors. It wasn't something I expected all the way out here. I guess there was a high regard for writers from my home state. It brought a smile to my face as I looked them over. They had all the greats—Faulkner, Grisham, and Eudora, along with a few more recent ones.

I could spend hours there reading and browsing. After finding a few and noticing how you couldn't make out the other buildings across the street, other than the lights coming from their windows, I decided it was time to check out and head home. I had three books in my hands, and I hoped they would allow me to stop staring at the blank page that kept plaguing me.

"You're Kodak," the shopkeeper said as I approached the counter. "This year's Alnwick writing fellow?"

She was probably no older than I was, with dark hair that was kept short. Her fair skin matched her simple shirt and jeans. The shirt read Novel across the front, and I had seen a display of them on the other side of the store for customers to buy.

"That's me," I replied, not making eye contact. I was the youngest winner ever at twenty-two. I'd never expected to win. I'd just been applying for everything towards the end of my senior year. To be honest, I didn't even remember applying for it.

"I'm Olivia. Welcome to Alnwick," she said as she handed the books back to me.

"How much?" I asked.

"No need. We comp the books for the fellowship, courtesy of the Condors."

I took the books and smiled. "Thanks," I replied, then turned and headed toward the door.

"Hey," Olivia called from the counter. "You coming to the gala at the Condor estate later? The writer in residence normally appears."

I knew of it, and they had formally invited me. I debated whether I would go. Whenever I was invited to a social gathering, I did the same thing—debate and try to find a million reasons not to go. I guess this was my push to do it. What harm would come from it? If anything, I would show my face, then fade away into the background before running back to my safe haven.

"I guess I'll see you," I replied, then entered the night to return home.

It took about fifteen minutes to return to the place that would be mine for the year. Perched near the coast, it came with an uninterrupted view of the Pacific—something I'd already grown used to during the cool spring mornings. My new home stood at the cliff's edge, a gray-blue craftsman with more rooms than I'd ever need. Four bedrooms, three and a half baths—too much space for someone who barely knew how to fill it.

Inside, everything looked just as I'd left it. The Condor estate loomed just down the road, its windows glowing like distant beacons. I wondered if they owned this house too. Probably. I needed to make an appearance tonight—at least long enough to be

18

seen. I opened my closet and pulled the suit down from its hanger. It was still pressed. A few unpacked boxes sat on the floor, waiting.

I should get to that.

Instead, I headed to the shower. The lukewarm water loosened muscles I didn't realize were clenched. Rain ticked against the window while wind howled softly beyond the glass. I'd need my raincoat—umbrellas seemed to be a myth out here.

After drying off, I groomed my hair, hearing my father's voice in my head. Had to look presentable. Couldn't show up looking like I didn't belong. I brushed it, added product, and hoped it was enough to pass whatever unspoken test lay ahead.

The Condor estate loomed larger up close—concrete and glass, all sharp lines and sterile elegance. Through the windows, I could see bodies in motion, voices mingling beneath the strings of a quartet. I hated gatherings like this. Back home, I always felt their eyes. Judging. Pitying. Staring like I was a ghost from a story they were too polite to ask about.

But I had to go. Had to let them meet the Writer's Fellow. Had to perform.

A clipboard check at the door. A nod. I was in.

No one noticed me at first. Perfect. I headed straight to the bar. Wine was safer than silence. I sipped and let the bitter red settle.

"Kodak, right?" a voice asked beside me.

I turned. Tall. Athletic. Confident in the way people are when they've never been shattered. Dark brown hair streaked with sun—natural or styled, I couldn't tell. He offered a hand.

"If we make it to dessert without small talk," he said, raising his glass, "I'll owe you a favor."

I blinked. Then laughed. He seemed too polished for awkwardness. But maybe that was the point.

"I'm Quinn," he said.

I shook his hand.

"So what brings you to this gala?" I asked.

He looked at me a little uneasily before the estate owners walked up to us. I had already met them when I arrived. Mr. and Mrs. Condor were widely respected for their real estate empire and deep charity work. Mr. Condor was tall, wearing a tux that was quite expensive, by the looks of it. His dark hair was hard to distinguish in the light. However, his wife's blond hair was a different matter. Their fair skin had a small amount of color to it—almost sun-kissed, yet not quite there. Mrs. Condor wore a blue dress that looked just as expensive as her husband's tux.

"I see you've met our son, Quinn," Mr. Condor mentioned as he shook my hand. His shake was as firm and warm as his eye contact was unnerving.

"Yes, I have," I replied as I glanced at Quinn, who now was more occupied by the drink in his hand. Almost like he was hiding in it, not wishing to be seen.

"Good. I was hoping you two would meet, being the same age and all."

I blinked. That was rather presumptuous, in my opinion; then again, I understood the need to connect people. It wasn't like I had friends or anyone out here, for that matter.

"I hope you enjoy the party and your time here. We look forward to seeing your finished work."

They left, moving on to their other guests, leaving Quinn and me at the bar. He kept looking down at his drink.

"So this is your house then," I said, trying to break the silence. I should at least try to be friendly.

"More like my parents. I just sleep here." He warmed up now. "Oregon's a long way from wherever you ran from."

Now he was taunting me, and I didn't appreciate it. Even if technically, he was right.

"I'm not running, I can assure you of that."

"You're from the South, aren't you?" he questioned.

I knew where this was going. I sighed "Yes," I said.

He smiled before finishing his drink, then he called for another one. He would have a hard time in the morning if he kept going at this pace.

I looked at the crowd, chatting with drinks in their hands; most must be townspeople or friends of the Condors. Some admired the artwork that hung on the concrete walls while others looked out into the night through the windows. I was glad to have found someone to talk to. Generally, I would just stand against the wall in situations like this, a wallflower of sorts, just noting each person to myself, taking stock of ideas to use for characters later.

"Oh good, you two found each other." Olivia walked up to us. Her dress was elegant, fitting her skin perfectly. Her short hair fell around her ears and a sapphire necklace hung across her neck.

"Olivia, you look beautiful as always," Quinn said, raising his drink to her.

She gave him a small laugh before turning her attention to me. "He means well, I promise. He wouldn't be my best friend if not."

By this point, he was looking a little worse for wear, and I was actually beginning to worry a bit. He had to already been on his fifth drink for the night. At least that was what I assumed at his current state.

"Is he always this – – "

"Drunk?" she stopped me. I worried that I might have uttered an insult until she grinned. "Only on nights like these."

Quinn seemed to ignore our conversation about him as he continued to drink. Olivia looked at me. I saw where this was heading. If we didn't do something, it would get out of hand quickly. He leaned forward—and didn't stop. I moved before I could think. Maybe I'd done that before, caught something falling.

"We need to get him to bed," I said, and for a moment, I wondered why I was even helping. I had just met him, her, for hell's sake. But, if I didn't, what type of human would I be? One that watched people suffer or fall to the floor drunk?

Olivia helped me pick him up so he was sort of standing as we tried to avoid being seen. "His room is down the hall," she said, and we slowly helped him in the direction.

By down the hall, she'd actually meant a rather long hike—at least that was what it felt like. Soon, we came to his door and opened it to find a relatively spacious room with large windows lining one wall, looking out over the dark sea. I was rather shocked at the state of it. The room itself was well-kept. Seeing him now, I would have thought it would be a pigpen.

We walked, trying to keep him from crashing into the ground. He was heavy, and it didn't matter that he kept talking, saying he was fine and could walk. Evidence proved otherwise.

Once we made it to his bed, he plopped down, and for a moment, he laid there before turning over. Olivia shook her head at him, and he smiled back at her, then looked over at me. It was a rather weird look, simple, no longer analyzing me.

"He's cute, isn't he?" he said.

Dear lord, how much had he drink? Honestly, I felt a little embarrassed standing there. I had just met him, and this was where the conversation had led.

"Yes, he is," she replied. "Now get some rest." She looked at me and muttered, "Sorry."

As we walked out, I glanced behind us. He looked fragile lying there. Like the driftwood on the beach—washed up, worn, still holding shape. I would hate to be him in the morning—I know I would hurt and regret everything.

Closing the door behind us, Olivia looked over at me. "Sorry about that. He never does well at these galas."

It felt nice to have a conversation; I had spent the last few days alone, not knowing anyone. Walking down the hall again, I gazed at the artwork on the wall. These were some of the most impressive pieces that I have seen. They must have cost a small fortune. Olivia pointed to a few of her favorites, describing the landscape that they pictured all with the initials of EK in the bottom corner. They looked expensive. Distant. Like everything here.

I stayed for maybe an hour more, talking to Olivia. She asked about my writing, and so did several other people who came to talk to us. Most asked how I had been enjoying Oregon, and I answered them with my typical response of how pretty it was here. I paid my dues and talked to people, introducing myself to everyone who wanted to meet the new Alnwick fellow. This was simply one of the political things you did during a fellowship—well, at least that was what I had been told by my mother.

Afterward, I said my goodbyes and grabbed my coat to return to my place. I was ready to be welcomed by the silence so I could rest and sleep, be prepared for what tomorrow would bring. I hoped I could at least write a damn line. I knew it was a common writer's problem, and I should be thankful for the opportunity. I was, but that didn't mean I still didn't want to come out of this with at least something written.

The house was dark and quiet as I locked the door behind me and headed to my room. I quickly stripped away the formalwear and curled up in my sheets. I curled into the silence and let the waves remind me I was still here. For now.

CHAPTER 2

I spent the morning at the gym, which made my entire upper body ache. I was used to it after all these years. It beat playing soccer in the dead of winter because the South thought it was a brilliant time to play the sport. Mind you, that meant you were out in the cold and rain with shorts. It wasn't pleasant at all, running the entire time. You still froze, and I remember coming home with blue lips—something which my parents were never happy about.

After the gym, I walked along the beach. The sky was clear, bright, and open, the shade of blue painted above me as if it blended into the Pacific. It was still brisk outside, so I resorted to a zip hoodie to go over my tank top. I was still sporting shorts, which I regretted the moment I stepped outside. Luckily, I had ensured the heat was on before leaving my place. It would embrace my entrance. I quickly learned to keep a fire going while I was at home. Everyone kept telling me about the summers here. They were still so far away that they were a dream even if it was only spring.

Once home, I sat and stared at the blank screen some more. After an hour of doing that with not a word to show for it or the effort given to it, I called my parents. I tried to call them every Sunday to catch up and keep my mother happy that I was still keeping in touch. She would tell me about everything going on back home—like how her students were acting stupid, or how one of the teachers had made a sly comment about another student that my mother didn't like. Sometimes, she vented about family members. Today, she told me about one of her brothers who was being stubborn. He needed to talk with his other sisters more, even if they made him mad. I rolled my eyes and laughed. Right after she asked how things were in Oregon, my father joined. We spent an hour or so on the phone each, just enjoying each other's company, even if it was only our voices.

Then when it was over, I went back to staring at a blank page while sitting at my kitchen counter. I don't know how long I stood thinking, occasionally writing a line before deleting it. It came to an end when I heard a knock at the door.

I walked over, wondering who it was. I opened the door to find Quinn looking sober, standing on his own.

"Hey," I said to him.

"Hey. Do you mind if I come in?"

"Not at all," I replied, moving aside so he could step in. I closed the door behind him, and we walked over to the counter where I was sitting. I wondered what he wanted. I hadn't been expecting a visitor, let alone him—a guy I had just met last night. Who also happened to know me because of his parents. Frankly, it was all a little weird, yet oddly interesting.

"Sorry about last night," he began. "I don't handle my parents well, especially at parties." He sat down, looking out at the sea, which, from the vantage point in the kitchen, went on for miles.

I grinned. "You're fine." The fact that Quinn was apologizing for this was funny. I didn't judge people for one drunk night. Three, maybe, but I would keep it to myself.

"I don't do parties like that well. I always feel like I get put into a box around my parents."

He didn't have to defend himself, but I could tell he wanted to. I grabbed a glass, filled it with water, and slid it over to him. He looked at me for a moment, then thanked me for it.

"I get it."

"Also, I'm sorry I called you cute if that made you uncomfortable." His face was red and it caught me a little off guard.

"I'm surprised you remember."

"I don't. Olivia told me this morning."

I laughed a little, and I couldn't help it. He looked so embarrassed by it, which was rather interesting and refreshing. I was used to people being fake nice—or outright hostile—towards me instead of seeing me as a human, so this was intriguing.

"It wasn't the first time someone's said that, and it won't be the last."

He grinned and his eyes sparkled. The same type of sparkle my mother would say he was up to something. I wondered if it was the only reason he had come over today. It seemed strange as I stood across from him near the island.

"Well, that's not the only reason I'm here. Olivia wanted me to invite you to our afternoon hike."

Now this made more sense. I thought for a moment about how I should answer. Getting out of the house wouldn't be a bad thing, and I knew I should explore more of the place I was living, not just the town and my home.

"I guess I should get ready then," I replied.

Quinn perked up at the answer. "Good to hear."

It was still rather chilly outside, so I added layers to my clothes. I also grabbed my dark forest-green jacket in case it rained. I had learned to always expect it out here, even if it was only a tiny drizzle throughout the day.

I came out to find Quinn sitting at the counter in front of his empty glass. Part of me wanted to pull back. My brain kept reminding me not to get close to anyone. You will lose them anyway. You don't plan on staying here.

I walked forward as I pushed all the thoughts away. I needed to be better; I needed to get out.

"Ready?"

"After you."

Quinn headed out with me behind him. As I closed the door, I saw him head to his car. I already felt my hand shaking. I couldn't do it, and I spoke before I thought it through. "I'll drive!"

Quinn stopped, looking rather startled. I hope I hadn't yelled it out. I probably did.

"But you don't know where we're going," he replied, his eyes squinting.

I had to convince him to let me drive. "Just show me the way. I learn better," I lied as my heart raced.

He looked at me for a moment, and I hoped he wouldn't ask.

"Okay, I guess you're driving," he replied cautiously.

Relief flooded through me as I led him to my car, the very one my parents had shipped to me days before.

He looked at me strangely as we drove down the driveway. Once we reached the edge, he gestured which direction to turn. It took only a few minutes before we were out of town. The buildings gave way to the dense forest that surrounded the landscape, lining the road with lush, green pine that went on for miles.

We were silent for most of the trip. Probably my fault. I had never known how to hold a conversation, and it was rare when I did, always coming down to luck. In school, I'd found it challenging. People would try, but I would either shy away or not have anything to say. That was why I had so few friends, among other reasons.

In silence, I took it all in—the coastline, the mountains, the trees. It all was perfectly mixed, like a painting. With its rich and full color, a picture wouldn't do it justice. I soaked it in for me to hold and use when I needed it—a memory to own and find comfort in when I was in pain. A place for me to escape to or maybe one day even use in my writing.

Quinn gestured for me to turn at the next right, and I did so, taking us further into the coastal mountain range. The road's incline began to steepen as the tall evergreen got thicker around us. After rounding a few turns in the road we found a small parking area. Olivia was waiting, leaning against her car. She looked confused at first, then she waved. She must have been expecting Quinn's car instead of mine.

"Well, hello," she said as we got out of the car.

The air was a little thinner here, crisper and lighter than it was down on the shore. The pine scent was thick in the air, and part of me wished I could bottle it up so I could take it home with me and have it to relax.

"Someone decided to drive and learn," Quinn said, already probably knowing what her first question would be.

I looked over him, trying to tell if his voice had any negative tone, but I couldn't tell with him. I smirked. "He seemed to get here in one piece."

Quinn gave Olivia a look that I couldn't read. "Come on, we want to show you something."

I was a little worried; I had only met them yesterday. They could lead me to some abandoned shack to murder me. Of course, that was the tiny and unconfident part of me trying to find a way to escape. Any excuse for me to return home? I silenced it and followed after them.

The trail was well maintained as it snaked its way up the mountain, weaving in and out of the trees. The parts near a sheer drop or steep incline had a wooden rail built next to them. As we headed up in elevation, I felt my thighs burn.

I'm going to regret this.

That thought always found a way through. This time, I was going to ignore it no matter how hard I tried, and I needed to.

"How are you liking Oregon?" Olivia asked, waiting for me to catch up to them.

"It's pretty." That was all I had to say at the moment. I hadn't gotten out of my house since I got here.

"Fair."

"How do you like working at the bookshop?" I asked, genuinely curious. I'd always thought it would be fantastic to work at one, but I'd never had the time to do it.

"Oh, I don't work there," she replied. "I own it."

For a moment, I was shocked. She was my age and already owned a business. Granted, I guess I hadn't really thought about it and had spent the last few years in college while she started a business.

"Wow, that's really cool," I replied.

"Well, we own it," Quinn interrupted.

"Oh yes, I forgot my lovely investor." There was a hint of humor in her voice as she said it.

Quinn smiled, probably enjoying picking on his friend and partner. "To be fair, I'm just the money, and she makes all the decisions," Quinn said, defending himself a bit.

I laughed a little. That was probably a wise choice. Quinn didn't seem like a literary person. Then again, I shouldn't judge.

After a brief rest and banter, we continued our trek up. This time, Olivia kept pace with me, with Quinn a few feet in front of us. There was a soft breeze as we walked, and the faint ruffle of the pines above us. Honestly, if you listened closely, it was like the forest was playing its own symphony for us to hear, to enjoy and savor.

"Did Quinn apologize for last night?" She kept her voice low.

"He did. He mentioned you reminded him about the cute comment."

She laughed a little. I think she enjoyed hanging that over his head for a reason, I didn't know yet. "He never handles those galas well."

"Why?" I asked. I was probably prying, but it maybe wasn't a big secret.

She looked over at me and was about to speak when the small path surrounded by trees gave way to a gorgeous clearing with a lighthouse perched on the other side. It stood tall and white. On the inside, you could see the large, rotating bulb, and by the looks of it, this was a working lighthouse. However, the lighthouse was not the star attraction here—it was the view.

I could see for miles out into the ocean, the coastline stretching endlessly. Waves pounded against the sheer cliffs while the simple clouds brushed up against the mountains as the breeze flowed in.

"What do you think?" Quinn asked.

"Well worth it," I replied, taking it in as much as possible. I thought back. How would they have liked this? Would they have loved this view, a view we'd always said we would see? I would just have to enjoy it for them.

"What are you thinking about?" Quinn asked.

"Nothing. Just taking in the view," I lied. No need to share my honest thoughts. What would they think of me afterward if I did?

We all stood there for a moment before I shamefully took my phone out to take a few photos. My parents would want to see them. They would be happy I had gotten out a bit to see a little piece of the area I now called home. Olivia and Quinn didn't seem to judge me for taking photos, even if I looked like a complete tourist doing so.

A few more people joined us, some with their families, others by themselves or with their partners.

"Do you mind taking a picture of us?" Olivia asked someone standing nearby.

They agreed, and she gathered us together with the Pacific to our backs. I was in the middle with Quinn and Olivia on each side. I couldn't remember the last time I took a photo with anyone other than my family.

The lady took the picture and smiled before giving Olivia's phone back to her. "A keepsake," was all she said.

Olivia pulled it up to show us. It was an okay photo. I never liked myself in them—in any image, really. This one, at least, wasn't the worst. Those had a special place where they would never be seen.

"How does coffee sound?" Quinn pitched.

"Always down," Olivia replied.

They both looked at me, and I nodded before we began our descent. I was usually not a coffee person, but I could at least have tea or something, and it was better than what was waiting for me at home.

I sipped at the latte Olivia made. It was pretty good and I would probably try it again at some point. I heard my mother applaud in my head. She'd spent years trying to get me to love coffee so she wouldn't be the only person in the house who drank it. I think she secretly wanted someone to have her morning coffee with. My father was not a coffee drinker, so she was always by herself in the morning.

Quinn sat across from me as Olivia made her rounds in the store. Learning Olivia owned it made me look at it differently, noticing the little bits of personality that brought the store to life. The wallpaper made it cozy. The subway tile behind the handmade counter was simple. It was all an extension of her. There was some of Quinn's input too, the light finishings, the shelves that held the books. It all screamed high quality, something I could tell was not optional if he was spending money on them.

"Is she going to sit?" I finally asked, noticing it was just Quinn and myself enjoying the coffee, while hers still sat on the table, full and getting colder by the minute.

"Maybe?" he said. After a brief pause, he called to her.

"What?" Olivia said as she came back to the table. Three books were now in her hands—classical works by Hemingway, Louisa May Alcott, and Jules Verne.

"Sit down," he told her in a rather commanding tone.

She glared at him for a second. For a moment, I thought she might actually yell at him. Then she placed the books on the table and sat down. I'd thought it would take more effort for her to sit and enjoy her drink.

"Sorry," she muttered.

"It's okay to stop working and enjoy the moment," Quinn said, smiling.

For a moment, I truly saw their relationship. One calmed the other, while the other was almost like a caregiver. I honestly would pair them as siblings if I didn't know any better. It reminded me of times when I wished I had a sibling of my own. Yet there I was, an only child.

I looked down at my drink. Steam was still lifting from it, warning of how hot it was, yet the liquid wasn't still. There were subtle ripples in it. I couldn't explain why it caught my eye, but it did. Then, just as they appeared, it stopped, and the brown liquid was still again.

"Everything okay?" Olivia asked.

I looked up to find them both looking at me. I must have been staring, probably for a while, for her to ask me that. They looked concerned, but I don't know why they would be. "Yeah, I was playing with a line in my head," I said. I knew it was a lie, but maybe it sounded better than what I was actually staring at. The little ripples fought for attention in my mind. Why would that be something to lie about?

Olivia and Quinn brushed it off, and the conversation turned to other things, like places they wanted to show me in the area. Apparently, they both had a laundry list. I couldn't name half the number of things back home to show them. Mainly because there was nothing to offer, other than a few things in Memphis.

I noticed it was getting late as the sun began to set. I would never get used to how early it darkened in the winter, and here, night fell earlier than usual. Olivia began to clean up, and I offered Quinn a ride home since his car was still in my driveway. He agreed since I was pretty sure he had no interest in walking back in the cold.

The drive was silent again, the air rushing past the windows, Quinn looking out the window into the town of Alnwick. As we approached the house, he thanked me for the ride, but once my car stopped, he sat for a moment. I half expected him to race out of my car into his, yet he was still sitting there, taking in the silent, cold night.

"I read your submission," he said, breaking the silence.

I looked over at him as many questions popped into my head. I hadn't expected him to say that, to have read some of my work. "Oh," I replied, not knowing what else to say as I pushed the real question out of my mind.

"You're really good, and I'm glad I picked you for the fellowship," he said.

Quinn had picked me? He was the one who chose the winner? It explained some things, yet made me want to ask so many more questions.

"You pick the fellowship winner?" I asked.

"Yes, I have for the past four years. It's one of the only things my parents have me do that I enjoy," he said.

"Can I ask why?"

Quinn looked over at me. For a moment, I thought he wasn't going to answer. "Your writing is raw and real. Plus, it didn't bore me to death." Quinn smiled, and I let out a little laugh at the last part. "Good night, Kodak."

"Good night."

JAMES UNGURAIT

Quinn left the warmth of my car for his own as I headed inside. As I closed the door behind me, I saw the headlights begin their way down the driveway.

34

CHAPTER 3

A few days went by without seeing them, but I was trying to actually write. It only turned out to be a line or two, then I erased them and went back to writing a line or two again. The same ritual over and over again. I didn't know how to start this piece. I never did; it was usually a freak accident when I finally finished something like the story Quinn had mentioned. It had come to me at the weirdest point, and by the time I was done writing it, it was like no time had passed. Part of me felt strange knowing Quinn had read it, maybe because it was a piece of work that was so personal. It was the one story that was almost true.

The rain had returned, and we were on the second straight day of it. You could barely distinguish the ocean from the house, as it was hidden behind the light rain that constantly fell, forming a fog-like sheet. That was half the reason I didn't leave the house. I didn't feel like being cold and wet, and I preferred the warm temperature inside, to be able to curl up in a blanket, as I was now, with a hot tea in hand.

The more I sat there, the more I thought of getting out and doing something. I knew I shouldn't sit there all day, yet I had no desire to move or enter the cold awaiting me on the other side of the door. I should go for a run, a coffee run, or a hike—well, maybe not the latter due to the rain, and I'd already done my gym session for the day. At the very least, I should take a shower so I would be ready if the motivation did arrive for me to go out. Maybe the rain would slow, giving me an opening to venture out.

I stripped as I turned the water on, letting the steam rise into the air. I let it embrace my skin as I entered the shower. The warm water fell over me, soaking me. The tension on my shoulders seemed to ease as the air warmed around me. For a moment, I let the world slip away. I thought about writing, of course, but the other thoughts began to creep in—the ones I tried for years to suppress. The eyes that blamed me stared, just as they always did anytime I entered the room. My parents had even considered moving because of it. They saw how the weight of it all was taking its toll, how I would dive deeper into things to keep busy.

Part of it was hiding, but the other? Grief.

I turned the water off and stood, breathing heavily as the water dripped off me. I've been running away from this for so long, but it still followed me wherever I went. Why couldn't I just escape it? Why did it haunt me?

I again tried to suppress it, all of it, as I dried my skin with a towel, rubbing myself down with as much force as I could. I changed back into sweatpants and a hoodie, but I barely made it out of the bathroom before there was a knock on the door. It was soft, almost like there was a hesitation. I paused a second to make sure I wasn't hearing things. It came again, softly, and I walked over to the door.

I opened it to find Quinn standing on the other side. This time, he wasn't smiling or embarrassed. His eyes were red, and he had a duffle bag in his hands.

"Everything okay?" I asked.

He stared at me for a moment, like he didn't want to speak. When he did, it took effort. "Can, uh, can I stay here for the night?" he asked.

I could tell he was trying to keep it together. There was almost a brutal honesty in how he looked. I couldn't leave him out here. He and Olivia had been so welcoming. Speaking of, why wasn't he going to her? Why was he coming here?

"Of course." I opened the door further, allowing him to come in.

His slow walk past me made me worry. What would push him to this? I followed him to one of the spare rooms on the other side of the house. He placed his bag down and looked over at me.

"Is there anything you need?" I asked.

"Just a long shower," he replied.

"Okay, I'll leave you then. If you need something, just let me know."

I headed to the living room, where my computer and phone were. I debated for a second if I should call Olivia. They were friends, but when I looked at my phone, Olivia had already beaten me to it. A message awaited, asking if I had seen him. I replied, letting her know he was with me. She quickly wrote back.

Thank god!

She was worried, that I was sure of. I don't know why and it didn't feel right to ask Quinn. Not now, at least. I could hear the shower running as I made my way back to my computer, hoping to come up with something. Instead, I stared endlessly out the window at the ocean, letting my thoughts wash over me like the waves.

I didn't know how long I sat gazing out the window. It had to at least be an hour, as it took me a minute to notice that I no longer heard the water running. When I turned, I saw Quinn standing behind me, mirroring my gaze. He was now in shorts and a T-shirt. His bare feet slid across the floor as he noticed me looking, joining me in a chair nearby. He sat quietly for a few minutes, his hair was still wet and unmade. This was the first time I had seen him like this—not his postured and well-groomed look. He looked normal.

He broke the silence. "I'm sorry."

"For what?"

"For just showing up here, begging." He looked down the floor as he spoke.

37

I paused, wanting to make sure I said the correct thing. I don't want to add any pain, but I couldn't think of anything else to say. "Don't be. Stay as long as you need."

A slight smile crossed his face, a soft one, one that was only there for a moment, then it faded back to the motionless face I had seen earlier. I watched him sitting there like I had been for the past few days, just looking out into the landscape. Except where I was looking for inspiration, I didn't know what he was looking for or thinking.

A few hours later, it was getting dark as the late afternoon sun sauntered down to the horizon. I was just getting back from picking up food for Quinn and me. He still hadn't spoken much, only enough for me to take his order. I still debated if I should try to ask what was happening. Something had pushed him here. There was still the question of why he had chosen to come here. Why me?

Entering the kitchen, I placed the food on the counter and noticed Quinn still by the window. Has he not moved?

"Food's here," I said, hoping it would get him to move.

He did, glancing back at me. Without a word, he got up and came toward the kitchen. I laid out the food as its scent filled the room. Quinn had wanted seafood, and Alnwick had no shortage of that. We both ended up getting salmon with sides. Mine was a loaded baked potato, his was grilled asparagus. I think it was safe to say that he had the healthier option. The food was well cooked and almost melted in my mouth. This had to be some of the best salmon I'd ever had, even if we spent the meal in silence. Salmon is available in Mississippi, only in some of the nicer restaurants. However, it's nothing like this.

"What happened today?" I asked, finally having the courage to do so.

We were sitting on the couch, and I had turned the fireplace on to warm the air. The light flickered in the dark, illuminating the floor around us in a slightly warm glow.

Quinn looked over at me and paused for a second as I wondered if he would even answer. Part of me felt like we stayed silent forever.

"I fought with my parents," he said. "Over something we've sparred about multiple times, and I couldn't take it anymore."

"I'm sorry," I replied, not knowing what else to say.

"They want me more involved in the company, and I told them no, which turned into a shouting match about how I'm nothing of what they wanted in a son. I told them I never wanted them as parents."

"Damn," I said, watching him as he stared at the floor. I couldn't imagine what that would have been like. I was lucky to have parents who had been there through the worst moments of my life. There were no expectations for me, other than being myself. My parents held my hand when I needed it, gave me the strength to continue when I desperately wanted to give up.

"I didn't mean the last part. I just got so angry. That was when I needed to leave. I couldn't be around them after that."

"Give it some time," I suggested. "It will get better, and they shouldn't force anything on you."

His posture improved a little, his eyes no longer staring at the floor. Now they were on me, and I understood him for a moment, and why he'd had so much to drink the first night I met him. He'd come here because he knew I wouldn't judge, wouldn't tell a soul. Mainly because I didn't know anyone else. Given some time, he would probably tell Olivia, if she didn't already know the situation.

"Thanks."

"You're welcome."

"How do you write?" he asked. "Like, how do you make your words sound so raw and powerful? How can you tell those stories?"

For a moment, I didn't know how to answer. How did I? "I write about experiences—my experiences," I began. "Then I create the story from there, changing things to make it more coherent, but the story's core always stays the same. I make the language clear and raw because stories should invoke emotion."

"So feeling torn between two different worlds? The story you submitted about the boy, the one where he felt isolated? Was your experience?" he asked.

I could see the confusion on his face. It was the same I'd seen since I'd left my small town. Like, how could I have possibly experienced something like that? Experienced hatred, discrimination, and judgment. How could someone who looked white, who had a white name, experience those things? That was the thing—I wasn't white. No matter how I looked on the outside. Inside, the truth was the same—I wasn't white. I wasn't anything, really, other than a boy who was torn between two different worlds.

"Yes," I told him, my words more aggressive than I meant them to be. "My father is from the Midwest, a typical white family with a standard white name. My mother, on the other hand, is Latina. So my identification says Hispanic/Latino, but I am neither white nor Latino. I sit on my own little island alone. Not belonging anywhere."

Quinn looked at me, wishing he'd never asked. I saw it in his eyes, at how they glanced over at me. "I didn't know," he said.

"Most people don't unless you grew up in a small, Southern town where everyone knows everything. They tend to make your life hell because you're different."

He moved closer to me, just inches away from me on the couch. His blue eyes stared into mine, looking like he wouldn't accept that. "Here is what I see," he began. "I see a person who is a brilliant writer, who deserves to be celebrated. I see a friend, and I see someone who cares and who is strong. I see you."

I had to take a moment. One, he'd called me a friend. He said he saw me. Maybe tonight, we'd helped each other. "Thank you. We should go to bed," I replied, changing the subject away from me. Plus, it was getting late.

He nodded in agreement, and I went off to ensure everything was locked and stowed away—my nightly ritual, which I had done each night of my life. With the fire out, the doors closed, and the lights off, I headed towards my room. Quinn was already in his.

Removing what I was wearing, I nestled myself in the sheets. The coolness spread across my skin as it began to conform to my body. I stared at the ceiling fan that sat motionless above me. No matter how much I wanted to close my eyes, I couldn't. Instead, my mind raced through everything that I had gone through. How lonely it made me feel—except for when I wasn't. But that short period had been taken away from me, and everyone blamed me for it. The pain that I tried to run from always found me.

I turned to my side, gazing into the dark abyss beyond my window. Quinn was probably already fast asleep, but I lay there awake like I did every night because it all haunted me. It followed me everywhere I went.

I hate this.

The tossing and turning, my skin rubbing against the sheet as I moved restlessly.

I eventually sighed heavily, frustrated as I pulled a pillow over my head. When I did, the cold air brushed my skin as it emerged from the warmth of the blankets.

I sat for a moment, hoping for a rush of tiredness. Instead, my mind races all over the place, unable to rest in a single spot. I take the pillow off my head and try to lie down in bed like a normal person.

This is my night, every night.

Until sleep finally decides to come.

I look over to the other side of my bed. It's empty, just like it is every night. For some strange reason, there are nights I wish someone was lying next to me. Someone that I could hold when I needed it. It was at night when I felt the most alone, when I sensed it lurking around me, trying to suffocate me.

So I tried to dream it away. Dreaming of that person next to me, how I held them in my arms, the endless whispers we would exchange. Their heartbeat would be in sync with mine as we were in each other's arms.

Sleep always arrived when I least expected it, and I greeted it warmly.

CHAPTER 4

It was dark, and my head felt weird as my ears rang. I didn't know where I was as I spun around and around. Dizzy and disoriented, I tried to move or yell, but couldn't. It was like my body wouldn't respond to the commands I gave it. As my hearing returned, I heard the sound of flames crackling in the air and felt the heat as it brushed up against my skin. I was confused at first, not understanding how everything had changed so quickly. I understood once my vision began to return.

It was slow at first, flashes of a scene. I was on the ground, pain erupting from my side. When I glanced at my hands, blood covered them. That was when I realized. The car in front of me was on fire, flipped over, mangled, and crackling with flame that danced over it. I stared into the car and I tried to scream, but nothing came out. No matter how hard I tried, my voice wouldn't work. All I could do was watch as it burned—as they burned. My life shattered in seconds.

Pain –

"Kodak."

I tried to move, but it felt like I was tethered to the ground. I was chained down, frozen. The dark swallowed me, and I couldn't do anything other than watch. Even as I tried to scream, hoping something, anything would change, hoping that I could move. How had I survived? How had I lived when they didn't? The same thoughts haunted me all these years, no matter how hard I tried to scream, say something, or move. It was useless. All I could do was watch.

"Kodak!"

Someone kept calling my name, but I couldn't tell where it came from. It was the only sound that pierced this awful scene, and I recognized the voice. But I didn't know him then.

I woke in the bedroom, already upright, sweating and cold. My skin was wet as the blankets shifted to the side. It was dark, but I saw Quinn sitting on my bed. His eyes were stern as he looked at me. His hand was on my shoulder; he must have been shaking me, trying to wake me. Dear lord, I could only imagine what he thought right now—me in full nightmare mode, probably lashing out at everything, unable to realize what was real and not.

"Kodak?" he said, his voice softer now that he'd noticed that I was awake and no longer dreaming.

"I'm fine. It was just a nightmare," I replied. I hated them, but it was something I lived with since the crash. Talking about things with him earlier must have triggered one, and I hated that he had to witness it. It was something that would scare people who didn't know why I got them. Hell, it scared my parents still. My mother worried about them since she'd learned I was moving. She wondered how I would handle them by myself.

"Are you sure? You were screaming. Kodak, you scared me for a moment. I didn't know what to do other than wake you. Also, who's Becca?" he asked.

I briefly shut my eyes before looking back at him. It must have been a bad one. I couldn't tell you how often my parents had given me the same look after running into my room and waking me from the nightmares that would take hold of me. Post-traumatic stress was what the doctors called it. To me, it was like the event haunted me. It scared everyone who'd seen me have one, and there was no way to prepare for one.

I didn't think I could get out of this without telling him. I couldn't lie, not about this. As much as I hated telling the story, I was going to have to.

"Becca was my girlfriend in high school," I said. "She died with three others in a car crash." There was no need to hide it. I'd probably said as much while I was dreaming. Honestly, there was no telling what I had said or screamed.

"Oh, I'm so sorry," he said. He glanced to my side.

I knew what it was he was looking at—the scar along my ribcage. It was small and healed years ago. I was thrown out of the car as it crashed, my side hitting a piece of metal. Most of the other scars faded, just not that one.

"I was the only one who made it out," I said before he asked. Now that I was more awake, I saw how close he was to me. Heat radiated off of him, and I couldn't help but notice that he was only dressed in black pajama pants. I could make out the definition of his torso as his head dropped, looking away.

"Damn, I didn't know," he muttered, moving a little further away.

"It's okay; I have nightmares from it still," I said, "but I'm going to try to sleep a little more."

"Okay. I'll stay with you. Just in case you have another one," he said.

I tried to protest, but by the glance he gave me, I was not fighting my way out of this one.

"Don't worry, I'll sleep on the floor."

"Okay."

He walked out to grab some blankets and pillows, probably from the bed that he'd been sleeping on. If I was honest with myself, part of me was glad he was staying. For once, I was not going to be totally alone as I faced the night. Nights like these had haunted me for years. The first couple nights that I'd had nightmares, my mother had stayed with me in a chair as I slept. She had been worried I would hurt myself while having one. I'd chalked it up to her worrying after the crash.

Quinn returned shortly and got comfortable on the floor, nestling on top of a few blankets, with one to cover him. I looked down at him as he curled up. His torso rose and fell with his breathing. It was comforting to hear, and part of me felt bad that he was on the floor and not in the comfort of the bed. I thought about having him sleep with me for a second, but he was already falling asleep—something I should try and do myself.

I opened my eyes as the morning sunlight peered through the open blinds into my room. For a moment, I look out into the room past what lies beyond the window. It took me hours to fall asleep after the nightmare, but I finally did as I focused on Quinn breathing on the floor, letting it guide me my eyes closed. For once, I hadn't felt alone while I slept. The mundane sound of him shifting on the floor, the breathing. It brought a comfort that I never felt. I turned over and glanced down, noticing him still asleep.

His chest was still rising and falling; he strangely looked comfortable on the floor, which was surprising as I tried to muster some motivation to wake up, but it took a minute as my sheets still had their hold on me. They wanted me to stay nestled there, to stare and think. However, the more I laid here, the more restless I got. I looked down at him again. I didn't want to wake him.

I slipped out of bed as quietly as possible, slowly closing the door behind me, and headed into the living room.

It was pretty and calm as I looked out at the blue sky that hovered over the waters while I waited for my tea to warm and steep. The sea was quiet today with no storm to stir it, just the soft, blue-green tint that seamlessly merged into the blue sky. The air was excellent as I turned up the heater a tad to ensure that the house stayed warm and cozy. I hated feeling cold, and even now, I wished I had grabbed a pair of socks before I'd left my bedroom. There was nothing worse than your feet being cold—other than maybe your feet being wet and cold.

When my tea finished, I again started at the blank page on my computer. With me wrapped in a blanket, sipping my earl grey, I found nothing to write about. Maybe there was something the more I thought about it, but I couldn't force it out. Not yet.

"Good morning." I heard Quinn's voice behind me. A faint shuffle echoed as he walked in my direction. I turned to find him dressed only in the pajama shorts he'd worn to sleep. I had a better view than I had in the dark. He must be—or was—an athlete. Yet what sport did he play? I couldn't see him as a football player. He didn't have the mentality for that, and his figure was leaner than what an ordinary footballer would be. That left a hundred other possible options.

"Sleep well?" I asked.

"As well as I could," Quinn replied, trying to tidy his hair.

"You didn't have to sleep on the floor," I said, making it known that he'd did that on his own accord.

"But I did. How did you sleep after everything?"

I didn't know how to take the first part. Then again, I shouldn't overthink it. "Better."

He glanced over my shoulder at my computer screen. All he saw was the same thing that had been there when I first arrived: nothing. I hadn't written in weeks.

I needed to change the subject away from writing. "Any plans today?" I wondered if he would be sulking around all day like yesterday, or if we had moved past that. It seemed that my nightmare turned the attention back to me last night—a fact that I was uncomfortable with.

"Nothing," he replied.

"There's this waterfall I've been wanting to see, but it's a bit of a drive," I told him. Honestly, I would like the drive—keyword: me driving. Maybe then I would get something out onto the page. I'd told myself when I moved that I should make the most of my time here, to explore the state and all the things it had to offer. This was my first time on the west coast, and I wanted to make the most of this experience.

"Then we should go. I'll go get ready," he replied as I smiled. He hadn't questioned it. I hope he was ready for the almost two-and-a-half-hour drive to the Cascades.

While he was in the shower, I looked at the weather to ensure we wouldn't run into snowstorms up in the Cascades. The last thing I needed was to be stuck in the snow. Thankfully, it was supposed the clear and calm, like it was here on the coast. A perfect day really to go see it.

Once Quinn was out, it was my turn to shower and change. I don't know why I waited for him to be finished, but I did. A habit I guessed, at my parents' house you had to wait for the water to reheat. I dressed in layers, since heading into the mountains would be colder than it was here, and I wore boots since the snow had been falling for a few months. When I returned, Quinn was dressed in a thermal that stuck to his skin under a thick flannel jacket. He, too, had chosen boots, which made me feel better about my choice.

"You look like a lumberjack," I told him.

He smiled at the comment. "You're not too far off. Ready?"

"Yeah," I said as we gathered hats and gloves before heading out into the day. I checked the map on my phone on my way to the car to make sure I knew the route. It would lead us through the coastal range and into the valley. Then we would head to Eugene before heading into the Cascades. This would be my first trip to them, my first trip to the real mountains, not the little ones found out east. These would be snow-capped, rough, and sculptured, and I looked forward to what it would be like to see the majestic formation of nature and its power over the landscape.

"Can I ask a personal question?" Quinn asked as we got into my car.

I glanced over at him, wondering what he wanted to know. He didn't need to ask me if he could ask a question. He'd already witnessed some of the more personal aspects of my life anyway. I nodded to him and waited to see what it was.

"Is that why you always want to drive? Because of the wreck?" he asked.

It was something I never recovered from. "Yeah, I think the control aspect is behind that. It was one way to overcome my initial fear of being in a car afterward," I said as we made it to the end of the driveway and headed out for the highway.

"Make sense. Sorry if I was weird about it at first," he said.

I smiled and told him he was fine, not to worry about it. It would have caught me off guard, too, if someone demanded to drive. If anything, I was surprised that it didn't scare him away.

We made it out of town and headed into the coastal mountains, which rose all around us. The road wove in and out of them as the tall pines seemed to cover them in a sheet you couldn't see through.

"So where is the waterfall at again?" he asked. Quinn probably knew it; he'd grown up here. I would be surprised if he didn't.

"Um, on the other side of Eugene?" I said with a question. I couldn't remember if there was another town before then.

"Oh, Sahalie! Good choice. Actually, it's two. The other is a short hike downriver."

I looked over him, unaware of the second one. "Then you know it?" I asked.

"Yes, and this should be a nice drive. However, we might want to stop in Eugene for lunch."

"I guess I can work that into our trip," I joked.

Quinn laughed before putting his feet up on the dashboard. I smiled as I drove. It seemed this trip was going to be an adventure for sure. Not sure why, but it felt so different with Quinn.

"You're going to love the drive up the McKenzie River. Very scenic," he said as he closed his eyes.

I think he was enjoying this too much—showing the tourist around. However, the moment he started giving commentary on every little stone and plant, I might throw him out of my car, making him walk the rest of the way back to Alnwick. Either that, or I might just find a way to make him stop talking—whichever was easiest at the time.

CHAPTER 5

Q uinn happened to pick a rather interesting spot to eat in Eugene. It was a sandwich shop near the University of Oregon, nestled along the road near other restaurants and shops. From the look of it, the place was popular among students. The nearby student apartment buildings looked nicer than any place I stayed at during college.

Eugene was beautiful, nothing like where I was from. The trees here were tall and covered the road. The streets themselves were well maintained, and the public transit options available to residents were plentiful as one of the buses drove past us—something the South knew nothing about.

As we ate, Quinn told me a few stories of his time at the university. It was crazy to think he had only graduated last year like I had. Maybe that was part of his parents pushing him. There were plenty of people around us, enjoying their food.

I ate one last bite of my sandwich. The food was actually delicious. I secretly wished we had a shop like this in Alnwick.

There was something that I couldn't figure out. The more I thought about it, the more I didn't understand it. I could sit there and talk to him like I'd known him my entire life. There was an ease of conversation flowing between us. Even the waiter made a comment that we seemed like we'd been friends forever. For some reason, it made sense.

After lunch, we drove towards the towering mountains of the Cascades. The massive mountains stood guard over the river valley as it snaked through the landscape. The highway took us up the pure, teal-blue river as it guided the road forward. The trees stood tall around us, blanketing the landscape.

On the drive, I saw my first covered bridge as it crossed the river leading to the other side, and as we got further into the mountains, the first snow-capped peak peeking through the trees. I couldn't help but wonder how nature had created such a perfect portrait.

The deeper we got, the fewer houses were visible. Once we passed McKenzie Bridge, we were in the national forest. The trees grew thick, and a spot of snow began to be visible. The road now was surrounded by the towering fir trees that seemed as tall as the mountains. Clouds drifted like feathers between them.

"The road splits up ahead," Quinn said. "Keep to the left."

As I did what he said, I noticed a sign. "Why is the road closed?" I asked, curious to know.

"They close it in the winter due to the snowpack. It's only open from May through October. It's a pretty drive; I'll have to take you in the summer."

"Interesting."

"Interesting?" His voice perked up.

"Yeah, that you plan on putting up with me until the summer," I joked.

Quinn grinned at the comment. "You'll have to work much harder to push me away."

The snow began getting thicker as we passed a sign that told us the elevation was above 2,000 feet. I felt the difference in how I was breathing, and I felt slightly light-headed. It was also a lot colder outside. For some reason, I found the mixture of green and white too pretty. Typically, when it snowed back home, everything was dead and nothing was green. Here, the pines effortlessly blended with the snowy landscape.

"We're here," Quinn said as we passed another sign signaling it was only a mile ahead.

The parking lot was covered in snow, but I did my best to find a spot with as little as possible. We luckily found one near the bathroom, and once we stepped out of the car, we could hear the roar of the water and smell the scent of pine hovering in the air. From where we stood, the cool mist in the crisp, thin air was already wrapping around me.

"It's right over here," Quinn began. "Watch your step." He pointed to patches of ice and snow that littered the path. The path had been cleared several times near the embankments on the side. Even so, we carefully made our way to the overlook. I tried my best not to fall, and when I did almost slip, I made sure to recover before he knew.

"Wow," I said as we came to the overlook. The falls rushing over the cliff were more massive and prominent than in the photos I had seen. Moss covered the ridge, making it green instead of gray or brown. Water flowed down the river, and from where we stood, the mist hovered over us as it landed on the wooden walkway.

"It's smaller in the summer, less melt. We came at a great time," Quinn said, standing next to me.

A few others leaned over the railing near us—an older couple, a group of students from the university by the looks of it. They wore forest green hoodies with the Oregon logo.

"You're such a good tourist guide. Maybe you missed your calling," I joked with him.

He just grinned—something he needed to do more of. "Come on, we have another one to see," he said as he began to carefully walk down the path in the snow.

It was clear to a degree because it had been frequently traversed, making the snow brown and compact in sections. I made sure to move carefully as I followed after him, watching my every step and trying to find the safest spots possible to step. When we came across the steps going down into the parking lot, I took my time, ensuring I had a sound footing at each step.

Quinn laughed at my slow steps, and in my head, I vowed to make him pay for that later.

"Taking it slow?" Quinn asked once I made it down to the bottom.

I looked over at him as he smiled again. "I hate you."

He shrugged it off as we continued winding our way through the patches of snow and trees, the rushing waters of the river next to us. The pale teal blue flowed fast. I didn't want to imagine how cold that water was.

"Can I ask you something?" I asked as we walked.

"What?" he replied, slowing down his pace.

"How do you know who you are?" I said part of me surprised I could muster it.

"I've been told all my life who I am. You?" His eyes were still low, back to how they had looked after the fight with his parents.

"I don't even know who I am," I said.

He stopped in front of me and paused before he turned around. For a moment, he looked like he would strike me, and call me stupid. Instead, his posture softened as he looked at me. "The only person that matters to is you. You decide that and no one else," he said, then began walking again.

"But what about who you are? The real you, not the one you've been told you are all your life?" I said, coming out rather forcefully. Then again, how could he say that he was what everyone told him he was while also telling me something different? "Because if I was that, I shouldn't be alive."

"I guess you'll just have to figure that out, won't you?" he replied.

I stopped to think that comment through, not fully understanding what he was talking about. When I sensed that he was looking at me, I shook my head and moved to catch up to him.

I was almost there when I hit a patch of ice that I must not have seen. Before I knew it, I was on the ground, pain shooting up my side. Except I didn't stop moving—I kept sliding down, hitting everything as the world around me shifted into clouds and blur. Then the cold—a bone-chilling cold that soaked me.

Water rushed around me, pulling and tugging me. I gasped, trying to pull air into my lungs but I wasn't breathing. My body turned numb to the cold that I knew surrounded me.

This was it. This was how I would finally die—in a cold river thousands of miles from my family. Thousands of miles from the people I once thought would destroy me.

Cold –

Silent –

I gave up, letting the river take me.

Something grabbed my hand and began to pull at me, eventually pulling my body to the surface, where the crisp mountain air greeted me. I was suddenly aware that my body was freezing, my clothes were soaked, and I could breathe again. I coughed out what little water I had swallowed during my brief swim, burning my throat.

"Kodak!" I heard Quinn yell. This was the first time he had yelled at me, each time, the terror in his voice intensified.

When I turned my head to locate his voice, I realized it was his hand on mine, pulling me. His strength had moved through me, through my arms. His warmth pulled me to the riverbank.

"Hey, I got you," Quinn said as he held me.

I began to shake as the air froze me. My muscles didn't know what to do, so they just shook, none of them following any command that I gave them. I didn't think I had ever been this cold, but Quinn began to guide me back up the path. He took it slow up the stairs and past the roaring waterfall. I still felt numb as we walked, and probably wouldn't be able to move without him forcing me. Eventually, we returned to the car, and he shoved me in the passenger seat and took my keys. Part of me wanted to scream at him, but my voice didn't work.

He got in and started my car. Fear took hold of me, I thought that was when my heart would stop. I couldn't; I needed to be in control. Yet there was no way I could. Not like this.

He drove fast. I saw how quickly the trees moved past us as I just sat, still shivering and wet. My lips moved in a motion I had never felt before, and my heart raced fast, trying to warm my body unsuccessfully.

"Stay here. I'm getting us a room," Quinn said as the car pulled to a stop. He was gone for a moment, and my eyes wanted to close, like my body was giving up, exhausted. I had never felt this tired. Well, that was a lie. Maybe when I was on that medication that I had taken only once after the surgery from the wreck. To be honest, it kind of felt like that now.

When Quinn returned, we drove for a few seconds before we came to a stop again, this time, in front of a wooden cabin. Its wooden façade stood out in the white ground and tall trees. He came around, opened the door, and lifted me from the seat. This was the first time I had felt his strength. He carried me, pushing through the doorway. Inside, the air was already warm, a fire burning. I barely made out the decor, but I presumed it was of rustic charm. He set me down, and I teetered on the carpet, unsure of what to do next.

With the door closed behind us, Quinn began to take his layers off, then pulled what he could off me.

"What are you doing?" I managed to say as he stripped me of my wet clothes.

"I'm taking your soaked clothes off so you don't get hypothermia," he said sternly.

I stood still as he did his work, moving parts of my body as he needed to. As uncomfortable as this was for me, I let him, eventually allowing him to strip me down to just my underwear. I didn't really know what else to do.

"Now, go sit over there." In full Boy Scout mode, he pointed to the bed, and I obeyed. He took the rest of his clothes off, down to his underwear, then grabbed a few blankets from one of the closets and came to me, wrapping himself around my body.

His skin was warm as it clung to me. I didn't move as he wrapped the blankets around us, enclosing us in a cocoon. It was like an embrace, except warmer and closer. As his skin touched mine, I began to feel better, the shiver slowly stopping. It was working; I felt the fire begin to burn again within me.

"How did you know what to do?" I asked as we sat there in each other's arms.

"Didn't they teach you what to do if you fall in a cold river down south?" he asked. I sensed he was joking. His tone was more playful than before as the worry had now begun to shed off him.

"No, just what to do if you get heat stroke or dehydrate," I replied.

He laughed a little, and I could feel it rumble against me. It was a little weird at first, with him on me like this. I felt everything—his heartbeat racing, beating against my chest. His breath was against my neck, shuttering through me. The longer we sat together, the warmer I felt as the fireplace radiated towards us. Then there was silence between us like we didn't know what to say.

"Thank you," I finally said. "For pulling me from the river."

"You're welcome. I wasn't going to let you drown. What sort of tour guide would I be if I did?"

I shook my head in disbelief at how this day had gone.

"We'll stay here tonight and head back in the morning. You need to rest since your body was in overdrive."

He was right; I was already tired. Which was probably why I hadn't fought him as he led me here. Not having the energy to, I didn't really know what was happening until he was holding me while we had almost nothing on. His body warmed mine as my hair began to dry.

With my body warming, I finally noticed the cabin. Small. Rustic. A single bed at the center of it all.

"Where are we?" I asked.

"Just down the road in McKenzie Bridge."

"Thanks," I said.

"You don't have to thank me twice, you know," he replied as he began to pull himself off me. My eyes drifted from his face down to his sculpted torso, as the chill returned. I yearned for the warmth of his body to be against me again.

"Quinn," I said. "Don't sleep on the floor tonight."

CHAPTER 6

For the next few hours, I laid wrapped in blankets, everyone that Quinn could find. The fireplace burned, and Quinn periodically stoked it, adding new wood to keep the flame hot. Outside, light snow began to fall from the sky. The flakes were small, effortlessly moving through the air. Snow was an infrequent occurrence where I was from. When it did snow, it would maybe last the morning, then melt by the afternoon. The only real snow I ever saw was when we traveled to my family near Chicago.

I remembered the Christmas breaks we spent up in Chicago. Snow up to our knees at times, blowing across the fields, drifting against anything it came across. However, here, the snow felt different, but I didn't know why. It looked softer, more peaceful. Maybe it was the landscape around us? From the vast mountains to the trees that covered them, the green of the pines was sharp, contrasting against the pearl-white snow.

As night began to fall, I felt more like myself, with more control over my body than I had earlier. I was no longer shivering to keep warm, and the feeling of cold no longer stuck to me. We lay facing opposite directions, like we were on a school trip, sharing a bed with each other, and careful not to touch like we would burn on contact.

Tonight, however, I felt back to my core identity—the one I hated and had tried to run from all these years. The scared boy who was "other." Yet again, I felt helpless when I should have been strong. Maybe I was precisely what people thought of me back home. For tonight, however, I need to rest, my body sore and exhausted from the day's events. I pushed away those thoughts, leaving only gratitude that I was still alive, thanks to Quinn. I owed him now.

I tried my best not to toss and turn like any typical night, staying perfectly still and careful not to make sudden movements. If there was one thing I could say, it was that I had made a friend—maybe even two!—out here—something I had never expected I would do. I was sure he would tell her everything. They seemed close. I wished I still had mine, the ones I had been close to, instead of being alone, bearing the pain without anyone by my side.

When morning came, Quinn had rolled over from the edge of the bed and was now next to me. I could once again feel the warmth of his skin. I didn't dare wake him as I slid out of bed and walked to the bathroom, ready for a shower and to fully feel like myself again. I took a longer shower than I'd meant to. When I got out, Quinn was awake and had breakfast on the table. He even had a bag of clothes for me to change into. I'd forgotten mine were probably still damp from yesterday.

"Where did you get these?" I asked, grabbing the clothes from the bag. They were nothing I would typically wear—a T-shirt, a flannel shirt, a jacket, jeans, and a new pair of socks. I was surprised he had gotten the right sizes, but then again, it was possible he had looked at my wet clothes for them.

"There's a general store next to us," he said.

I faintly remembered seeing one on the drive up, before we crossed into the national forest. I quickly changed into what he'd bought, and then we sat and ate breakfast before heading back to the coast.

"Well, that was an adventure," I said as we got into my car.

"You said it."

I laughed a little. Part of me was glad he had gotten to see this part of me and not the one that laid next to him last night—the person who still struggled with who he was.

"Hey, I want to show you something when we get back," Quinn said.

"What is it?" I asked.

"A surprise."

My eyebrows raised a little. I didn't think I could take any more surprises after yesterday's fall into the river. I would prefer to go home and rest, but I guess I should give him this.

"Should I be scared?" I asked.

"Not at all," he said.

I nodded as we began to drive off toward Eugene.

The drive itself was peaceful, our conversations switching between different things. Our time in college. A few political discussions we surprisingly agreed. A little gossip about our families: I learned his mother was an avid activist who sometimes attended protests against the wishes of his father. I could tell from the conversation that his relationship with her was more substantial than with his father. There was a smile on his face as he spoke of her.

Before I knew it, we were already making our way through the coastal range and coming to the outskirts of Alnwick. The Pacific spread out in the distance as we came down from the hills, the blush teal in contrast to the green of the trees.

"Stop by the bookstore on our way in," Quinn suggested as we entered the central part of the town.

I nodded and headed towards it, wondering what this surprise was.

"You're still not going to tell me what this is?" I asked as we pulled up.

"Nope, you just have to see it," he replied.

I shook my head, knowing he wasn't going to reveal it. Part of me worried because I hated surprises. I couldn't control them.

The store was busy as we walked in. Customers browsed the selection of books and a few sat sipping coffee at one of the tables. Olivia was serving customers at the counter. She waved as we entered, and she came up to us after she finished.

"There you are!" she said to Quinn, then directed her eyesight to me. "Hopefully, he hasn't been too bad."

"I'm doing great, thank you," he replied. "I actually saved his life yesterday."

Olivia paused for a second and looked at Quinn, then at myself, before staring at us with her mouth slightly open.

"Long story," I said, trying to see if we could move past it.

"I expect to hear it later; what are you doing here anyway?" she asked.

"I'm showing him upstairs," Quinn said.

"Oh," Olivia started, somewhat surprised. "Okay then. Dinner later?"

"Sure," Quinn replied.

Olivia went back to her customers as Quinn led me towards the back of the store and then into a stairwell that led to the upstairs part of the building. The stairwell was unfinished with exposed brick on the exterior-facing wall and dim lights cast above us. He better not be leading me to my death, I thought. I was getting a serial killer vibe by the look of the place. However, we soon came to a door, and when Quinn opened it, I was shocked.

The room, stretching the length of the entire bookstore, held paintings on easels and walls. Some were blank, others in progress, and a massive amount of paint all over the floor.

"Is this yours?" I asked as I glanced around at the paintings. This was like nothing I had ever seen. Some were massive landscapes I assumed were around Oregon, incredibly detailed and vivid with mixes of colors that seemed to blend perfectly.

"Yeah," he said. "This is one of the Three Sisters. We saw those mountains on the drive up to the falls. That perspective is on the eastern side, where you can see them more clearly."

At the corner of the painting, I noticed some initials, but they weren't Quinn's unless I was missing something about his name.

"Who's EK?" I asked, pointing to them.

"Elias Kerner. That's the name I sell under," he said.

I looked over at him, somewhat surprised. I did a quick Google search on my phone and found several news articles and a gallery that mentioned the name. "Why not your name?" I asked.

"If my father knew, he would find a way to kill me," Quinn said. "Come here, there's one I wanted to show you."

He guided me past more of his work, stopping near some of his works in progress. In the center of the easel, with a station next to it full of paints and brushes, stood the piece he wanted to show me.

I couldn't help but gasp—not at the beauty, but at the meaning. The painting was of a teenage boy, his face separated into two halves by a thin, black line. One side was of ivory skin, and the other was light tan. His brown eyes and dark brown hair were detailed and blended with the handsome face that stared back at us. It was an awe-inspiring work, and a little weird seeing a likeness of myself in it. However, the words that were painted near his body held the true meaning.

I'm the same

"When I read your story, I got inspired. It was finished before you got here in Oregon, and I named the same as your story."

I stayed silent, looking over the work. I didn't know what to say. Here was this person who was nothing like I thought he was. Maybe we both had two worlds that we tried to straddle. Yet perhaps the battle was what made us who we were, as we bore the burdens of belonging to two sides of ourselves. Part of me wondered, as those eyes stared at me, what did they see?

"I don't know what to say," I replied.

"Thanks." He blushed.

"Wait, that painting at your parent's house, the huge one. Is that yours?" I asked, remembering it suddenly. Olivia and I looked at it after we dragged him to bed. It had the same style, and if my memory served me well, the same initials.

"Yes, it is. My mother convinced my dad to buy it from a gallery in Portland. My dad likes the piece, yet he has no idea his son was the one who created it."

I couldn't even imagine how that must feel—to have someone love your work but not even know it was yours because he would disapprove.

"Does your mother know?"

"Oh yes, she was quick to realize it. Mothers know these things, I guess. Part of the reason she steered my dad towards it. I donated all the money from the sale—well, all the sales, really—to charity."

"So you're an heir to a massive fortune, an investor, a lover of writing, and now a famous painter?" Summing him up at this point was hard. Seriously, was there something else I was missing?

"I guess so." He laughed, and I was glad he showed me the other side of him. The honest Quinn was both him and Elias put together. I wished I knew who I was, but the more I tried to find him, the more I felt lost.

"What's your plan with it?" I asked, curious as to what he envisioned for the painting.

"Don't know yet," he said. "Come on, we should meet Olivia for dinner. She'll want to hear about your fall in the river."

Dinner was next door at a restaurant that I really didn't know how to place. It had a mixture of different things, and they all paired incredibly deliciously. Quinn told Olivia all about our adventure in the mountains, including how he'd saved me from the cold river. Olivia laughed through parts of them. I defended myself by reminding them that our rivers down south were not that cold, or too dirty to see, and I wouldn't want to swim in them anyway.

Olivia also asked how Quinn was doing, knowing full well the fight he'd had with his parents. I didn't think he gave it any thought these past few days. Maybe everything else had kept him preoccupied, his mind on other things. The one part Quinn didn't explain was my nightmares. I was glad he kept that between us. I still was grasping them, despite spending several years in therapy trying to overcome them.

Towards the end of dinner, Quinn had to run to the bathroom, which left Olivia and me alone at the table.

She took the opportunity to talk to me while he was gone. "Seriously, he hasn't been a total wreck? Normally, a fight like that takes it out of him pretty hard."

"The first night, he was quiet and to himself, but he's been fine since then. I think getting out of the house helped."

"You're sure he's been sober the entire time?" she asked.

"Yes, the whole time," I replied.

Olivia smiled. "I'm glad to hear it," she said as Quinn began to approach from the bathroom.

Once he was back, we paid for our meal and headed out. By the time we made it back to my place, it was already getting dark outside and the streetlights were beginning to turn on.

"Hey, I'm going to stay here again tonight, if that's okay," Quinn said as we exited the car.

"Yeah, of course," I replied.

"Thanks. I need to go do one thing first," he said as he headed over to his car.

I had a feeling I knew what it could be, and I knew that Quinn needed to do it. He knows he needs to at least tell his parents why he was upset. Maybe that would help them start to heal. He wouldn't be able to live with it if he didn't—something I understood all too well.

As Quinn drove down the driveway, I went inside back into the warmth of my house. I was alone again, yet I smiled. Maybe my friends were looking down on me, watching, happy to see me moving forward. Who knew, maybe they had even helped Quinn save me in the river. Perhaps I was never alone.

CHAPTER 7

In the next five days, I wrote a few things. Nothing I would share, mind you, but it still beat just staring at an empty page. For a while, I wondered if it was mocking me, waiting for me to write something that would embarrass me. Yet when the words came, they flowed like an endless rain.

Quinn moved back with his parents but was now searching for a place to call his own. I thought it was a smart move. Maybe their relationships would be stronger if he didn't have to live with them daily. The downside was that he left me alone in the house again. Even after a short time, his absence felt weird, but like everything else in my life, I moved forward.

Now I found myself getting out of the house, as I was supposed to meet Olivia at the bookstore. She wanted me to help with an event for a traveling author along with allowing me to talk about my work.

When I arrived at Novel, the store was already busy. Several people had taken seats in an area that was cleared out for the event. Olivia waved me over to where she was speaking with the author.

"This is Kodak, the writing fellow this year. Kodak, this is John Spencer," she introduced.

"It's a pleasure to meet you," John said as we shook hands. "I hear many good things about you. I'm looking forward to working with you tonight."

"Thanks, me too," I replied before he went off to speak with more guests before the event started. We would have plenty of time to talk after.

"I'm excited to finally hear you talk about your work," Olivia said once it was just us.

I smiled, trying to mask the anxiety I felt. Part of me was scared to talk about it, mainly because I felt like they would ask what I was working on now. Which was nothing. I hoped the conversation would stay around Mr. Spencer. I already prepared my questions to ask him, and counterpoints if the conversation drifted my way instead.

"I just hope we stay on my past work," I said.

Olivia looked over at me and nodded as I worked to slow the tremor in my hands. "No one will ask what you're working on now, and they know it's a work in progress. Though they will ask about the short story. I know a lot of people have questions about it. Good ones, I promise."

That made me feel a little better, but I was still nervous. "Thanks," I said as I tried to smile, probably failing miserably at it.

"It's time. Now go get 'em," she ordered. I felt her hand on my back, pushing me forward.

We were both introduced to the crowd of people, which extended almost outside of the store itself. It had to be the most visited book event I had been to. Granted, they were mostly here for the guest author, not me—which was perfectly fine.

The event started with me describing the book Mr. Spencer had written. Thank god I had been able to read the entire thing before the event, otherwise, it would have been a challenge. Then I asked him about the book and writing in general. After the second question or so, I got more comfortable being in front of all those people. It helped that the guest speaker was also excellent at keeping the conversation going.

"Now I have a question for you," John said.

My heart stopped.

"Your short story, 'I'm the Same.' It's about a biracial teenage boy growing up in the South. How did you develop the concept, and did you ever feel pressured afterward?"

"For me, I wrote about my own experience," I started, choosing my words carefully. I didn't know how this crowd would react to me being anything other than white. "I framed the story in the struggle of the character feeling like he was on this island, always torn between the two different worlds, but never fully belonging to either of them."

I hope that will do.

"When you say your personal experience, what do you mean?" he asked.

I paused for a second, trying to again think about how I wanted to say it. "My mother is Hispanic, and my father is white. So for me, the character was easy to relate to and write about because many of his struggles were mine. Of course, with the story, I took a little creative license on things to make the story interesting."

I watched as the audience took it in. The general acceptance had me uncomfortable, unsure of what to do or think. There was none of the subtle disdain or disgust I was used to. At least that is how it always felt back home.

"I think that's incredible; you crafted a powerful read that I think reflects something not a lot of people think about—what it is to be biracial in America," he replied.

Applause rang out in the room.

Part of me was relieved, and the other part was scared. I had opened the door for something else to happen. Now the town knew I was different.

The rest of the event was pretty straightforward. He did a book signing and talked with people, as did I. I had several people come up to me, asking about the story and my own experiences. I was surprised by how many "I'm so sorry for your experience," comments I received. It was a head scorcher to have people acknowledge such a thing. Maybe Oregon was different from what I had come to know in the South. I guess only time will tell.

"You did a great job," Olivia said to me afterward.

"Thanks," I replied. "Hopefully, I didn't scare anyone off."

She laughed, which helped relieve me. "You didn't."

I still felt like I had, but I took the encouragement. I needed to stop being so hard on myself. Years of dealing with it had taught me otherwise.

"Also, I'm inviting you back once something of yours is published," she casually mentioned.

A smile crossed my face. Of course, that would mean actually finishing something to be published. I guess this was a little motivation that I needed.

"I also expect to be somewhere in the acknowledgment section."

"Of course," I said. "Now, please tell me food is somewhere?" I was hungry and needed to move this conversation forward before I sold the rights to everything I would ever write.

"There is, don't worry," she responded, and ushered me towards the café. There, she had an arrangement of little sandwiches and appetizers, and both non-alcoholic and alcoholic drinks to choose from. I decided water was best, at least for now. I wasn't promising to go after something else later.

I found a place that wasn't as crowded before I began to stuff my face with food, enjoying the peace and quiet after the event. Olivia was making her rounds, talking with people as the author continued to sign books. The bustle of the people talking reminded me of my dad's work events that my parents had taken me to as a kid. With him being a member of one of the local college faculty, we frequently went to things that the college hosted. Mostly for fundraising events and so forth.

"I see you're hiding again," a voice said, and I almost dropped everything I was holding.

I turned my head and quickly relaxed. "I see you're doing the same," I replied to Quinn, who stood beside me.

He was dressed in dark jeans and a pressed shirt with a blazer. In his hands, he held a small glass of punch, the stuff I tried to stay away from. The last time had not been a good experience. Let's just say, at college parties, it turned out that it only took two cups of punch to put you under. Then you're the talking point for a week on campus, without even remembering a single moment. So I stayed away from the punch—especially if it was blue!

Quinn grinned as we waited for our opportunity to exit. The event died down after another hour or so. We helped clean up and close the store, most of which consisted of putting up chairs and cleaning the food area of the café.

Stepping out into the wind as Olivia locked the door behind us was chilling. It had really picked up since earlier in the day, to the point that even the lights began to sway along with the trees. I looked up to the sky at the clouds in the dark, shadows that trailed across the horizon. Wind like this, where I came from, meant one thing—a storm, a bad one, the type that made you hide in your home, waiting for a wail to startle you into taking cover, praying you would be spared from the destruction.

"A storm coming," Quinn said, glancing up at the sky with me.

"You get storms out here?" I joked sarcastically.

"Yes, and they tend to be windy," he replied, but I didn't think he'd picked up on my sarcasm.

"I'm going to go home, and you should, too, before the rain starts," Olivia suggested as she wrapped herself in her wool coat.

Quinn just smiled as she turned the other way. "I guess that leaves us then," he replied.

I shook my head at him as we walked toward my car. I could smell and hear the ocean from where we stood, which was unusual. The Pacific had to be angry to hear it from here. I wondered if the waves would reach my place.

Standing there in the cold, I couldn't wait until I was back in the warmth of my home. I already planned to have the fireplace running as soon as I got there. I wonder how intense the storms were out here.

"Hey, I can stay at your place tonight if you want," Quinn said.

Had he noticed me questioning the sky? Storms here couldn't be as bad as they were back home. Those suckers were intense when they wanted to be. Maybe he just wanted some time away from his parents again.

"If you want, but if it's because of the storm, I think I'll be okay," I replied.

He grinned, confirming my suspicion that he just wanted company, and that was something I didn't mind.

"I'll bring wine," he said, which made my ears perk up. I had been meaning to try some Oregon pinot—I heard it was some of the best.

"I expect a good wine," I told him.

He laughed. "I'll grab a good one., he replied before he headed towards his car, which was on the other side of the street.

I'm going to hold him to that.

As he drove off, the first little sprinkles fell on my windshield. They stayed light until I pulled up in my driveway, and it was then that it decided to come down heavier. My typical luck. As I went inside, I heard the waves crashing on the shore again. The Pacific didn't sound happy. I could picture the waves even without being able to see them in the dark—crashing, spraying water into the air as they hit the rocks of the cliffs, angry as they came, ashore one after another.

Thank goodness I had left the heat on. It instantly melted the cold off me as I removed my outer coat. Without turning the light on, I looked out the window to see more of the sky, to witness the power that was being brought ashore, and I knew then that it was going to be a long night. Looking at that monster of a sea, I was happy to have someone to brave it with. I wouldn't be alone through it all.

I thought about the lights and how much wind it would take for the power to be knocked out. I remembered some candles that I had seen underneath one of the kitchen cabinets, and I quickly ensured that I knew where they were, just in case. My mom had always prepared for the power to be out—what to have, what to save, and what to organize. Thinking back on them like a laundry list, I went on autopilot and did them all—made sure appliances that weren't in use were unplugged, secured all the doors and windows, prepped the candles and dug out a lighter, found a flashlight with batteries and an old weather radio. Better to be safe than deal with the consequences if I wasn't.

Once done, I turned the fireplace on; it was gas and would keep the place warm if the heater went out with the power. The warm light filled the room as the flames danced.

An outside light flashed through one of the windows. Quinn was here.

I headed to the door, ready to open it so he wouldn't have to wait in the rain. When I got there, he ran right in with a bag.

His jacket was soaked as he tried to brush the water off his face. "Well, it's definitely storming out," he said, placing the bag down.

"You think?" I replied.

He grinned and pulled out two bottles of wine. "The finest Oregon pinot that I could scavenge from my parents' stash," he said, placing them on the counter.

They looked expensive, but I was eager to try them. I headed to the cabinets and found two wine glasses. It took me a second to remember how to pull the cork out, but once I did. I poured us two full glasses, and we headed to the fire to begin our night.

CHAPTER 8

We sat on the floor with the fire in front of us. Our gazes fixated on the flames as we listened to the rain pelt the side of the house while the wind howled. It was a terrifying sound that pierced through me. The wine helped, keeping my nerves on edge. I never handled storms well as a kid. My parents told me I would hide from the lighting, not the thunder. At least I hid from the thing that could kill me.

To help with this, my parents made me learn all about the weather. They thought I would be less afraid by knowing how it worked. It may have helped some, but that didn't mean I didn't feel my stomach turn when I could tell a storm was coming.

The strange thing, at least for me, was the lack of lighting and thunder. This storm was just wind and rain, yet it kept me on edge. At least I had Quinn, his back against the couch next to me. He wasn't more than a few inches from where I sat, and I felt the same feeling as I did a few nights ago, when we shared the bed in the mountains, inches from each other, but not moving, not touching.

"You did great tonight, by the way," he said, breaking the silence that had fallen over us.

I thought for a second, realizing I had never noticed he was there, that I had only seen him at the end. I'd assumed he'd gotten in late or had other places to be.

"Thanks," I said, trying to stall while coming up with something better to say. A sizable crash threw my train of thought out the window, spurring me from my seat and nearly spilling the glass of wine. Quinn jumped up to look too.

Water crashed along the window and back down to the deck. Luckily, it held, and no water went into the house.

"That was a close one," he said as he sat back down.

I did the same, noticing how he was now closer to me. I smiled at the thought that maybe I felt safe for him. We went back to watching the flames dance, taking in the warmth as it radiated outward. My thoughts moved to tonight, about what I said, how I explained the story I had written, looking into a crowd of people who didn't know who I was. Then I said it.

"Do you think they see me differently now? Do you think they're judging me?" I said it before I realized it was out loud.

"What are you talking about?" he asked as he glanced over at me.

There was no getting out of this, and I had already opened the door for it. "The people at the event tonight. Now they know what I am."

"Why would you even think that?" His entire body was now turned to me, his eyes concerned.

"Experience," I said. That summed it up. It was my experience that when people knew I was mixed race, They hated me. I was other. I wasn't pure. They didn't know I felt safe when they just assumed how I looked from far away.

"This isn't the South. I don't hate you, for the record," he said.

"I figured."

He smiled.

"That you didn't hate me, I mean. The jury is still out on the first part."

"Don't bet against Oregon just yet," he replied.

I took another sip of my wine, knowing full well I would need it for the coming conversation.

"What did they do to you?"

His question sounded like one my parents had asked over and over when they knew something was wrong but didn't know what it was. He knew they hurt me, but didn't understand how. Should I tell him? I wondered. Should I tell him the stories, the ones that hurt? The ones that haunt me still now?

"I was in first grade the first time I felt it. The teacher across the hall came to our classroom and asked for me. I remember she sounded frustrated. I followed her down the hall toward the bathroom." As I spoke, I still smelled the cleaning solution used in the school. "We stopped at the water fountain, where another kid was standing there looking at the teacher, confused. He was tan and had black hair, and I didn't think anything of it. I was a kid. She turned to me and said, 'Ask him if he wants water.' I looked at her confused, then asked him if he wanted water. She scolded me. 'No, ask him in your language, not English.'"

I stopped for a second to collect my thoughts. It was to make sure my emotions were still held together before I continued.

"I remember being so confused, not understanding what she wanted from me. Not to mention that she was angry at me because of something I didn't understand at the time. 'Don't you speak Spanish?' she asked me, probably after I stared at her. And then I shook my head because I didn't. My mother never taught it to me. 'What type of Mexican are you? You don't speak Spanish?' The teacher yelled at me, and I wanted to cry because I didn't understand what was happening."

"A teacher did that to you? Said that?" Quinn asked, shaking his head.

"Yeah. It was the first time I was··· other. I wasn't white like the teacher, but I also wasn't like the other kid," I said. My chest tightened. There was still pain here. I had just been a kid. "The worst part was everyone staring—all the kids were waiting to go to the bathroom." I looked away. Some of these kids were the same people who had hated me from that moment on, even to this day. Because I was different from them.

Quinn was silent as he took what I said in.

"I don't even know what to say." I looked over at him.

His face said it all. The disgust.

"It got worse as I got older. From one side, I got racial slurs from people who didn't know any better. On the other side were people who didn't accept me because I wasn't one of them. I was alone."

Quinn grabbed my hand and squeezed it. "I can't and don't want to imagine what that felt like, but it's not what the people think of you here. Give them a chance. They are some of the nicest and most accepting people. Hell, they accepted me," he said.

I couldn't help but laugh. "Yes, they did," I replied. "Though, who couldn't accept you?"

He gasped, then laughed louder than I think I'd ever heard from him. He looked at me and shook his head, still grinning.

Another wave crashed, reminding us that a storm was still unleashing its wrath outside.

"I'm sorry, I didn't expect you to say that," he replied, his gaze back on mine.

"That's your excuse? Sorry, not good enough," I joked.

He shook his head again. I hope he knew the more he got to know me, the more open and··· well, this would happen.

"What do you want me to say then?" he asked. "You surprised me with your candor, and I had no choice other than to almost spill wine all over me."

"I mean, that would work." I was feeling the alcohol now, as it slowly clouded my head. I always chatted when I drank, which was why it was almost always in a social setting. I guess it was too late now; I might as well go along with it.

His hand playfully pushed at my shoulder, slightly moving me to the side. I smiled. I couldn't remember the last time I'd had this—a night with company that I enjoyed. Thinking back on it, I didn't think I'd had this since high school—since they died.

"Do you miss them?" he asked, and I sensed the change in tone.

For a moment, I understood he knew where my mind went and what I was thinking of at the moment. Maybe my face had given it away. I'd never had great control over it. My emotions and thoughts seemed to always show, which landed me in trouble more times than I could count.

"All the time," I replied, almost like a whisper.

The sadness in his eyes told me he'd heard me. "Here, let me refill your wine," he said, grabbing my glass. He headed to the kitchen, and I heard him pour more into both glasses. I think it was safe to say that we would be drinking 'til we fell asleep. I, for once, was okay with that, even if I knew I would regret it come morning. My one hope for possibly being drunk before I slept was that it would keep the nightmares away.

Quinn returned and handed me my glass, filled almost to the rim. He was trying to do me in tonight, and he was doing the same to himself by the looks of it. I took a swig and felt the wine go down with a slight tingle. The same clouded numbness washed over me as I sat back and watched the fire.

The drinking continued as we talked about various things, including childhood stories that would probably have best been told by our parents. I ended up going on an entire rant about the South. Like, I spilled it all—all the things I hated, like the humidity, the racist-minded people, the damn racist system that made up our society as a whole. It would have been enough to scare any sane person, yet Quinn sat there and cheered me on, agreeing with me on everything, even asking how I survived when I mentioned the humidity. I promised I would take him so he could experience what hell actually felt like. All he had to do was go to Mississippi in August.

I probably should have stopped drinking at that point, but he refilled my glass again, and we kept going. We talked and talked, learning more about each other. Apparently, Quinn even had a sports scholarship for college. However, he neglected to tell me which sport. I might have to bring that back up once he is sober again. Through the fogginess of the alcohol, I sensed Quinn getting closer to me—or maybe I was getting closer to him. I wasn't very sure about it as the distance disappeared between us.

It was after maybe our fourth or fifth glass—I honestly lost count—that I felt him against me. It took me a minute to make sense of what I was feeling—Quinn's head was now on my shoulder, using me like a pillow. His wine glass was empty and on the table. I looked over at mine with only a tiny amount left of the red liquid. I quickly downed the rest, placing my glass next to his on the table, and for a moment, I just sat there. I had no desire to move; I was a little afraid I might not be able to walk straight. I also didn't want to wake him. He was already fast asleep. So after thinking it through, I decided it was best to stay.

I reached over, careful not to wake him as I grabbed the soft throw blanket from the couch and wrapped it around us, snuggling us in together. His heartbeat thudded against my shoulder as his chest moved up and down with his breathing. Honestly, it was calming. Something I would have guessed was awkward or weird was, in fact, comfortable to the point that I let sleep wash over me.

I laid my head upon his and slowly fell asleep together—well, more like I fell asleep. I already lost him, who knew when? As I drifted, part of me wondered what people would think. Caring about other people was something I tried to push out, but it was there. Then I asked myself—what is this? Why was I okay with this? Maybe it was the wine talking, but part of me wanted this—the closeness, the warmth, him. I wanted it every night. I felt safe for once. I felt accepted. What the hell is going on with you, Kodak?

Could this be?

I felt nothing.

Stop it! I need to stop trying to overthink this.

We were drunk and tired, and that was where I needed my mind to stay.

Sleep –

Warmth –

When my mind finally did slow, I focused on the rain still falling outside against the side of the house. I slowly began to feel my eyelids close just as my heartbeat began to sync with his, bringing me closer, until finally, I was numb to it all as I drifted off.

CHAPTER 9

When morning came, we were still on the floor with the blanket wrapped around us. I opened my eyes to find that we were no longer upright, but horizontal on the floor. Surprisingly, my head was on a pillow, and I was unsure how it got there. Quinn's head laid on my chest, and my arms wrapped around him. He was warm and still fast asleep as my head began to hurt. I knew I was going to regret the wine.

I didn't have the strength to move, so I laid with him as the sunrise erupted in the distance through the same windows that the water had crashed along last night. The sky was painted this pinkish-lavender color that was slowly getting brighter. A faint blue tint mixed in as the sun rose higher into the sky. I was lucky the sun rose on the other side of the house so it didn't blind me.

A few times, my eyelids closed for a second, only to open a couple of minutes later. The one thing I could think was that this felt – – right. Because I wasn't alone on an island here with him, and he didn't judge me—okay, maybe a little. Kidding. He was indeed a friend, a kind I didn't think I'd ever had.

"What time…?" Quinn mumbled as he shifted on me. I think it took him a second to find his bearings, as his eyes were barely open, staring out into the room. Then he finally looked up at me.

"Good morning," I said as he lifted his head, then laid it back down again, this time, facing me.

"We drank too much, didn't we?" he asked, still sounding dazed.

I nodded and smiled. We had, and there was no hiding it.

"You're a great pillow, by the way."

"I've been told that before," I joked.

"Liar. I'm positive I'm the first person who's done this," he kidded as he began to get up off the floor. To be fair, he wasn't; Becca was the first. She was the only person I had on my side while I was growing up, other than my family. It was probably pathetic. I found it hard to trust people, never knowing if they were being true or using me.

"We should get up," I said as I slowly moved out from under him. The tense muscles in my back stretched out once I got to my feet. Then, the full impact of all the wine—pain shot straight to my head. My first thought was water, as I became aware of the dryness in my throat, which was probably half the problem with my head.

I grabbed two glasses and filled them, placed one on the counter, and quickly drank the other. Refreshing, yet my head still hurt. It would probably take another hour or two before that stopped. Quinn took his glass and did the same.

"Hey, can you hand me my phone?" I asked, gesturing to where it lay on the end table.

Quinn nodded and handed it to me. I went through my emails— nothing in them—and ensured I hadn't missed any calls or texts. No notifications. I pulled up social media and scrolled through. It was better than reading the news. I stopped when I saw a post from my aunt.

I dropped the glass of water, splashing water all over my legs and floor.

"Kodak, what's wrong?" Quinn asked.

I couldn't speak as he came closer. I swallowed and tried again. "My mother is in the hospital," I replied once I ensured that I was reading it correctly. All the post said was that she was in the hospital and needed prayers.

I pulled up my contacts, quickly scrolled to my father's name, and clicked the call button.

No one answered.

"What do you need?" Quinn asked, but I ignored him as I tried to call my aunt, desperate for someone—anyone—to answer the phone and tell me what was going on.

Yet I was met with the same voice. That infernal robotic please leave your message after the tone. I finally got to the point where I was yelling in one of the voicemails I left for my father. Telling him to call me now, I kept saying it. It wasn't coherent by any means. Honestly not sure why. Frustrated at him for not answering his godforsaken phone. He promised to be better at answering his phone.

Quinn walked over and grabbed my phone and placed it on the counter. He then looked me in the eye.

"I need to go home," I said. My mother was in the hospital for some reason, and she could be dead for all I knew. Apparently, no one in my family answered their damn phones. I couldn't believe that no one had called or texted to keep me informed. I was in the dark, wondering what was going on.

It was noon in Memphis, so I called a family friend. She, however, was in the dark just as much as I was. She said she would find out and call me back as soon as possible. Until then, I needed to find a way to get to her—back home, back to Mississippi.

"Where do we need to fly into?" Quinn asked. This time, he caught my attention.

"What?" I asked, trying to make sure I'd understood him correctly. We?

"What airport is nearby?" he asked again. I noticed now that he was on his phone. Maybe he was looking at flights?

"Memphis," I said.

He went right back to his phone while I paced back in forth in the kitchen, waiting for my phone to ring, for something, some godforsaken news about my mother.

I was startled when he put his hand on my shoulder a few minutes later. "I got a flight for us; it flies out of Eugene at three. We need to go now to make it."

"Wait, you bought a flight?"

"Don't worry about it, come on," he said, almost pushing me out the door.

It took me thirty minutes to pack light—just the essentials. Luckily, I still had plenty of things at my parents if I needed to stay longer. Quinn had his bag with him already, and I looked at it as he placed it in his car.

"You're coming?" I asked, slightly confused.

"Yes, I bought two tickets. I'm not letting you do this alone," he replied as he got into his car.

I hesitated slightly; he was driving, but I was in no condition to thanks to the hangover and the state of my mind. My head was still swirling. I would just have to live with it again.

For Mom.

Quinn drove fast—faster than I was comfortable with. The power lines moved to the speed of the car, as I followed them with my eyes. I watched the lines move up and down and across the road. It kept my mind focused, so it didn't wander, or make me feel. For moments, they would disappear behind the trees, and those thoughts would creep back in—the ones that scared me. What if she was already gone?

On the way, he called Olivia and let her know what was happening. We would be out of town for a few days. He even called his mom, and I think he did it to hear her voice. I know I would have.

I finally got an update from the family friend. My mother had collapsed at home. Knowing this didn't make me feel any better. Nothing good came from that. She was still trying to get ahold of my dad, but he was with mom at the hospital. The one good thing, I now knew what hospital she was at. It was in Memphis—midtown, to be exact. It was never good when they transferred you up there.

I told myself I should be comforted that she hadn't been flown into The Med. The Med was reserved for patients who needed a miracle to survive. I had been flown into The Med after the wreck, but I didn't remember much of the trip. All I remembered was waking up to my parents at my bedside. They looked awful and had been crying after several sleepless nights. It was there that I learned I'd survived, but no one else had. Safe to say, it wasn't my fondest memory, if not my worst.

Then it hit me. I knew precisely where I was going, and I felt it. The anxiety of it came over me as I thought about home. I tried to focus on the good about going home—the rolling hills and soft sunsets, the endless songs sung by the bugs on summer evenings, the humid air that holds you together.

The drive was silent as I looked out into the landscape. I still had not heard a word from my dad. Maybe he, too, was still learning from the doctors what it could be. Perhaps he was doing the same pacing I had done back at the house, except in the waiting room, waiting on the news about his wife.

It took me until the outskirts of Eugene before I noticed Quinn had his hand on mine, rubbing the back of it softly. I let him continue, returning to the scenery as the land became flat. The connection brought me some peace. I hope he knew what he was getting himself into.

"Have you ever been to the South?" I asked as we pulled up to the airport.

"Um, no," he replied.

I smirked. Lord, help him. "Well, sorry it's under these circumstances," I said. I didn't think I could accurately describe what he was about to experience. It was better for him to see it himself, and then he might understand.

It didn't take us long to make it through security—a feat I was impressed with. Granted, the Eugene airport wasn't big. Once through, we got to our gate and sat down. Quinn went and grabbed us a bite to eat and something to drink. All I'd had was a glass of water, which was still shattered on the floor in the kitchen.

I didn't even notice what he brought back, but it tasted fine. I inhaled it, then drank the soda he had bought for me. No word from my mother, or anyone for that matter. I sat and looked out at the tarmac, waiting for our plane to arrive. I listened to the random announcements on a loop and the soothing jazz that played in the concourse.

Quinn watched me; he tried to look away when I noticed him, thinking I wouldn't see. I did, but I knew he was worried. I had seen it in his eyes all day. I honestly didn't understand what I did to make him care so much. However, I wasn't going to stop him. Maybe I also cared back.

"Hey," he whispered to me. "Your mother is going to be okay."

"I hope so," I replied. I really did, but it was hard to keep my hopes up since I didn't know what was happening. I was stuck thousands of miles away, still hours away from landing back home. "You didn't have to come with me," I said as I looked over at him.

"Yes, I did. You needed me, and you've already been there for me," he replied.

I tried to smile, but it wasn't successful. "Thanks for coming."

Soon, they called us to board. Our boarding group was first, and Quinn led the way as we walked across the jet bridge. This would be the last of the Oregon air I would breathe for at least a few days. The flight attendant ushered us to our seats in the first-class cabin of the plane.

"First class?" I asked as we took our seats.

"Yes, did you think I was going to book us in coach?" he replied as if I should have known better.

"Yes, that's exactly what I thought," I replied.

"Oh, just enjoy it," he joked, but I could tell he was serious.

I had never flown first class, so I wasn't sure what to expect. Honestly, I just wanted to close my eyes for a bit.

The flight was short, as it was just a connecting flight into Seattle. Then we had to wait a few hours before our next flight into Atlanta. A red eye would have us arriving in Memphis at like five in the morning.

We took a seat at a restaurant near the gate as we waited for the flight to Atlanta. Quinn tried to cheer me up, but I was still worried, still wondering what was happening back home.

Once we were on the plane, I slept most of the way. Even Quinn closed his eyes for a bit, and I only knew because when I had to use the bathroom, his head was on my shoulder. I carefully moved him, trying not to wake him. When I returned, his head again found my shoulder as I laid mine against his.

I tried to sleep again, but couldn't. I wrapped one of the blankets they gave us and wrapped it around me. I tried to close my eyes, letting the sound of the air rush past us as we flew through the night sky. The more I thought about it, the more I was glad he was with me. It would have been weird doing this alone. Who knew where my mind might go? Now, I could touch him next to me, and it calmed me, kept me grounded—well, as grounded as I could be on an airplane, 30,000 feet in the air.

I drifted a little towards the end of the flight until they came over and announced we were landing soon. I reached over and pulled the window shade open. The sky was still dark, but on the far horizon, light began to shine over a sleepy Atlanta. The streetlights were still lit, forming a grid of the city, a grand design that was visible this far up in the air. Quinn woke as we prepared for the landing.

"One more flight," I said as he rubbed the sleep from his eyes. It would be short—I had done this flight several times during travels, including on my trip out to Oregon.

We had an hour before our next flight, which would rush by like seconds while we tried to find our gate in Atlanta. Luckily, we got there right as they were boarding.

Our next stop was home, and hopefully, news about my mother.

CHAPTER 10

As the plane began to descend, the pressure changed in my ears. Quinn let me have the window seat this time, and the morning sky began to clear as the city of Memphis came into view. Tints of blue and pink were painted in the sky. Everything was so small. It put everything into perspective to see it from up here—how small we were, how little our lives were. I could feel the weight of it. I felt hopeless. There was nothing I could do. Just like I hadn't been able to do anything while I watched my friend die.

Quinn looked over at me. Part of me wanted to push him away still. No one close to me ever survived or stayed. His hand touched mine, and all I wanted to do was be with him. He made me feel more alive than I had in my entire life.

His hand was on mine until the moment the plane hit the tarmac, and the city of Memphis was in our view as we approached our gate. I was home.

We arrived at the newly renovated concourse. The modern finishing and openness were much better than the classic gray brick concourse, which had been a staple at the airport for many years. I noticed some new places to eat, a nice expansion from what used to be only a sandwich shop that was okay at its best.

"Welcome to the South," I said to Quinn, who looked around. I wondered what he was thinking. To be fair, this was just the airport.

"I don't know why, but this is not what I expected," he said.

"Did you think it would be more rundown?" I asked, confused.

"Kinda," he said, unsure. He was trying hard not to offend me, which he wasn't, by any means.

"To be fair, this is a city, and it's not quite Mississippi," I replied as we walked to baggage claim. Granted, the state line was almost a stone's throw away from the airport. Even then you would be in the suburbs surrounded by homes and businesses alike.

It took us almost twenty minutes for our bags to arrive. We headed out to the rental car Quinn had secured. The air was pleasantly warm for this time of year, and that concerned me. Warm weather during the winter meant only one thing: storms—and not the fun kind.

"I'm letting you drive, otherwise, we might get lost," he said when we got to the car, tossing the keys to me.

"Hope you're ready for this," I said, knowing how Memphis drivers were. They were awful.

We drove out from the airport and I headed out to the expressway. A few cars passed us as we merged onto the highway, heading into midtown Memphis. It took us about fifteen minutes for the downtown skyline to come into view.

"Is that a pyramid?" Quinn asked, pointing towards it.

"Yes, it's a Bass Pro Shop," I said.

Quinn looked confused as I exited. A few minutes later, I parked in the hospital parking garage. I still hadn't received any word from anyone about how my mother was doing.

We approached the receptionist at the front desk. I was a little out of breath as I began to speak. "I'm looking for my mother, Maria Palin," I said as she looked towards her computer.

"Okay, sir, and who is this with you? Only family is allowed at the moment," she said, giving me a somewhat confused look. It was full of attitude and snark, something I don't miss about here. Her face gave it all away.

I honestly didn't have time, and I spoke without thinking. "This is my fiancé. Is that a problem?" I replied. I was ruder than I intended to be, but in my defense, it didn't matter who he was. She was being disrespectful.

She looked back at me for a moment before shaking her head and giving us the room number. Mom was up on the seventh floor.

Once inside the elevator, Quinn looked at me. "So, when's the wedding?"

"Not now, Quinn," I said.

He smirked. I was going to make him pay for that later.

We arrived on the seventh floor. I walked down the hallway until I got to the correct room. I peeked my head in to find my mother alive and watching TV. Her long, curly, brown hair was messy, and her tan skin looked darker than usual against the white gown she was wearing.

"Kodak, what are you doing here?" she said with a smile.

"Do you think being on the opposite coast would stop me? What happened?"

"It wasn't a big deal," she said, giving me a "stop worrying" face. "Who is this?" Her eyes moved over to Quinn, who was standing near the door.

His eyes shot to me. He was slightly uncomfortable with my mother's stare.

"This is Quinn," I said, trying to move the conversation along. I paused, wondering how to properly introduce him. I couldn't understand why I had let him come, and why we had grown so close since the move, but I still didn't know. "He's a friend."

"It's wonderful to meet you, Quinn. However, I do wish it wasn't in a hospital."

"It's a pleasure, and I hope you get better," he replied, stepping into the room a bit more.

"Oh, they're just going to install a pacemaker. The doctor said it wasn't a big deal," my mother said.

I gave her a look. "A pacemaker is a big deal, Mom," I reminded her. "What happened?"

"I felt sick all day, I thought it was just a stomach bug, but then apparently I passed out a few times." She spoke. "Your father grabbed our neighbor; you know the nurse. My heart rate was super slow, so she said go to the hospital."

"You passed out, Mom that not normal."

Her hands went up into the air. I could practically see it go in one ear and out the other. I was not going to get through to her—many years of experience told me this.

"They said it will be a quick and easy surgery tomorrow, and I should be back to my students a week later."

Of course, her first thought was her students. It made it hard to be mad at her.

"You could have at least told me. I found out from my aunt Maria on social media." I laid the last part on pretty hard. I was upset about being left in the dark to wonder, to feel helpless, not knowing what was going on. That was what irritated me the most.

"I'm sorry. We didn't want to wake you and your father has not handled it well."

"You're allowed to wake me for this!" I said. "But I am glad you're going to be okay.

"Thank you, honey and I will next time. Now, why don't you go get some rest? You look exhausted, and so does Quinn." My mother was still being my mother, and she wasn't wrong—I was exhausted.

There better not be a next time!

"Wait, where's Dad?" I asked, realizing I hadn't seen him.

"Oh, he went to grab something to eat. He was here all night and will probably be here again tonight. I'll let him know you're in town and to call you. I assume he never answered his phone."

"I called about a million times," I said.

"His phone died," she clarified, pointing to his phone, which was plugged into the wall.

I let out a small laugh. Of course, he didn't answer. It had been sitting on the floor, charging, for who knew how long.

"Go sleep!"

I sighed and looked over at Quinn. He looked tired but was trying to hide it. "I'll see you later. We'll crash at the house," I replied.

"I would expect nothing less. Sweet dreams," she said with a smile.

Minus the hospital, I was happy to see her.

Quinn and I left and began our drive to my parents' house. It was about thirty minutes south of Memphis in the state of Mississippi. Even as we crossed the state line, part of me feared the fact that I was going home to a place that hated me. The other part of me didn't know how I felt about it. I couldn't help but think of the things I enjoyed and missed, yet the pain still lingered.

The familiar landscape of rolling hills and trees reminded me of everything as we drove. Even having only been gone for a few months, I felt it—the longing for home, the familiar sway of the trees, the roadway we traveled, the scent right after it rained, the way the sky looked at sunset.

Quinn was quietly looking out the window, and I wondered what he thought. Did he hate it? Feel weird about it?

"It's different, isn't it?" I said as he glanced over at me.

"That it is, but it seems peaceful and laid back." He returned his gaze to the landscape.

He wasn't wrong, it was laid back, and it could be peaceful at moments. There were good people here, ones who cared and tried to make it a better place. Others didn't care, and didn't try to make it a better place, and sadly, sometimes you could only really see them and all the things they did. It was hard to see or appreciate all the good that was happening because of the stupidity that overshadowed it.

We crossed a small river and its floodplain. The water filled in between the trees, but I had seen this area low to the point where grass grew at its bottom. At other times, I'd seen it just an inch or so from the highway. It was the back end of a large lake that had been created when they dammed the river. Now, it was a recreation area where people boated and fished. You could even camp if you wanted.

Finally, we came to the town of Bend, Mississippi. Home.

Bend was a small community. It had grown over the years due to its proximity to Memphis, yet it still kept its small-town culture and an extensive tree canopy that shaded it from the sun. Over the years, the town's historic district had added many restaurants, coffee shops, and boutiques, and even a few hotels had been built towards the expressway. We drove past the downtown area, seeing the green spire of the red-painted brick courthouse rise above the tree canopy. It was a unique courthouse; to me, it looked more like a church on the outside than the boxy, dome-topped courthouses you saw all over the state. However, it was still beautiful—the pride of the town.

The city was also home to a community college. It looked more like a four-year university than a community college with its neo-classical buildings, tree lines, courtyards, and streets. It was where my father worked, and thanks to the countless hours I'd spent there after school, it felt like a second home to me.

We came to the drive I knew so well, and soon, the white siding with a stone accent came into view. My childhood home sat among the trees and other houses on the road.

I was home.

"We're here," I said, pulling into the driveway.

"It's so quaint and cozy," Quinn said with a smile as he got out of the car.

We were greeted by a lingering humidity in the air. It wasn't as bad as it would be in the summer months, but I still felt it, along with the familiar scent of fresh-cut grass and a sweetness that I had never traced. The sky was still sunny, with clouds building in the distance. The street was quiet, nothing stirred. Not even a car passed. The only sounds were the tree branches moving in the wind.

Inside, the house hadn't changed much other than a few new things I saw here and there. I walked back to what had been my room. It was still the same as I'd left it, except now, my mother had placed a few things in here. I moved out, and my mother had turned it into a storage room. I should have known she'd do that, with all the years she'd complained about not having enough storage.

Placing our bags down, Quinn headed to take a shower, and I found the comfort of my bed. The familiar, firm yet plush feel began to take its hold. My eyes already felt heavy from the day's worth of travel, even if it wasn't noon yet. My head rested on the pillow as I felt the weight of everything coming down.

I laid there for a moment, taking the moment for myself. I hadn't had that, hadn't asked myself how I felt. My mind had been hyper-focused on one thing: my mother—who, at the moment, seemed fine, other than the scare. Granted, I was still furious that I had found out from my aunt on social media and then gotten no update until I showed up. Communication wasn't a strong skill in my family.

I heard the shower stop as sleep got closer. Yet the more I wanted it, the more my mind wouldn't let me. Thoughts just raced through me, keeping me awake.

The door opened, yet I stayed still. I wanted him to think I was asleep, so he wouldn't worry. I had seen the look on his face the entire time we traveled—the worry. I listened to the shuffle of his feet as he moved around the room. He was probably looking through his bag, finding what he needed. Soon, he would leave me alone and let me sleep.

Except, the bed shifted, the sheets moved, and he climbed in. Then Quinn was against me, his arms wrapped around me. He was warm as my body relaxed, conforming to his. The fresh scent of eucalyptus engulfed me. I felt his strength as he held me, his head against mine, lying next to me. My heartbeat synced to his. Time seemed to stand still as he held me, letting his body comfort me.

"It's okay. You can rest," he whispered into my ear.

Tears formed. Maybe it was okay for all the walls to come down, to just be my true, authentic self—the one that was adrift, the one who was always in pain and hiding it from the world.

I turned to face him, burying myself in him and letting out all the stress, worry, and anxiety that I had bottled up for the last day. I cried as he held me.

"You're safe with me," he said, holding me tighter.

Eventually, we fell into a deep sleep that I hadn't had for years.

I was safe.

CHAPTER 11

It was about four in the afternoon when we woke. We were still in the same position that we'd been in when we fell asleep together. As I moved slightly, Quinn's eyes slowly opened. He stared at me for a moment, his breathing was slow and steady. Part of me wanted to be closer, but I didn't know why. There wasn't much space between us as it was. Then again, I wanted him next to me every night.

"What's for dinner?" Quinn asked, still drowsy from the nap.

"Honestly, we'll probably need to eat out," I said, knowing my parents probably wouldn't have much food in the house since they'd been at the hospital. Plus, even though I'd grown up here, it felt weird to eat their food.

He shifted slightly, laying his head on me for a second before looking back at me. "Any good spots?" he asked.

"I might know one," I said, "but it will require you to get dressed."

"Fine," he grunted and moved away from me.

I got out of bed too and did the same. It took about ten minutes or so to be more presentable, getting rid of our bedhead from the nap. I looked over at the dresser and noticed the picture of my friends was still there. I remembered removing it at one point, and my mother must have put it back up. The photo was taken at the lake on a summer day. I missed that day. It was one of the only ones where I'd felt normal like I belonged somewhere.

"Hey, give me a minute before we go to dinner?" I asked Quinn, who was in the middle of putting his shoes on. He stopped in a rather weird position and almost lost his balance. "I need to do something."

"Do you want me to come with you?" he asked.

I looked over at the photo again. "No, I think I need to do this one alone," I replied.

I caught his eyes looking over at the photo, and I was sure he'd pieced two and two together. "Okay, I'll wait here for you," he said with a smile.

I headed out the door to the car, picking up the keys on my way. The air was still humid and warm, but the clouds were darker now. I hoped the rain would wait until after dinner. I looked up at the sky before getting into the car, giving it my warning. You better wait!

I drove to the local florist, just down the street from the house. It was a modest establishment, but the smell of flowers started before you even entered the door. The walls were ivy-covered, with only bits of the brick showing. Ashley recognized me as soon as I entered from the many times I would go before I left for Oregon.

"Hey, Kodak," she greeted me. "Your usual?"

"Yes ma'am," I replied.

She smiled and headed back to gather the flowers. She came back a few minutes later with a small assortment of flowers in individual, small clusters. Four in total.

"How is your mother?" she asked. "I take it that's why you're back."

"Doing better; it ended up being just a scare," I replied. I knew better than to give away too much information. If I said it to one person, the whole town would know, then my mother would never hear the end of it. She would, of course, make sure I never did because I told the town her business. Oh, the ways of a small town.

"That's good to hear. It was good to see you," she said.

I paid her before leaving the store.

Now, I headed to the gravesite. The cemetery was on the edge of town, covering several hills, and had been there since before the Civil War. There were grave markers from soldiers, both Union and Confederate. The saddest part of the cemetery was a small section on top of a hill covered by a large oak tree; there lay several children who died from yellow fever. The names were worn and weathered, making them hard to read these days.

I headed to the newer part of the cemetery, to the gravesites where my friends lay. They were spread out in different sections, some near family members, others in plots their families had bought next to where they would lay once they died.

I came to the first. She had been one of Becca's friends that I had grown close to over the years. Her name was Grace, and she had been a year younger than the rest of us. I laid one of the flower assortments next to the marker. I stayed to pay my respects before moving across a few rows to the next.

Jack had been one of those people who made everything fun and lit up any place with his energy. It was sad that the world had lost a soul such as his. I missed the jokes that would make me laugh. He never was afraid to attack anyone or anything. Sometimes, that would anger our classmates. However, he often spoke the honest truth, and I respected that. I placed my hand on the stone for a second before I headed to the next one.

Jordan's grave was next to a large sycamore tree, and the branches swayed in the warm breeze. I bent down as I laid the flowers on the ground. He had been one of my oldest friends and one of the only ones who knew the truth about me. The other was Becca.

"Kodak, is that you?" I heard a voice speak behind me. I turned to find a dark-skinned lady looking at me. Little lines of gray were starting to show on the sides of her long, dark hair. She was wearing a simple dress, probably coming straight from work. It took me a moment to recognize Jordan's mom.

"Mrs. Walker. How are you doing?" I said, getting up from the ground. She also had flowers in her hand.

"I'm doing good. It's good to see you," she said, giving me a hug. "How is your mother doing? I heard she was in the hospital. She's been in my prayers."

Mrs. Walker worked with my mother at the school. Those two were thick as thieves. She actually cared, not the fake caring we got around town.

"Doing better. They're saying she should be back home in two days," I said. "They're going to install a pacemaker, so she has to take it easy."

"You know very well she's not going to do that." She laughed. "But that doesn't mean I won't look after her for you."

I smiled. She was probably one of the only people other than me that could scold my mother into taking care of herself. She had been a good friend of the family for a long time, and one of the few genuinely nice people in town. Granted, they were also outcasts in town, being that they did not belong to the correct race or church.

"Thank you, I really appreciate it," I replied.

"Of course. I come at least once a week to see my son, and I guess it gives me comfort. I know he's still here with me," she said, patting her heart.

"I was in town, so I had to stop by and update the flowers," I replied.

She wrapped her arm around me as we stood there.

"It just felt right to come."

"Jordan would be proud of you—your writing, what you've done with your life. Also, a little jealous you're living in Oregon now. We all are."

I took a moment as I felt my emotions flare. Even after all this time, it still hurt—seeing them lying in the ground when they should still be here for me to talk to and spend time with. Instead, they were dead, and it was my fault.

"Thank you," I said. "I'll leave you to it. I have one more to see." I looked over a row to Becca's.

"Of course. It was good to see you. I'll make sure to check in on your mom for you." She gave me one last hug before I walked to the last gravestone.

Becca's grave was alone, with two empty plots on either side of her. This was where her parents would be buried when they died. I hadn't spoken with them in years. I hoped they were doing well and had found some peace. They'd retreated pretty far into themselves after she died.

Her flowers were different than the rest—favorites: white lilies and lavender. She would have found a way to haunt me if I put anything else at her grave. She loved their smell, and white and purple were her favorite colors. I sat them in a stone planter next to her name after I pulled out the dead flowers. They were the ones I had placed there before I left.

I sat down next to her gravestone. I guess it was my way of spending time with someone I loved. She had been my first and my best friend, one of the only girls that would talk to me. She had been honest, not fake like the others who would be nice to you, but say bad things behind your back. She had been taken way too soon.

I still held one secret about her, one thing I never told anyone. She hadn't died on impact like the others. She was still holding on as she crawled to where I was lying. We waited for help to arrive as the car burned next to us, its heat unbearable. She died in my arms. Her last words still whispered in my ear—Be yourself. You do belong.

I wiped away tears, remembering the moment. The pain, the heat, was still there. I would do almost anything for one more day to hold her, to be with her.

"I know you're proud, and I'm so sorry I couldn't save you," I said before I got up. "Love you, always."

On my walk back to the car, I waved to Mrs. Walker, who was sitting next to her son's grave. She waved back.

I knew what would come tonight, and I was prepared for it.

It was still overcast when I arrived back at the house. It seemed the storms were holding for now; either that, or I'd succeeded in intimidating them to not come 'til after dinner—a feat I would be proud to boast about.

Quinn sat at the counter, looking at his phone. He was dressed casually, and it took him a minute before he noticed I had returned. He looked at me and smiled.

"You ready?" I asked.

"Yes, I'm starving."

"Well, come on, then. Before it storms."

He got up and headed toward me. I grabbed an umbrella next to the door as we headed to the car.

"Why are you going to use one of those?" he asked.

"Because when it rains here, it pours," I replied.

He shook his head at me. He had no idea.

We drove to a local spot, a steakhouse. I always ate here when I went home. It was the one spot my family could agree on. It was located downtown, next to some shops that wouldn't be open much longer. It was also one of the only places in town that served alcohol. I remembered the days when possessing alcohol in the county was illegal. Yes, we had been backward here until they'd finally allowed it. We were a good Catholic family that didn't mind a good drink.

We were seated shortly after we arrived, as it wasn't busy. I had guessed as much since the storms were heading in. Everyone would probably be ordering their food to go so they could take it home. It was perfect—I wouldn't see anyone knew me.

The restaurant had old beams that crossed the ceiling and high walls. We were seated by the window, with a view of the town hall across the street. The smell made my stomach grumble. I could already taste the food before the waitress came over and took our order. Quinn got a glass of an Oregon wine. I chose a beer, which was rare for me, but it was my favorite craft brew from Memphis, and I couldn't resist.

"You must have had perfect grades, definitely in English," Quinn said after taking a sip of his wine.

"Why would you say that?" I asked.

"Because you seem like you were a great student," he said. "Look at your writing for a prime example

I laughed. I couldn't help it.

Quinn gave me a puzzled look.

"I was a great 'C' student in high school," I replied. "For the record, my worst grades were always in English."

"Are you serious?"

"I struggled in school for the longest time, some of it, not my doing." I lowered my voice at the last part. "I did much better once I got to college."

"Why would it not be your fault?" he asked, sensing something.

I paused for a second to think how I could explain it. "I wasn't always given the same sort of⋯ instruction, I guess, as the other kids." I kept my voice low.

His face darkened, probably putting it together. "Because you weren't white enough," he whispered.

I nodded.

"That's sick."

"Welcome to the South," I said. "I would spend hours with my mom and her friend trying to improve my grade in English."

"Was some of it the language barrier?"

"Actually, I don't speak Spanish. My mother didn't teach me," I said. "She feared it would be used against me." She had been right, of course. It would have made it worse if she had. Even if now she bugged me to learn it, saying it was something we needed in the world. Granted, I had taken a few classes in college, mainly because of my degree requirements, so I at least could navigate the language. By no means was I fluent or could hold a conversation.

"Wow, I'm sorry," Quinn said as he took another sip.

I didn't have the heart to tell him everything. I had been excluded from things because only certain kids could do those things—at least, that's what I was told. I hated part of myself because it was what everyone hated. I'd thrown my own culture out the window so I could fit in and not be despised. None of it mattered to them. I was still the mixed, half-Hispanic boy who didn't belong to the Mexicans or the white kids.

"I published the piece you read and studied writing in college because someone told me I could never be a writer since I was mixed," I told him.

He smiled. "You showed them, didn't you?"

I shook my head and smiled. "It's just one short story. It's not like I won an award for it."

"It was critically acclaimed," he said, not letting me get off easy.

Thankfully, our food arrived, and our attention turned to it. It was just like I remembered it: every bite savory, and the loaded baked potato melted in my mouth. I wished I could have this food shipped to me. I would pay a fortune if I had to.

Quinn was halfway done with his before he finally said anything. "This is incredible. They can definitely cook, I'll give them that."

"Very true. It's one of few things they do well," I said. "I'll have to ensure you get some Memphis barbecue before we leave." I watched the joy explode on Quinn's face.

We spent most of the meal silently stuffing our faces with the food. I switched to water, but Quinn ordered another glass of wine. With the steak and potato he'd had, he wouldn't feel it. I knew I was driving, even if it was just a mile, so water was a better bet.

Outside, it was still cloudy and getting dark. I was honestly surprised the rain had waited this long, but I knew it would soon find us. The wind had picked up quite a bit—a sign it was near.

When our waitress came over, Quinn paid. He didn't have to keep paying for everything, but I didn't say anything. I let him have it. I think that was the only way he believed he could help. He had joined me on this trip to find ways to help. He cared.

After he paid, we sat there while he finished his glass. The conversation continued to be mostly questions about my life in Bend. I told him all the good memories and a little of the bad. I don't want to get too deep, mainly surface-level stuff, as that got into the trauma—some of which I still hadn't recovered from.

Once the last drop of wine left his glass, we got up from the table. The air outside was thick with moisture as the wind brushed us in waves. The sky grew a dark, menacing gray with the low rumble of thunder in the distance. The tug in my abdomen intensified, bracing for what would come later. Mother Nature was not happy tonight.

"Look who it is," said a voice I wished I could forget. The thick, country accent gave it away. I turned to find Henry Watson standing tall, walking towards us. His fair skin looked dull, those green eyes staring at me, full of hate.

"Hello, Henry," I said, rather rudely. Nothing good could come from him.

"Did you go see the people you killed?" He smirked as the blood rushed to my face. For years, everyone had blamed me for the car crash, like I was just the easy person to pin it on. Thankfully, the police knew it was an accident, but that didn't stop people in the town from making my life more a living hell than they already had.

"What the hell, man?" Quinn said, stepping in front of me.

"Quinn, don't. Let's just leave," I said, pulling at him. There was no point in arguing with Henry. The truth didn't matter to him.

"Surprised you would be with little mixed Kodak." Henry laughed. I'd honestly thought we would grow past the little pokes.

"Just shut up, Henry," I said, mainly because I was trying to shrug the entire conversation off. No point in dwelling on it. The hard part was pulling Quinn away. His face was bloodshot red as he began to inch toward Henry, fist balled and ready.

"Quinn, come on."

"Better listen to the little colored boy."

I shut my eyes at the last part, mainly because of the memories it brought back. They had long called me that, even though my skin was a light olive, even though they knew my father was white. That little bit of brown was enough for them.

"That boy is better than the man than you think you are. So go fuck yourself," Quinn spat.

Henry laughed it off and headed inside the steakhouse.

I began to walk to the car, trying to forget the conversation even happened. But it had already built inside me, waiting to come out.

I got into the car as Quinn followed. Once inside, we began to drive toward the house.

"You shouldn't have said anything," I said.

Quinn looked over at me, confused. "What? Why not? He was being a racist jerk."

"Because it's not worth it. They're all racist." My voice elevated a little. "I don't need protection."

Quinn looked at me as we pulled into the driveway, and he seemed annoyed by the last part.

Little rain droplets began to fall, hitting the windshield as I got out of the car. I ran towards the door as the rain got heavier by the second. Thunder rumbled across the sky as the storm blew in.

Quinn grabbed my shoulder just inside the doorway. "What's going on with you?" Quinn asked.

"What do you want? A thank you? A thank you for dealing with Henry, the racist bitch?" I yelled as my anger flared.

"No, but you don't have to be angry about it."

"That's not what I'm angry about."

"Then what is it?" This time, he was yelling as the rain pelted against the side of the house. It seemed that our moods matched Mother Nature's. "Because I could buy this entire town that that little prick thinks he owns and then flip it for a profit."

I looked at him, dumbfounded. That was his answer to all of this? To just throw money at it? Like he'd been doing this entire trip— throwing money everywhere, hoping it solved the problem.

"We get the point, Quinn; you're rich. You're white and rich and have a perfect life, where no one hates you!" I screamed at him, my face hot as my anger flared more, coming out in full force for the world to witness.

Quinn's face said an entirely different thing. Now he was mad— not at Henry, but at me, because of what I said. Well, sorry, it was the truth. "That was low, Kodak. All I'm trying to do is help," he said, trying to keep his voice low.

"Then don't," I yelled back at him as I began to walk away.

"No, you don't get to that. All I'm trying to do is help, be here for you, and care for—" He paused for a second. "Why are you so upset about this?"

"You want to know why I am so angry right now?" I asked. "Well, I'm angry that no matter what the hell I do, how much progress I make, how much I give, that I'm never enough for any of them!" I screamed. "To them, I'm a colored boy, just like he said, nothing more. I'm less than a life, and it doesn't matter that half of my being is the same as them. Because they can't recognize that I'm the same!" My eyes began to water. "I'm the same human they are, but no, I'm different; I'm other. I'm the person they blame for killing my friends because that's how the world works. That's how this whole damn white world works. We are the problems, not them. So yes, I'm angry because I have to live with this rage that boils inside me. After all, I don't belong anywhere. I'm not good enough for the white people or for the Hispanics. I'm better off dead!"

I was crying now, while he just stared at me silently, his face solemn, unable to process. He'd finally seen the other side of me— the one that had no control, the angry side. I didn't think he fully grasped how I was one, yet torn in two, unable to mend my parts no matter how hard I tried. They were at war, with no peace in sight.

Our phones rang, the chilling alarm piercing the tense air. I already knew. Years of conditioning had taught me so.

"Come on," I said, this time more calmly, trying to keep my heart rate down. "We need to get in the closet."

"What?" he said, looking at his phone. He seemed still in shock, unable to process what had happened.

The piercing wail of the siren sliced through the air, sending waves of fear down our spines. That's when Quinn began to panic, his hand shaking. It probably didn't help that I had yelled at him, but I couldn't leave him out here if there was one coming.

"Have you never been in a tornado warning before?" I asked. The wind howled and the light began to flicker.

"No. What the hell is this?" he asked as I pushed him inside the interior walk-in closet. It was a safe room built from concrete that my parents had installed years ago for situations like this. I closed the door as the sirens still sounded, then dropped onto the floor next to Quinn.

"I'm sorry I took it out of you," I said.

"It's okay; you have a right to be angry," he said. "All I want to do is be here for you."

"I know; I'm sorry," I said, as a loud crash of thunder shook the house.

Quinn jumped straight into me. "This place is hell," he said, and surprisingly, all I did was laugh. Mainly because he wasn't entirely wrong. He was wrapped around me as we held each other, bracing for it.

"It's going to be okay," I said calmly, my hand running through his hair.

He looked up at me. "For the record, you belong with me."

I stared at him. I felt it again.—I wanted to be closer to him, even with us arm-in-arm. I wanted to be closer.

"Quinn – – " I began, but I was cut off as the sirens stopped. We sat there in silence, waiting for the bomb to drop. I pulled out my phone to look at the radar and was relieved to see that the storm had passed. It was safe to head back into the rest of the house.

"Is it over?" he asked as we walked out of the closet and into the kitchen.

I looked outside at the light rain falling. It was dark now, the streetlamps illuminating the wet street outside. I opened the door and felt the cool breeze flow in. We were on the other side of this system now.

"Yeah, it is," I said. "It should just be raining now."

I began to walk toward my room, eyes heavy and exhausted from tonight already.

"Wait," Quinn said, grabbing my hand.

I turned to him, confused.

"I need to say this, and I know I could ruin everything right now," Quinn said.

"What are you talking about?" I said. "I'm the one that just bit your head off."

"I care for you, Kodak. That's why I came and have tried to help in all the ways I can. Because I care. I⋯ I know I might never be enough or what you want, but I have to say it because I want you to know there are people out there who believe it doesn't matter what you are. You're enough for them. You're enough for me."

I stared at him, my jaw open. This guy had been nothing but friendly to me. He'd even pulled me out of a freezing river and fought to keep me warm. He'd shown me a side of himself only a few people knew. He'd shown me his true self.

I pushed everything else from my brain as I walked up to him and kissed him, pulling him into me. His lips were soft and gentle as his arms wrapped around me. For a moment, I let the world melt away around us. Only we mattered.

As quick as it began, it ended, and we broke apart.

His eyes locked onto mine as he processed what had happened. "Did you just—"

"Kiss you?" I interrupted. "Yes."

"Oh, okay. I'm confused but happy. But also confused."

"I like you, you idiot. What is there to be confused about?" I said, unable to believe he still couldn't grasp it.

"You did just yell at me," he said with a grin.

I just shook my head at him, then grabbed his hand and pulled him with me. "Come on, let's go to bed. We need to head to the hospital early tomorrow."

Once we were in my room, I kissed him again as I pulled his shirt off, and he did the same to me. I let him pull me close as we cuddled together in the blankets, falling asleep to the gentle rain and low rumbles of thunder in the distance.

CHAPTER 12

When morning came, we hurried to get ready, leaving the house before dawn broke. My father texted me the time of Mom's surgery, which was to be right at eight. We needed to get there a few minutes early to see her before she went under.

Anytime I found myself out this early, I always noticed how calm and quiet everything was as the world slept or was just beginning to wake. On our short drive into the city, the sun began to rise, lighting up the eastern sky, while the west stayed locked in night. The highway was the dividing line between the old day and the new day that was starting.

Quinn closed his eyes on the way up, leaving me to drive alone in silence, other than the sound of the car and road. With it being early, traffic wasn't bad yet, and I was able to make it into the city with ease. Once we arrived at the hospital, I woke Quinn, who mumbled at first before finally waking as I parked the car.

"We're here. Time to get up." I said softly.

"I hate mornings," he replied, rubbing the sleep from his eyes.

"I know you do."

Inside, my father was sitting on the chair next to my mother's bed. My mother was being her usual self.

"Make sure the kids eat, and text the family when I go in and when I come out. Otherwise, my sister will worry and no one will hear the end of it," she said.

"I know. It'll all be fine," my father replied.

"Oh, and let Mrs. Walker know that the worksheets are on my desk. She should know which one to give to the sub." She continued giving him a list of things to do, telling him to make sure they let her go home afterward. Most of the things she told him were information to give to the school so that her students would still be receiving the best education possible while she was away.

"Kodak," my father said, turning his attention away from my mother for a second.

"Hi, Dad," I replied as he pulled me into a hug. Dad was going gray, his glasses giving him a studious look that fit a college instructor. The old BMW he drove fit the part too. I hated that thing, but he loved it. His fair skin looked tan for once. He must have been doing yard work while the weather was unseasonably warm.

"Please tell your mother to relax a little," he joked.

My mother glared at the comment.

"I know better than that," I laughed.

"See? He knows," my mother cut in.

"You must be Quinn," my father said as he reached out to shake his hand. My mother must have told him that I had someone with me, no doubt speculating as they always did. It was with love, I knew, but still.

"Nice to meet you, Mr. Palin."

"No need for formality. Just call me Derick."

Quinn smiled as we moved towards my mother.

"Do you mind coming with me to grab some drinks while we wait?" my father asked him.

"Sure thing," Quinn said, and then they left me with my mother.

"He's lovely, mejio," my mother said as I sat down next to her. I'd known she was going to go there, but she was also right.

"Mom," I said, giving her a look.

"You haven't opened yourself up to anyone since Becca and your friends died. You deserve to be happy." My mother grabbed my hand, holding it tight.

I looked away. I knew I had put up a wall for people since then, mainly because I didn't trust anyone. Nor did I feel like I could love like that again. Maybe that was the pain talking, the grief that still washed over me at times, never fully going away.

"Is it really worth it?" I asked, knowing that I would only be out there until the end of my fellowship.

"It's always worth it. I want you to be happy. I want to see your smile back."

"Thanks," I said. "Oh, I have Mrs. Walker looking after you to make sure you take it easy."

My mother smiled at the mention of her friend. She also knew I was very serious. "You must have seen her at the gravesite."

"I did. It was good to see her. I had to replace the flowers on the graves."

"Still caring for them, even after death. That's my Kodak. I'll have to call her when this is over," she said. "You and Jordan were inseparable as kids, not to mention how much trouble you two could get into."

"Yes, and it was you that always caught us."

"Of course, you two weren't as sneaky as you thought," she laughed. "Then when Becca joined, it was a little power group that kept us busy."

"I miss them," I said.

"I know, but they're still here." She placed her hand on my heart. The nurse came in and began to prep her.

Now the waiting began.

We waited what seemed like days for the doctors to come out. My dad held a Coke in his hand, while Quinn and I sipped on coffee. The hospital moved around us, like gears working in complete harmony, while we just sat still, frozen to the rest of the world. I kept trying to think of other things so I wouldn't focus on how nervous I was. I hated waiting.

A person in a white coat approached, her face emotionless. At first, I thought they were just passing by until she came up to us. She let us know how the surgery went, and that it was successful. I felt like I could breathe again. She did, however, mention that my mother should stay another night just to be safe. She was not going to be happy about that.

Quinn grabbed my hand and nodded. He knew this made me feel better, knowing that she was indeed going to be okay. I wish I could have believed her when she told me that, but I knew my mother would put on a good face, even if it was bad.

"She's back in her room if you'd like to see her," the doctor said.

My father thanked her before looking at us. "Come on, you better see her before you two leave," he said, knowing soon we would make our journey back across the country.

In her room, my mother was awake and rather coherent, even if she was on all kinds of meds. She smiled as we all entered. "See? I told you. All fine!" she exclaimed.

"You still have to stay overnight," my father replied.

My mother grunted her displeasure. "I would like to appeal that."

"No, you are going to rest and leave tomorrow," I ordered.

She glared at me, but eventually conceded. "Fine," she said.

We stayed with her for most of the morning, laughing, talking, and catching up. Quinn even got a few embarrassing stories about me. My dad went and grabbed us lunch, then brought it back to the hospital. Thankfully, my mother was able to eat now, so she scarfed her food down as the rest of us ate at our usual pace. It also kept her quiet from complaining about the situation.

"You two should get going. You've been here all morning," my mother said.

"Mom, our flight doesn't leave until tomorrow morning."

"All the more reason to take your friend around the city," she replied.

"I mean, I haven't seen much of Memphis," Quinn interjected.

I looked over at him and smiled. "Okay, fine. Get better. We should have time to see you one more time before we go."

"Go have fun," she ordered.

I grabbed Quinn's hand and left the hospital, heading back out into the city.

I took Quinn to see the highlights—that was all we really had time for—including Staks pancake house, Crosstown Concourse—he really liked that one—a stroll through Overton Park, and lunch at an Irish pub in Cooper-Young. Then, of course, I took him down Beale Street and to the Peabody Hotel. For some reason, he was impressed by the ducks. I just laughed. I think he secretly wanted to put an Oregon jersey on one of them. I couldn't bear to think about the poor thing wearing a bright green and yellow shirt with a giant O on it.

Later in the afternoon, I finally escorted him away from the bustle of Beale Street and walked him down to the river. The Mississippi was a mighty one, with the M-shaped bridge in the distance. As the sun was about to set, it soon would be transformed by lights that had been installed a few years ago. We were near the landing, where the riverboats would dock, letting off their passengers. There was the port which was used by the river boats. Some new replicas of the old steam-powered ones that once roamed these waters.

"This is so neat," Quinn said, taking note of how one of the buildings had a grass roof and slope that made it easy to walk above it to the other side.

"I find you easy to impress," I said, finding a bench to sit to down on.

Quinn joined me, sitting close as we watched the sun begin to set. "No, I just love to travel. I've learned to just let life take me where it wants me to go," he replied. "It's how we learn to let go, learn to not expect what's next."

"Didn't realize you'd go all philosopher on me. We can add that to your masterful resume," I replied. I noticed how he was just staring at the river as it flowed past us, and I spoke without even thinking. "You should tell him. Your father, I mean, about the artwork."

Quinn turned to me. I thought he would rip my head off at the mention of it. Instead, his gaze was soft, almost like he was thinking the same thing. His eyes turned to the ground and I watched patiently for his next words as his eyes walked along the groves of the pavers under us. "What would I even say?" he asked. "I don't want him to force me to stop."

"He can't make you stop. Only you can make that decision, no one else." I grabbed his hand. "Besides, you're basically a prodigy. If he's upset with that, then I don't know what will please him."

"Me, closing a real estate deal below the asking price then selling it for a hefty profit five years down the road. He might take a skyscraper development as a highlight," Quinn shot back rather playfully.

I just shook my head, some of that going straight over my head. I didn't even know how I would buy a house, let alone rent an apartment, once this fellowship was done. "If you don't mind me asking, what do you want? What do you want your life to look like?" I asked. Even though I felt like I was lost, not really belonging anywhere, I always knew what I wanted, or at least what I used to want to do. I wanted to write, to tell stories. I didn't even know what Quinn looked forward to. I felt as if he was just there, going where life took him as he worked in secret, within the bounds of his family business.

"I don't know," he replied as he again looked to the river. The lights of the bridge were beginning to come on, changing colors in a synchronized pattern.

I laid my head against him as we sat there, watching the colors change and the lights of the city moved around us. A slight chill began to creep across our skin, bringing us closer together to stay warm.

"Kodak, when we get back, I want to take you somewhere," he said.

"Where?"

"It's a surprise."

I looked at him in shock and, to be honest, a little fear. Mainly because I had no idea where he would even want to take me.

"Trust me, you'll like it."

"Okay, just don't murder me, please."

He laughed at that. "Why would I murder you? If I wanted to do that, I would have let you drown in the river."

I just looked over to him with a rather unsatisfied look. He was never going to let me live that down. "We should get going. Long day tomorrow."

Night had taken hold of the city. The buildings of the Memphis skyline lit up the sky, and the low, warm glow from the streetlamps covered the city in an orange glow. The Bass Pro pyramid had turned on a greenish glow that mirrored the water of the Mississippi.

We walked a few blocks up the bluff to the parking garage where the car was parked. As we climbed into the car, a trolly passed, ringing its bell.

"Thanks for taking me around today," he said as we pulled out of the garage and back onto the street.

"You're welcome. Sorry, it was more of a crash course in Memphis."

"You'll just have to show me more next time we're out," he replied.

The drive itself was easy. Quinn kept asking me questions about the city, then he told me how much he wanted to show me Portland and Seattle, mentioning a bookstore that caught my fancy. Apparently, it was an entire city block and four stories, all full of books. That was something I could be on board with. I wondered why he hadn't taken me there in the first place. It was practically a requirement that one should always take the writer to a bookstore.

When we arrived back, Bend was quiet and still, as it always was at night. The town basically died once the sun went down and everyone went back into their homes. It was one my favorite times, because no one was out to say anything to me. I could move through town undetected.

The house was dark as we entered. Once the lights were on, I headed to the bathroom and when I returned, I noticed Quinn looking at some of the things my mother had around the house. She had collected many different art pieces from Hispanic artists, not to mention her plethora of aloe vera plants.

"Your culture had always fascinated me—how family-oriented it is, how full of life everyone seems," he said.

All I felt was shame. "I wouldn't know." I kept my voice low, part of me hoping he wouldn't hear.

He turned to look at me, and his eyes said it all. "Why?" he asked.

I sat down on the couch, trying to think of a way to make it sound less shameful, less all my fault, less horrible. "Because I ran from it. I tried to fit in, thinking that would make people accept me. I completely disowned half of myself for the longest time. I hated that part of me. It was the thing that people couldn't understand, the part they hated. So I hid from it. I wouldn't even eat the food if I was out in public. I never learned some of the customs that people expected me to know. I tried to be fully white. But now, I hate that I didn't love what's supposed to be my culture too."

"Kodak—" he began, shaking his head.

I didn't want to talk about it. "Can we just go to bed?" I asked.

"Promise me something," Quinn said. "Don't run or hide away from who you are, all of you."

Part of me wanted to agree, but I couldn't really promise him that. When I was here, in this place, all I wanted to do was hide.

"Okay," I said, just so I could get him to move past this and get to bed. My eyes were already feeling heavy from the long day.

He shook his head as we headed to the bedroom. Once again, I let him hold me as we fell asleep, resting up for our travels away from this place. Part of me couldn't wait to leave Mississippi behind—I didn't like the version of myself when I was here—but the other part of me didn't want to leave home.

CHAPTER 13

I said goodbye to my mother on our way to the airport. The flight was early, but luckily, I was able to see her leave the hospital, which made me feel better that I was leaving her at least at home. Now, I just needed her to take it easy and go to her appointments, like the doctors had requested. As the plane ascended into the sky, I felt a tug in my chest. The city disappeared beneath the clouds, the window filling with white before moving above the cloud bank, which stretched endlessly out beneath us. I think I knew that I was truly saying goodbye to the place I had called home for many years, and part of me mourned. The first time I was running, now it will only ever be a place to visit. Oregon is home now.

This time, the flights were so much easier, with only one stop in Salt Lake City. On our approach, the mountains were glaciered with ice, poking up from the earth. Once we landed, Quinn, like always, found a place to get us something to eat. I was far more relaxed this time, and we chatted during our lunch, unlike the silence that had been between us on the way over. Thinking on it, it was strange how we had become so close. We were from two different worlds, yet I felt like I had known him all my life. Honestly, I couldn't really picture my life without him.

It was just a short time before we were back in the air, heading for Oregon. This was the same flight I had taken all those months before when I moved. It was a quick flight of an hour and a half or so. Soon, as we made our way down from the sky to the Willamette Valley, wet and green came into view. The Cascades looked down from their perch as we made our way into Eugene. We were home—at least, almost.

It was now just an hour or so drive before we would arrive in Alnwick. I let Quinn drive, since it was his car. It felt weird, and I still jumped at almost every bump, but I had started to get used to not being in control of the car. He was also a good driver, for the most part. There were a few turns he took rather quickly on our drive through the coastal range, but I kept my comments to myself and just let him drive as I enjoyed the view. I still wondered what place he wanted to take me. While we ate in Salt Lake City, he mentioned that it would be later this weekend and that Olivia might join.

On the side of the road, we passed several little waterfalls as water cascaded down the sharp cliffs that bordered the road from the rain earlier in the day. I don't think there is really any place like here anywhere else. Coming back from the south it was so jarring, the drastic change of scenery, each had beauty in its own way.

We rounded the last few curves and began our descent to the coast and the town of Alnwick. Just past it was the vast Pacific, its blue tint shining in the sky, spread out to the horizon. It was a clear day, yet still a little cold. Apparently, we would have our first warm weekend of spring. Strange to think we were almost done with the cold. I was ready for a summer that didn't feel like a sauna.

Then there it was, the town nestled into the mountains, the quiet that I had come to enjoy. With the tall Douglas firs towering above us, I felt like I could breathe once again. For some strange reason, I was safe here.

Quinn drove us first to the bookstore, where we were greeted by Olivia with rather big embraces. The bookstore was busy with customers, and for a moment, Olivia spoke with Quinn while I perused a shelf of new books. Once they were done, he took me back to my house. I sat in the car as we drove, wondering what they had talked about. Maybe it was about this place he was planning on taking me. Maybe he had told her about the one thing we hadn't spoken about the kiss. Frankly, I didn't even know what I wanted to say.

When we pulled into the driveway, Quinn hesitated. "Hey, I have a few things to do, but I'll pick you up next week for that trip."

"Okay, what's with all the cloak and dagger?"

"Just adding suspense."

I couldn't help but smile. "Maybe you should be the writer then, and I the painter."

Quinn laughed as I got out of the car and walked back into the house, welcomed by the familiar scent of it.

About a week later, Quinn came to my house and picked me up. We had talked and had lunch a few times between then. He'd had some things to handle business-wise—at least, that's what he'd told me. I assumed it had to do with his paintings. Maybe he was securing another gallery or something. On Friday, he sent me a list of things to pack. It was detailed—like hiking boots, the number of sweaters and shirts to bring. He even mentioned bringing one formal outfit and swimwear. This made me really want to know where we were going, and also a bit confused.

The first thing I noticed was that he was driving. His car was already packed from the looks of it. I had gotten better about him driving, but it was still weird, still nerve-wracking to sit there with no control.

"You ready?"

"Where is it that we're going again?" I asked, trying to see if he would slip up.

Of course, he just gave me a look that said nice try. "As I've told you before, it's a surprise," Quinn replied as he picked up my bag and fit it in with the others that were crammed in his car. Why was he bringing so much stuff?

"You know I hate surprises, right?" I poked at him as he began to drive off.

He set off out of town in a direction that I hadn't been before, up the coast of Oregon. As we drove, I watched the waves of the ocean crash against the shore. Every so often, the road would curl back into the tall trees and mountains, embracing us as we wound through the curves of the road. Everything seemed so alive. I felt it in my veins. It all moved around us, giving me a rush that warmed me, and for the life of me, I couldn't even truly explain it, other than Oregon knew how to surprise me.

"We have to stop first in Portland," he replied.

"What are we going to do in Portland?" I asked, looking over at him. None of the trip was making sense to me—mainly because he still hadn't told me a damn thing about it.

"Remember that bookstore you wanted to see?" He glanced over at me while still keeping his eyes on the road as we rounded the curves.

"Wait, really? We're going to Powell's?" I asked, excited.

"Yes, yes, now calm down. It's just a bookstore," he joked, laughing at me. He really didn't understand how excited I was, because I could already picture myself dragging him in every direction in this place—not to mention probably buying too many books that I didn't have room for at home.

A smile was what I got from him, and I took it, not caring if I embarrassed myself with how excited I was. I didn't care. Plus, it was Quinn. He knew what he'd signed up for when he decided this part of our trip.

We cleared the mountains and the land flattened as we came into the valley. The Cascades bordered the other side as we found our way to the highway and made our way past Salem and onto Portland. We rounded the curves of the highway, and soon, Mt. Hood loomed large over the sprawling city, its peak still white with snow. To the north, Mt. St. Helens showed her broken top, like an upside-down funnel that had been cut off at the top. I wondered what it was like here when she blew, how terrifying it must have been to see the column of ash rise into the sky.

My face pressed against the glass of the window as I looked out into the city. It was different than Memphis, where we had a total of two bridges that crossed the river. Here, there were several, and the city still spread beyond it and up into the hills.

The sad part, even with how beautiful it was, there were the tents underneath bridges and hard-to-find places. People just wandered around their clutter, the homes sitting in plain sight. I honestly didn't know how they did it—survived in conditions like this. Frankly, I didn't think I could.

Once we parked, we walked a block or so to the store. The buildings rose all around us as we waited for the signal to turn, allowing us to cross the street.

"Here it is," Quinn said as we walked up to the front door. "The largest independent bookstore in the country, all four floors of it.

Inside, it was bustling with activity. The store went in two directions, one leading to a room with literature, and the other to a pink room with children's and young adult books. I beelined right for the literature room.

I pulled books from the shelves, looked at them, and then moved down through the narrow line of bookshelves. They were tall, completely enclosing me in the smell of paper. I had three books in my hands when Quinn found me.

His hand touched my shoulder as he came up behind me. "Hey."

"What are those?" I asked, pointing to the books he held in his hand.

"I read too, thank you." He laughed, then showed them to me. There was a Stephen King novel, which surprised me, along with a few other fiction titles. I think I spied an Agatha Christie in his hands too.

"I take it you're ready to get going?" I said, noticing that he was hovering a bit.

"We do have a drive still," he replied.

We headed to the front desk to check out, then walked back to the car before getting back onto the road. I tried to see which direction we were going but was turned around until I noticed we were crossing the Columbia River and passing a Welcome to Washington sign. I looked over at him to see if I could once again get a hint. Quinn just shook his head.

We drove on north, passing by small towns. The trees grew thicker and greener.

"So it's in Washington?" I poked at him.

"You don't give up, do you?" Quinn replied with a smile.

"Nope."

Quinn laughed as he kept his eyes on the road while we rounded the curves on the highway. We passed over a few bridges, huge steel trusses covering them, giving them character as they blended with the landscape.

We traveled north to Olympia, then veered off onto a smaller highway. It curved as the Olympic Mountains came into view. They stood tall, their peaks covered in snow in perfect lines. The road began to turn towards the shore as we traveled past a section of the Puget Sound, water to one side and the tall mountains on the other. It took me a second to realize where we could be going. There was only one thing that I could think of—the Olympic Mountains.

"Wait, are you taking me to Olympic National Park?" I asked.

His face began to turn red, suggesting I'd nailed my guess. "To a degree yes," he said. "My family has a cabin up here, and I wanted to spend some alone time with you." He was seriously blushing, like he was scared that he may have gone too far in this endeavor.

I smiled to reassure him that my shock was, in fact, a good thing. "I think it's sweet," I replied. "Plus, I've really wanted to go here for a while."

"Good!"

The sky began to darken as we passed bays and through thick forest. On the northern side, we passed a small town with a casino outpost, the tall tribal totem poles illuminated with light. It took us maybe an hour or so more before we came into Port Angeles, a small town on the border of the national park and the Strait of Juan de Fuca to the north. A dense fog rolled in as we made our way into town.

I couldn't tell where we really were, but the cabin was by no means small. It was large, well-lit, and modern—something I should have expected since it was part of the Condors' real estate holdings.

"Here it is," Quinn said as we walked inside. The wooden beams smelled of pine and the large windows on the far side had a view, I just couldn't see anything in the night. "You're going to love the view." Quinn came up behind me and placed his arms around my waist.

"Is this what you meant by alone time?" I asked, letting him hold me as we stood there. I could feel his heat all around me.

"We never really talked about what happened," he said.

"I know. I'm sorry about that." I turned towards him and looked into his eyes. I kissed him back in Mississippi after I tore into him. He had witnessed me at my worst, yet he was still beside me.

"I wanted this weekend to be about us," he said. "I know how complicated all of this is, but I want to see if, well···"

"I know, and this is so sweet of you. But I need you to stop throwing money at me," I said laughing. I didn't want him to feel bad, but the whole money thing was something I was still trying to get used to.

Quinn blushed and tried to apologize, but I shook my head. "So what's your plan for this trip?" I asked.

"Well, spend time with you, enjoy the lake, see the park. Ask you out on a da···"

I smiled. "A date?" I poked.

"If that's okay with you," he said softly.

"That is perfectly okay with me."

CHAPTER 14

Quinn wasn't wrong when he'd said the view from the front window was going to impress. The cabin sat upon the shore of Lake Crescent, an alpine lake bordered by the mountains. It seemed like a scene straight out of the Lake District in Italy or the planet of Naboo in Star Wars—and yes, I knew those scenes had been shot in Italy. The water of the lake was pure teal blue that reflected the clear sky. It was nothing like the brownish mud-filled one we had back home.

I spent most of the morning on the patio, sipping hot tea as I waited for Quinn to wake. I had seen the exhausted face he'd had the night before. He deserved a little extra sleep after handling the entire drive by himself. I'd handled the entire thing by not jumping at every bump for once. I guess that's what they called growth and overcoming trauma. I still had so much more to sort through. Part of the reason I had woken up so early was because I'd had a dream where I'd heard them screaming. I really couldn't fall asleep after that, and it haunted me until the sunlight began to rise beyond the mountains and I'd crawled out of bed.

The air was warmer, just like they had said it was going to be, but I still found it a little cool. I guess that might be the Southerner in me coming out. I was used to the heat, making this weather still feel cold. Sitting in the sun helped, even with a light hoodie on. The breeze was soft, swaying the pine needles in the tall trees around me. These mountains were not snow-capped, as their peaks did not extend high enough into the sky. Instead, they were blanketed by a lush, evergreen rainforest. Moss hung from their branches, and the ground was moist.

I looked down at the computer open in front of me. I wrote a few lines, then stared out at the lake again, collecting my thoughts, before doing it all over again. Line by line, taking advantage of the brief moment that the words seemed to flow from my hands. I knew there would be many hard months of writing ahead. I just needed to take it chapter by chapter, word by word.

The door slid open behind me as I heard him walk out. I turned to find him in just his pajama pants, rubbing his eyes as the sun glared in them.

"You're up early," he mumbled.

"It's ten in the morning. You slept in," I said.

He stared at me for a moment, still looking tired. He sauntered over, grabbing the chair next to me. I honestly didn't understand how he wasn't freezing. "Oh, well then. Good morning."

"Go get some caffeine, please. You like someone just ran you over," I said.

He laughed and smiled. "I could just take yours," he said as he grabbed my drink. I tried to warn him, but was too late. His face squinted when the taste of tea grabbed him. "That's not coffee." He placed the drink back on the table, very unsatisfied.

"Nope, it's Earl Gray." I smiled.

"I'm going to make coffee. I don't see how you drink that."

He got up and left as I went back to writing. About ten minutes later, he returned with a steaming mug in his hands. At his first sip, he closed his eyes and smiled at the taste. I just shook my head at him. That would teach him to take my drink.

"Better?" I asked as he sank into his chair.

"Much."

"I have to ask, how are you not cold?"

Quinn looked at me, dumbfounded and surprised that I was being serious. "It's warm outside and summer. How are you not hot?" he asked, seeing what I was wearing.

"It's not freezing, but still a little cool."

"Such a Southern boy," he taunted me.

I glared at him. He knew I hated being called that, yet it had become his favorite way to be playful. His smile kept me at ease. I knew he meant no harm by it—if anything, it was done with care.

We sat there for an hour or so before Quinn went to fetch something to snack on, bringing back some fruit and bread. I nibbled on a few grapes and pieces of pineapple.

"How does canoeing this afternoon sound?" he asked in between bites. It was already warmer than it had been when I first came out, as the sun rose higher in the sky.

"I'm guessing on the lake?" I replied.

"Yes. No river to canoe here," he laughed. "Try not to fall in this time." He was taunting me again.

"Sounds great." I smiled back. "If anyone falls in, it should be you. To make it even."

"Oh, so now we have to be even, eh?"

"Why, of course. Can't have you holding that over me forever," I said as I shoved his shoulder playfully.

He just laughed at me, smiling big.

We sat out there for a little longer before we headed in to get changed. Quinn gave me marching orders on what to wear. Apparently, he already had a plan for that too. I wondered how much of this weekend he had planned out. I had a hunch I was going to figure it out, and maybe find a way to change it here and there, just for the heck of it.

It was a little after lunch when we headed down to the dock. Quinn had made sandwiches for lunch. For some reason, he felt he had to cook for me. Granted, I didn't mind—he didn't do a bad job. It was tasteful and filling, which was what you needed from lunch. Then again, it was a sandwich. I would be scared if he'd messed that up.

A canoe already sat in the water. It was a two-seater with a wooden hull and oars—and it was painted green and yellow. I had already gathered the references, and I could say that I still preferred the Yale blue and Harvard crimson of my school. Why they had to put two Ivy League names in front of the colors is beyond me.

Quinn noticed me looking at it. "Sco Ducks!"

I just shook my head. All it needed now was a damn duck on it.

He handed me a life jacket before hopping in. The canoe swayed a bit as we shifted, trying to balance, and then we were facing each other.

"Easy there," he said.

I reached into the water and splashed him.

We laughed before pushing our way out into the lake. The air was so clear and light. Before long, I felt my arms and back burning from the rowing. The view from the lake was even better than it was at the house, the water cool and clear. In the shallow parts, I could see all the way down to the rocky bottom. Even in the deep sections, I could still see far below.

Quinn grinned at me as we made our way to the other side of the lake, the sun warming our skin. There were others out on the lake, paddle boarders and canoes and boats in the distance. From where we were now, I could see that the lake still stretched far to the other side of the hill that was in front of us. I wondered how far it went.

"It takes a good twenty minutes or so to drive around the lake," Quinn said.

I swear he must have read my mind. It was a little creepy.

"It's incredible," I replied.

As we rowed, I told him how the lake was where I grew up. He was surprised to find out that people actually swam in them, not to mention fish. To be fair, I preferred this lake.

As we neared the other side, I could feel sweat beading on my forehead, and my arms were sore from the strain of pulling the boat through the water. I was about to reach into the water to splash myself when we passed underneath a pedestrian bridge that was a rusted red color. On the other side of it was a small bowl-like pool area. It was quiet, with no one around, and I could make out the bottom of the lake. It seemed maybe eight or so feet down. There was a little shade here, at least on the edges of the pool.

Quinn brought us to a stop and looked at me. He pulled his life jacket off, exposing his bare chest, and placed it behind him.

"What are you doing?" I asked.

"You think I told you to wear swim shorts just to go canoeing? We're jumping in! Come on," he said as he dove into the water, which sprayed everywhere.

"Are you crazy? The water has to be freezing."

"Kodak, you're literally sweating. Don't make me pull you overboard," he said with that mischievous smile.

I didn't want to give him the satisfaction of that. I pulled my life jacked off, along with my tank. I braced as I jumped in. The water at first was indeed cold, shocking me. Seconds later, however, I found it refreshing, remembering how warm my skin had gotten out in the sun. I swam up to the surface, where air once again graced me. Quinn smiled in front of me as we treaded water.

"Okay, this does feel pretty good," I said.

We had the area to ourselves as we swam. When I noticed that I had an opening, I took it, splashing him.

He pulled back, startled at first. "Oh, so that's how you want to play," he said, splashing me back.

"Well yes, what else could we do?" I said, joking.

"Oh, I could think of something." He gave me that smile as he swam closer to me. He pulled me towards him until I was an inch away, and his arms wrapped around me. I placed my hand on his chest, feeling his heartbeat as his eyes stared into mine, sucking me in.

His lips pressed against mine as he leaned into me. We moved like a dance between us as I placed my arms around his neck. The warmth of his body embraced me, even in the water. The water seemed to boil around us as I lost any semblance of place. All I could do was think about him.

He broke away, but his eyes showed that he hungered for more. This time, I moved, locking myself against him as he pulled my body to his. I could feel his strength as he held me. My lips found his over and over again. We pushed and pulled at each other, and I didn't want to stop. I wanted to just be here with him.

"I've been waiting to do that since we got back from Memphis," Quinn said, breaking away.

I smiled at him, still in his arms. "Me too," I replied. "Not a bad way to start the weekend."

He grinned. "I want to wake up every morning and see you, kiss you, hold you." He pushed a piece of my hair from my face. "No matter what I need to do for that to happen."

"You've already done enough," I said, kissing him again.

We stayed there for a while, just being together, enjoying the moment. Finally, I had a question I wanted to ask him. I had been thinking about it the entire way up here, but hadn't really known how to bring it up, or if I had already pushed things too far. Now, I knew this was my chance.

"Quinn," I said.

"What?"

"I don't want you to be just my friend," I said. "Can we be more?"

He smiled at me with a big smile, not like the others I'd seen all day. "Like a couple?" he asked.

"Yes, a couple. Two people who like each other a lot."

"I would love that," he said, then pulled me again into a long kiss that melted the world around us.

I could honestly stay there all day. We played around for a while, splashing each other, laughing, and talking endlessly. On our way back across the lake, there was one thing on my mind as I looked over at him. Each time our eyes locked, a grin crossed his face. He was mine, and I finally felt something that I hadn't had for years: I felt loved.

After the lake, we changed. Quinn took me on a hike just down the road. We pulled up to the Crescent Lake Lodge before turning further into the dense forest, then parked in a small parking lot next to a ranger station. We walked past the main path and through a small tunnel that went underneath the highway. On the other side, we headed further in between the mountains. The tall evergreens towered above us with moss and vines hanging. The path was well-worn.

"If you want a challenging hike, we can go up to Mt. Storm King," Quinn said.

"I take it we're not going that way, then?"

We walked past several large trees, some of which had fallen over the years. Nature was slowly beginning to retake them.

"No, not today," he replied as we made it to a river snaking its way through the hills just as we were. The trickling sound of water bounced off the trees.

We stopped at an offshoot of the path on the bank of the river. The small sandy area was at a bend where we could see as it approached the lake on one end and up to its source in the mountains in the other direction. There was a small bridge crossing the path ahead. It was simple, constructed of wood, probably hand-crafted by the park rangers.

Quinn grabbed my hand as we walked back to the path. His hand was warm and firm as we moved underneath the canopy of the trees. The cooler here than at the lake, the air thinning as we traveled upward in altitude.

We came to the bridge, which was only wide enough for one person to cross. Quinn went first, pulling me behind as he guided us across. On the other side, we were greeted by a small section of rough trail, then only a few feet later, wooden stairs that were built into the landscape.

"You're really working me out today," I said, knowing my thighs would be burning by the end of it. At this point, I could probably expect my entire body to be sore in the morning.

"You thought this would just be a sit-at-the-house type of trip?" he joked as we began our ascent. The path was thin, and we often stopped for other couples and families, giving them room to pass us on their way down. Most thanked us, and a few kids waved. I think that was one of the more remarkable things about out here—how genuinely nice most people were. It was jarring for someone so used to people being fake, seeing scowls as I walked past.

We traversed up each step as it curved with the mountain. The trees were thick, hiding the sun, and the ferns were green and moist. I tried hard not to make a fool of myself and trip. It was a contestant struggle, and I half the time, I was just hoping that Quinn wasn't looking at me. I didn't want to make him save me from falling down a mountain.

As we climbed, I could make out the sound of rushing water. I knew now what he was showing me, where this hike led to. I found it ironic, since last time, it hadn't ended so well.

As we ventured through the last curve, there it was—the thin stream of water falling high from the cliff face. Moss covered the stone, turning the area near the water green, and a cool mist hung in the air.

"Try not to fall in," Quinn taunted me.

I just grinned. "No promises."

We took pictures, mainly because my mother would want to see this. Quinn made us take a picture and had some random person nearby take it. It actually looked pretty good. For once, I didn't look haunted or sad.

"You look happy," Quinn said as we looked at it.

"That's because I am," I said, leaning my head against his shoulder.

We made our way back down, and I did not fall, thankfully. I never knew how clumsy I was until I came out here. Either that, or I'd hid it well. Then again, I wasn't used to the topography, so maybe that was the culprit and I could still keep what little pride I had.

We walked past all the same trees and that narrow bridge as we slowly made it back to the tunnel that went under the highway. Once there, we were in cell service range. I hadn't realized it was already late in the afternoon when my stomach began to rumble. The sky still looked like early afternoon to me. We found the car, but as I made my way over to it, Quinn stopped.

"Come on, we're not driving back yet," he said waving me over to him.

"What else are we doing?" I asked. "I'm getting hungry."

"Good," he said. He wrapped his arms around my waist, looking straight at me. "I still have that date to take you on." He leaned in and kissed me. Oh, he was good at that. I should have known he had something up his sleeve.

"Still hoping this date has food," I replied.

"It does. Come on."

He walked me over to the lodge we'd passed earlier on our way in. It stood two stories tall, with a tower that reached to a third. It was in a craftsman style with shingles that covered its façade as it faced the lake. From the shore, a pier stretched out into the teal-blue water. There were several people around, some lying out by the lake. Others were in the water on paddle boards and small boats. Behind the lodge were several rows of cabins with front porches. People were sitting out and enjoying the day, letting time just slip through their fingers.

The inside of the lodge was all wooden with old pictures hanging from the walls. There was the front desk buzzing with activity, and a gift shop to the left. On the right was an enclosed terrace, its walls of paned glass looking out into the lake. Quinn gestured me towards them, and we sat at a table that was covered with a white cloth. It was set with two plates, candles, and two glasses of wine, with a bottle nearby. He was too good at this.

"You really planned this out, didn't you?" I said as I looked around.

He gave me that smile. "Of course. Would you expect anything else?" he said.

I just rolled my eyes at him.

The terrace was busy with other people enjoying their meals. I took a sip of the wine, which was absolutely incredible—no doubt, it wasn't cheap. Then again, nothing with Quinn ever was.

"You outdid yourself with this," I said, looking at the menu.

"Did I?" he joked, giving me that playful side-eye.

I shook my head with a grin.

"By the way, we're going to need to have dinner with my mother when we get back."

"Okay. Any reason why?"

"She wants to have dinner. It's a normal thing for the fellowship."

"Oh, so not because we're on a date?" I said. I wanted to see what he thought about that comment.

Based on the redness building in his cheeks, he was a little embarrassed. "We can tell her if you're okay with it," he said slowly.

He was treading carefully, trying not to misstep, and I honestly didn't know why. I found it adorable the way he wanted to make sure that this wasn't moving too fast.

"I'm playing, Quinn, it's okay," I told him.

He blushed, almost looking like a damn tomato. At least I knew he cared what I thought.

Dinner was served shortly after, and the conversation softened to silence. The food was fabulous as the sun dropped lower in the sky, but it was still daylight as we approached eight. The air was getting colder thanks to the draft that blew in from the doors opening.

When we finished with dinner, Quinn had dessert planned.

"You're going need a wheelbarrow to get me back from this," I said as the waitress laid a cheesecake in front of us.

"I can arrange one if you'd like," Quinn replied with a laugh.

"Haha."

When we finished, I felt full and unable to walk, but Quinn and I kept talking, letting the food and wine settle. Our conversation led in different directions, full of laughter and joy, and piece by piece, the layers peeled back on us.

Then we headed back to the car, and I couldn't stop smiling, even though I was cold as we walked. Quinn had an answer for that, too, once we got home. He lit a fire outside as the sun began to set over the lake, and had us cuddled in a blanket as the smell of burning pine embraced us, his warm body next to mine as we rested our heads together, just enjoying the serenity that the blue hour gave us.

I'd never thought I would have this again, to be loved. I'd thought I would be alone because that was how the world saw me. Then he came.

CHAPTER 15

I woke to screams—the kind that sent shivers down your spine and pulled at you, making it to where all your mind could focus on was it, freezing you where you stood. Yet all I saw was darkness, my head spinning, hurting, even if I couldn't see where the screams originated from. I was unable to move, panic began to set in as I tried to figure out what was happening. The screaming intensified, the fire crackled, and the wind blew through the trees.

I wanted to see, to understand, yet nothing gave me the opportunity other than the sounds I could hear and the faint feeling of heat and rough, moist dirt beneath me. A warm liquid soaked my clothes. My mind could only think of one thing—I was hurt and in pain.

That was when I saw the fire that had scorched the earth and the black bark of the tree where a car lay broken and smashed. Black pieces of metal and plastic twisted, having been thrown in all directions. Smoke rose into the dark night sky without a moon or stars. Someone lay dead next to it, bloodied, gruesome. I tried again to move. Pain shot up my side as I crawled toward the heat of the fire.

Pain—

Death—

I crawled to the person lying face down. My body moved slowly, agonizingly slow, as my skin burned, rubbing against the ground. I had no strength to pull myself up and walk. I could only feel pain, and nothing would move except my hands and upper body. When I arrived, the man was dark-skinned and young. He was hard to recognize for anyone who didn't know him, but I did. It was Jordan—the person I had basically grown up with. We were thick as thieves as kids and kept close as we grew older. Now, he was dead in front of me, his eyes wide open as his body lay still. There was fear in them still, his last thoughts—fear of death.

Death—

Fear—

Pain—

I looked at the car and found others dead and dying. Their bodies burning from the fire, and all I could do was watch. Not able to help them as their screams echoed in my ears, and I could never forget them. They're the ones that haunt me. Burned into me till the day I finally will perish.

Next to the tree was another body, a girl. It was Becca, her brunette hair giving it away. Her eyes were closed and peaceful, but her body didn't move. In the back of my mind, something didn't feel right. I didn't remember this. She had never laid against a tree. She hadn't already been dead. She'd survived the initial impact, just as I did. She'd crawled to me despite being impaled by metal that would eventually take her. I remembered holding her as she died, crying, preserving what little strength I had while I waited for help, waiting for the world to find out about this tragic moment—the one that they blamed me for. The one I blamed myself for happening.

None of this made sense now, because the trees were not those of the rural Mississippi road I had traversed many times. These were tall evergreens, the air cold once I moved away from the flames. The ground was moist and full of moss, pine needles, and ferns, while also jagged and rough with rocks. This was not the South, not

Mississippi. The accident didn't happen here. This was something else, something new and frightening.

Fear—

Pain—

Death—

I couldn't breathe or think. None of this made sense. None of this was real. Yet I could feel everything, all the pain erupting around me. What was this? How was this?

I tried to scream, yet my voice was broken. Nothing but air exited my mouth as I tried, frustrating me further as I kept at it, worsening the panic inside me as it spread. Then I heard a scream from a voice that triggered something worse.

"Kodak!" it said. "Help, please!" The pain was evident in its desperate call to me. The voice was low yet rasping as I searched for its origin amongst the wreckage. I crawled toward its sources as it continued to call out to me, avoiding hot metal and flames that were spread throughout.

"Kodak!"

There he was—the person calling my name. His head was bashed and bloodied as the fire spread toward him in the car's back seat. Fear and panic set in as the flames reached him, burning him. He called and called to me as I tried to crawl towards him, making little progress, and the pain inside me spread. When I got closer, his screams intensified. He was dying, burning. The agony in his voice was unbearable—and that was when I recognized him.

Quinn was burning. Quinn was dying. This was Oregon, not Mississippi. This was real—it had to be.

I screamed, finally finding my voice. I screamed loudly as I crawled inch by inch to him. He begged me to save him, and I couldn't. There was no way that I could, not in my condition, and I stopped and screamed.

Kodak!

Help, please, I beg you!

The screams finally stopped after minutes of suffering. That was when he died, and everything felt numb. My mind was lost, unable to muster a single thought. I lay there, blood pouring from me, waiting for the moment that death would greet me too.

The longer it took, the more I wondered if I was just there to suffer, suffer through all that pain and agony. I screamed, pushing everything out, wanting everything to stop, for the world not to hate me—so that maybe I could live, live where I was no longer in this awful pain.

Quinn was holding me from behind. I was hot, soaking in sweat, breathing hard, my throat burning. His arm was around my abdomen, his head was next to mine. He kept calling my name calmly for a second as I tried to orient myself to my surroundings. We were in bed, the covers pulled away. It was still dark, but I could see the moon shine off the lake in the distance.

"Kodak, it's okay. It was just a dream," he said as I turned my head to him. I had to make sure it was actually him, and it was. The heartbeat against my back was his, as was the warmth of his skin.

I stared out towards the lake nestled in the dark. I couldn't get it out of my head—the screams of him dying, cries of the person holding me.

I can't do this.

My head began to spin, and I couldn't breathe as I lurched forward.

I can't do this.

I reached the floor and grabbed a zip hoodie as I ran out of the room into the dark that seemed to enclose me. I could hear Quinn call after me, but I kept going, making it to the door. I pulled at it, the cool night air embracing me. I couldn't lose him. I couldn't do that again. It had been so real. I didn't know if I could survive that again.

So I ran—ran away into the woods that surrounded the house, sprinting my way to someplace other than here.

The moon rose high into the sky as I raced between the thick ferns and evergreens. They scraped at me, leaves brushing against my body. I wanted to scream because my heart ached, wanted to push through my chest.

My foot found a root and I tripped, falling to the ground. I landed almost straight on my face. I lay there for a second before mustering the strength to pick myself up and continue. Dirt covered my arms and knees. This time, I moved at a brisk walk instead, now feeling the cold as I let the calm night take me.

I found a clearing, small but enough that I no longer felt trapped by the forest. There was no view of the lake here, just the tall trees that towered to the sky, where the moon and stars shined. How had I let myself get here? How had I been so stupid to think that I could ever do this again? Everyone would blame me if something happened—me, the person that was other, even if all I wanted was to be seen as a human.

I sat down against a tree, unwilling to move. Why should I? If I moved, it would just let the world tell me what I was, to say this was what I could do because of my pedigree. Was it easier to stay here, away from everyone, to be alone? Just like the world wanted me to be—alone and sad, out of everyone's view, where I belong.

"Kodak?" I heard Quinn's voice say. It was rushed, in between breaths. I looked up to find him standing over me. There was worry across his face, but I could only stare at him. "You have to let me help you."

"Why?" I asked.

"Because I want to, Kodak. You're hurting in ways I can't understand, but you don't have to do it alone. Let me in."

"I can't," I said, my head still feeling dizzy, unable to make eye contact. "I can't let you in because I can't lose you."

Quinn dropped to his knees in front of me, placed his hand on my face, and rubbed away the tear that had slipped down my cheek. "Kodak." He just shook his head.

"You died, Quinn. The same way as they did. I heard your screams; I still hear them. I can't do this again, and I can't know that pain again," I told him as sternly as I could manage. I wanted him to understand what I felt. I wanted him scared because it was easier than the other, easier than the fear of losing him.

"That was just a dream," he replied.

"Not to me. I can't do this, Quinn. I'm just meant to be alone," I said, getting up and trying to walk away.

Quinn grabbed my arm, and I tried to pull away from him. "Stop running away. Stop running from your fears," he said.

I snapped. "Quinn, I can't, okay? I watched them die right before me. I heard their screams, and I couldn't do anything to help them. I saw the life exit the person I loved while I held her. Then everyone blamed the colored boy for it!" I screamed at him.

The moment he let go, I began to walk away, hoping to end this conversation, but he spoke, stopping me.

"No!" he yelled. "No, I'm not letting you push me away because you're scared."

"Quinn—" I began, but he still had more to say. He was stern, and his voice carried in the dark. His features were stone cold in the moonlight.

"No, I'm not letting you be scared of us. You're the best thing in my life, Kodak. I'm not letting you walk away, not when I care for you like I do. Your dream be damned, for all I care, because I will fight for this."

I looked at him as he walked up to me. I honestly wondered if he was going to hit me. He seemed that angry.

"So you are coming back with me, and we are going back to bed, where I will hold you until you feel safe until there is no more fear in you. Let me be there for you, because I need you." His voice broke at the last part. This was the first time I had seen him like this, where he was almost broken, as I had been. I could only stare at him as he grabbed my hand and pulled me towards him.

"Quinn, I'm sorry," I began to say, realizing that I had hurt him through my fear of losing him.

"Save it. Just come back to bed," he replied, then pulled me back through the woods to the house.

His hands were warm as we returned to the deck and then into the house's warmth. Once inside, he pulled me to him and we stood in the living room in the dark. He pulled the hoodie off me, and I did the same to him as he kissed my forehead. I knew now what was really happening here. We were just too afraid to say it—what we truly felt. Now, I remembered why I couldn't lose him.

As we returned to our bed, I wanted to only be with him, no matter what my brain and dream had done to me tonight.

We loved each other. We had fallen hard and not realized it until now. At least I did. I feared losing him like the others because I loved him, and now I could only see myself with him.

I looked into his eyes, holding his sad gaze. "I'm sorry I snapped. I – "

"You don't want to lose me, I get it. Just let me in, Kodak. We need to do this together."

"Okay," I replied as he kissed me, pulling my body into his. His hand rubbed my back and I felt like I melted into his skin. Eventually, he pushed me back onto the bed, the cool sheet spread against my back.

"Just don't do that again," he said as he climbed over me, locking us together. He curled into me, wrapping me in a cuddle as we pulled the comforter over us. Quinn now held me, just like he'd said he would. I knew as I began to feel sleep come over me again that I had fallen in love with Quinn Condor—a whole new experience for me, yet all I could do was sleep.

CHAPTER 16

We laid in bed for most of the morning, my eyes opening around nine. Okay, maybe it was ten. Quinn was already awake but still in bed, holding me across my waist. I turned to face him, staring into those blue eyes that felt like looking into the ocean itself. I could lose myself in them. I wondered what he thought as he looked back at me. There was a soft smile on his face as we laid there. He probably thought I was crazy after last night, when I panicked about us, about losing him.

"Good morning," he finally mumbled.

I just laid there, leaning into him, not wanting to let go. The sun was bright as it entered the room, and I didn't dare look away. The lake was probably a bright blue as it spread in between the mountains. I would be able to do that all day, but in that moment, I just wanted to be there—cuddled together, not worrying about the world around us.

"So what's our plan today?" I asked, wondering if Quinn had it all planned out like yesterday.

"For right now, just being here. We might go up to Hurricane Ridge later," he replied.

I nestled further into him, not wanting to move. "Sounds good, as long as I don't have to get out of bed yet," I mumbled, closing my eyes.

"We can do that," he replied.

I honestly had no idea how much time passed. It felt like time was still, as it was just us and the faint sounds of the outside that we could hear—the simple chirp of the birds, the rustle of pine needles. My thoughts would wander into the sky, into us. Why did we ever have to leave such peace, only to return to the chaos surrounding us? It was something I used to think about as a kid. Why did I have to leave my safe space, to venture out where people hated me?

I always felt safe under the sheet on my bed, where no one could hurt me. Now, I laid there with someone who made me feel loved and even safer than I had felt in years—in a decade, really. Also, I had never really gotten to do this last time. Becca and I had been so young; it was only on a rare occasion that we had shared a bed, shared each other in a way that was more than holding a hand or a kiss here and there.

From where we laid, I heard a door opening, then the shuffle of feet sounding louder with each passing second. Then a knock on the door, and we both shot our heads up before it opened, and in stepped Olivia.

"You two are still in bed?" she asked.

I felt embarrassed about someone walking in on us, even if we were just lying there, even if we knew her. She seemed calm as she looked at us. There was a bit of sternness to her voice, like she'd half expected us to be up and ready. If only she knew how late we'd been up last night. I was happy to rest, as I'd spent most of the night restless after the dream that had shaken me.

"Yes, Olivia, we are," Quinn replied, pushing himself back down into the covers.

"Well, hurry up and get ready. We got things to do," she said, closing the door behind her.

We laughed and proceeded to get out of bed to get ready.

Quinn shook his head as he got changed. "I should have known she would do that," he said.

"That she would barge in like that?" I laughed.

"Yes, she does it all the time," he replied.

When we finished, we were each wearing a T-shirt and shorts. Quinn's shirt was dark green with a yellow O on it. I rolled my eyes at it as he grinned. On the other hand, I had just found a black tee. I low-key wished I had brought one of my own school shirts just so I could pick at Quinn. However, I would have to wait to do that, but I looked forward to the day I would be able to.

"It's about time. I could have cooked an entire meal by the time you guys got up," Olivia said, her arms crossed as she waited for us in the living room.

"What's got you in a hurry?" Quinn asked as he made his way toward the kitchen. He was most likely looking for coffee so that he could fully wake up.

"There are things I want to see while I am up here, thank you." She smirked, and Quinn shook his head as he made his coffee. "Plus, this is Kodak's first time here."

I didn't know why she'd invited me into the conversation, so I just shrugged and kept my voice out of it, even if it was just a playful argument. It was safer that way. I sat at the counter and waited to hear what the plan for the day was. I assumed there had to be one, as it seemed most of this trip had been pre-planned.

Quinn had that playful smile on his face as he talked with Olivia. He enjoyed picking at her; I could tell he was more awake than he was letting on. "Kodak, you better get ready. Someone has wheels on their ass this morning," he said.

Olivia glared at him before picking up a kitchen towel and throwing it at him. It landed on his shoulder perfectly, as if he'd placed it there himself. Quinn just laughed, and Olivia eventually smiled and shook her head.

"Where are we going exactly?" I asked, curious to see what they would say. It had taken Quinn almost the entire drive up here to finally let me in on the secret of where we were going. I don't see the need for secrets, and it wasn't like I had seen any of this before.

"We are going to hike 5,000 feet into the air. So wear something warm and bring lots of water," he replied.

Olivia rolled her eyes. "We're going to Hurricane Ridge, which has a good view of the mountains." She looked over at Quinn with a glare. "You could just say that instead of being so cryptic."

I laughed.

"Where's the fun in that?" Quinn said, finishing his last bit of coffee before placing his mug in the sink.

Olivia just lifted up her eyebrow before grinning and shaking her head.

The drive up to the ridge was nothing like I had ever seen. We had to first drive into Port Angeles, then we started our ascent, winding in between trees and houses until it was just the natural landscape that surrounded us. Once we passed the park's boundaries and paid the fee, the forest became thick and lush. Each clearing allowed us to see just how much elevation we had gained. On one side was a downward slope to the strait. On the other side, the Olympic Mountains rose high with their thick, evergreen coats, their peaks hidden behind a layer of light gray clouds that hovered like fog.

About a quarter of the way up, just before a tunnel, was a small parking area with a viewpoint. Quinn pulled the car in so we could see the view. I could see all the way down to a body of water, but I couldn't tell what direction we were facing, so I had no idea what it was. Regardless, it looked pretty from the high viewpoint.

"What do you think of the view?" Olivia asked as she came up behind me. The air was already more relaxed up here. It was still rather pleasant, but I knew the higher we got, the colder it would get.

"It's pretty cool."

"Hey, over here," Quinn said, waving us over to the edge of the parking area. A couple was emerging from a small path that seemed to go into the forest.

"It's a pretty good view over there," the man said as his partner nodded her head in agreement. "Enjoy!" they said as we ventured on.

We hunched down under some tree branches before we came to a circular section of concrete with an overlook. It extended over the edge of the cliff face, allowing us to see into the mountain range. Gray and green mixed together, little sections of clouds moving like feathers between the trees. The air was fresh here in a way that made me feel free. Not bogged down, almost like I could lift into the sky.

Quinn went up the edge of the lookout, eyeing out the small valley between the mountains. Olivia took photos as I just took it all in, letting it soak into me.

"Do you mind taking my picture?" Olivia skied, handing me her phone camera with a smile.

"Sure."

She posed, and in the background, Quinn sat down next to the railing, his arms spread out. I shook my head as I snapped the picture, trying to get at least one without Quinn. I handed the camera back to her and she turned it over to see the photo.

She laughed when she saw Quinn posing in the background. "Really? You just had to?" she said to him.

"It was an opportunistic moment, and I had to take it," he replied.

"There will be a day that I finally kill you. Please know that" she joked with him as she looked at some of the other photos that she had taken.

"I look forward to it," Quinn joked back before smiling at me. I swear, he was enjoying this too much.

I shook my head before walking over to where he was standing. I came up next to him and looked out into the small valley. The gentle sound of the pine needles moving in the breeze was soothing. That, mixed with that pine smell that seemed to hover over this entire state, made it different from anywhere else I had been.

"You can be such a joke sometimes," I said to him.

He just grinned at me. "We can't always be serious; there's no fun in that," he said.

I guess he was right to a degree. Then again, I'd never really done anything that made me feel outright joyful, or at least not where other people saw it. Then again, I never let anyone see what I was feeling.

"Are you two ready? We still have a good ways to go," Olivia called after us as she began to walk back to the car.

When we were on our way again, we passed through the short tunnel, stopping a few more times on our way up, taking a few minutes to take in the view. It wasn't until we were almost to the top that the first snow became visible. By this point, I could already feel how light the air was.

We stopped behind several cars in the middle of the road. At first, we couldn't really tell what was going on until we saw a black figure on all fours run across the street.

"Is that a bear?" I asked, curious.

"Yes, it is. A baby, by the looks of it," Quinn replied.

"Which means Momma is nearby somewhere," Olivia chimed in, looking out the window to see if she could spot her.

Once the bear crossed the road into the woods, the cars began to move again, and the snow became thicker as we drove. Luckily, the road had been plowed and was only wet in parts as it had been melting, making it an easy drive to the top of the ridge. I knew we were there once we passed through the clouds and saw the peak open up to the blue sky. The valley below was covered in clouds, a scene I could have never imagined. Sometimes, I wondered if humans were ever supposed to see these sights. Then again, maybe we were so that they could inspire us.

I'M THE SAME

The white of the snow formed a perfect line straight across the range. Today, it hovered just above the clouds as the sun reflected off them. Quinn pulled the car up next to the visitor center; on the sign, it told us the current elevation of 5,242 feet.

We took turns running into the lodge to go to the bathroom, then returning to the parking lot, where we could look down at the forest below. It seemed like we were on top of the world. A few feet away, Olivia stood on the edge of the curb, lost in thought as she looked into the distance.

"Everything okay?" I asked as I approached her.

She looked at me for a second, then back at the landscape. "You make him happy," she said. "That's all I have ever wanted for him, even if it hurts."

I was confused, but as it sunk in, I remembered how she looked at him, how they were together so often. I'd seen her give him the same look I gave him now. Had she always had it?

"You love him," I said softly.

I knew I was right when she closed her eyes briefly. Perhaps I was the first person to actually say it out loud. Now it was real, and someone else had noticed it.

"Yes, I do, but I'm not the one who makes him happy. You are. That's all I need, even if it's not me." She turned pleading eyes on me. "Please continue to make him happy. Give him someone to live for, and love him like I do."

I nodded my head in understanding. "He loves you, too, you know that, right?"

She smiled just as I heard Quinn's footsteps behind me.

"What are you two talking about?" he asked.

Olivia looked over at him with a smirk. "Plotting your demise, of course."

Quinn shook his head at her sarcastic comment and gestured for us to continue walking.

As we began our hike, I wondered where Quinn planned on taking me next. We moved between the tall evergreens, the snow covering the ground, and looked out into an endless sky of mountains as we walked upon the top of the world.

The sun was setting as we sat next to a burning fire. The crackling of the wood created a symphony with the faint waves from the lake and the breeze against the pines. As the blue hour approached, the sky turned a soft shade of blue which created a relaxing mood. Paired with the faint smell of the fire and trees nearby, it was calming to just sit there in silence, yet not alone.

Olivia sat bundled with her legs to her chest, looking into the fire. Quinn lay nestled against me, curled together with the throw wrapped around us, snuggling us in to keep warm. As the moon started to rise in the sky, my legs felt sore from all the walking. Quinn had literally made us hike over three miles in changing elevations. I couldn't remember the last time my legs felt this sore or my lungs were so out of breath. Despite all that, however, I'd enjoyed every second. I felt as if I had walked upon the top of the clouds as I looked down at the Olympic Mountains. Their majestic white peaks seemed like another world to me.

"You seem lost in thought," Quinn whispered.

I shifted and gazed into his eyes. "I was, to a degree," I replied with a smile.

Quinn held on to me a little tighter as the fire danced in front of us. It was a weird sensation that I wasn't used to feeling, but it felt right.

"You're always lost in thought," Olivia interjected jokingly.

"It's a hazard with writers, I guess," I joked back.

She laughed softly before turning her gaze back to the flames.

I smiled as I followed suit, gazing into the fire and thinking about the people sitting beside me. I hadn't realized what I was missing all these years. I'd avoided people, hiding in the shadows, hoping no one would see me, avoiding the hate and judgment that seemed to follow me. Now, I felt free, but I wasn't sure I knew how to live in the moment.

Tomorrow, we would head back, ending our little retreat up in the mountains. Olivia would return to being the bookseller, and Quinn, the investor-slash-artist-in-hiding. Lately, he'd been opening up more about his artsy side. On our hike, he'd gone on a whole rant about the different vibes you could create using watercolors or acrylic paints. I shook my head, not knowing the difference between the two. Art had never been my thing.

Olivia seemed to know more than I did, so she could interject her opinion on the matter. I just listened and watched the argument. It was funny to me to watch them go. This would be how they felt if I went on a tangent about writing prose and style, or maybe grammar and syntax. They would probably be just as lost as I was listening to them. Then again, maybe they would just enjoy seeing the joy that someone's passion brought out in them—just like I felt with them.

"So tell me, what are your plans after the fellowship?" Olivia asked.

I could feel Quinn glance at me.

"I honestly don't know. I haven't planned that far ahead, I guess," I replied. It was the truth—I had no idea what I would do after it. I had thought of MFA programs, maybe, or just writing, finding a job. I should probably figure that out now rather than later. However, I had a feeling that question was loaded—there was now another factor to contend with.

"You're welcome to stay, you know," Quinn whispered next to me. "With me."

I smiled at him and laid my head on his shoulder. "I know."

I wondered what I would do. Would I stay and make a living? Would I leave and move on? That was something I would just have to figure out. For now, I just wanted to enjoy what time I had left.

A little while later, we put out the fire and headed indoors for the night. I followed Quinn to bed, and we lay snuggled together. More and more, I felt like, just maybe, I'd found where I was supposed to be. I could stop running, stop hiding for once, and just live. Maybe I had finally found the place I belonged.

"Quinn?" I whispered.

He shifted his eyes to me. "Yeah?"

"Whatever I do decide, I want you to be there."

"Every step of the way."

I smiled before closing my eyes and waiting to sleep to find me. I was ready to continue on to wherever life would take us next. Right now, that was back to Alnwick, where I needed to finish this story and write the words that drifted into my head.

CHAPTER 17

We woke up early—too early. Olivia was already gone, and Quinn was rushing me. I didn't think he'd gotten the memo that I wasn't a morning person. Granted I'm talking like 3 am. Like, please let me sleep. It was the one small favor that I asked for; it wasn't that hard.

"Will you hurry up?" Quinn said to me as he took his bag to the car.

I was still trying to pack my own bag. drowsy still, wanting desperately to not be awake. The plan was to get in the car, get comfortable, and then sleep. The sun wasn't even up yet, for god's sake. "I'm getting there. You do realize it's dark outside still?" I asked him, putting the last of my things in the duffle. I could still see the damn moon. There was no light other than the car lights and the ones in the house.

"Yes. That means we'll hit less traffic," he shot back, coming back inside to grab what I had ready. "So come on, sleepyhead."

At that moment, I did not like him. We could have at least waited for sunrise, and that would have given me another hour or so of sleep, which would have also put me in a much better mood.

"You can sleep in the car. Come on," Quinn ordered. His gaze was rather intense, and I could sense he was getting frustrated.

"That was the plan," I replied. I finished gathering what was left of our belongings before marching to the car. Hopefully, we could get on the road so that I could once again see the back of my eyelids.

Once we were both in, we began to move, pulling away from the cabin, from the memories we had made there. We started on our venture south as we drove down the winding road. When we came to Port Angeles, the town was quiet and dark. The world lay sleeping, dreaming still before they woke. It was weird being up this early, to feel everything so calm, but there was also a peacefulness that was hard to explain.

I never saw the sunrise, as shortly after making it through Port Angeles, I drifted back into sleep, coming in and out of consciousness. I'd see the road for a moment, Quinn driving, and then back to the darkness. It wasn't until we stopped somewhere outside Olympia that I was fully awake and noticed that the night had turned into day.

As Quinn pumped the gas, I looked out into the dense forest. It was gray, beginning to rain again. The chill was also coming back. It did this back home in Mississippi too—tease you with a little warm spell before thrusting you back into the cold, making you yearn for it again.

In the background, I could see the mountains rise above the trees, their peaks still white.

Quinn glanced at me and smiled. "I see you're finally up."

"Yes, I am," I replied.

"Better mood, I hope."

I just grinned. knowing full well he was probably still annoyed at me from this morning, but he would have to get over it. He should know by now that I hated mornings. "I hope so too," I joked.

He just shook his head as he finished putting gas in the car.

The rest of the drive was filled with us talking, the conversation taking us in different directions. We made a wish list of travel spots that included Rome, London, Japan, Tanzania, and for me, Hawaii.

Quinn had already been several times, while I had only dreamed of it.

Quinn casually mentioned that flights were never that expensive from Portland to Hawaii. I found it odd that he never worried about money. Meanwhile, I was on a student's no-salary budget, so I always worried about money. Both our trip to Memphis and our trip to Port Angeles had been on Quinn's dime, and I wanted to find a way to at least do something for him—for being nice, paying for my trip home to see my mother, and being with me.

Our conversation switched to things he wanted to do, like paint. He mentioned the national park residency as something he wished to do—to be able to paint some of the country's most prized natural wonders, all while immersing himself in them. His favorite parks were Olympic, Grand Canyon, Yosemite, and Crater Lake. Apparently, Oregonians were very fond of their national park. Quinn went on a whole tangent about how beautiful and peaceful it was to be near Crater Lake. I was honestly surprised by how many words he used to describe how blue the water was.

It was about another two hours before we made it to the Columbia River and crossed into Portland. Quinn stopped so we could eat. After that, it was just another two and a half hours to Alnwick. When the Pacific came into view, I knew we were home once again.

Quinn drove to my house, and as we pulled up the driveway, I felt something that I hadn't felt in a long time—the feeling that I belonged here. I felt almost at peace, even as he pulled the car to a stop and smiled. We got out, and he headed to the trunk, pulled out my bags, and began walking them into the house. It felt domestic like we had done it forever. Quinn placed the bag on the floor next to the couch.

I walked up to him and kissed him. "Thank you," I said.

"You're welcome," he replied as he wrapped his arms around me. "Don't forget dinner at my parents' next week."

"I won't," I said. I knew he wanted to tell them about us. I understood. If I told my mother, she would probably say something along the lines of, "I called it!" She had started to notice what was forming before I even knew, all while lying in a hospital bed. She had a habit of that, and I loved her for it.

"Do me a favor?" Quinn asked.

"What?"

"Come to bed with me."

"It's the afternoon?" I questioned.

Quinn stared at me intensely as he held on to me tighter. The space between us warmed as I stared back. His hands made their way under my shirt, touching my skin. "That doesn't mean we still can't go," he whispered.

His touch sent shivers through my body, and I leaned up to touch his lips with mine. We wobbled our way down the hall, our lips still feeling, only breaking to breathe. We stumbled a few times, hitting the walls, laughing, then going straight back to touching each other, moving through the threshold to my room.

The deeper our kiss got, the hotter the air seemed to feel, and the more it felt like our bodies knew what to do, and how to reach each other. Quinn stripped me down to my boxer briefs, touching my skin with his warm hands, feeling every fiber of my being down to my very core. I could feel the strength of him as he held me. I turned my gaze to him, releasing him from the soft cashmere that hid his skin from me. As I explored every muscle of him, he pulled us down to the bed and we laid arm in arm together.

All I could think about was him as we pulled at each other, longing for more as each second passed. The pull and tug were in constant harmony as we explored each other.

We stayed there all afternoon, not caring about the world that lay outside the walls.

I'M THE SAME

Later that evening, after lazing around in bed and eating pizza when we were famished, we sat around, talked, and enjoyed the sunset from the house's balcony. I found it hard to imagine not being around him; I couldn't really see what life would be like here if Quinn hadn't come into my life. What if I hadn't moved to Oregon? As the sky erupted into color against the sea below, I wondered where my life would go, and what journeys lay ahead. For once, I felt I had a future that could be bright, not one that was so broken and harbored in pain.

"You're deep in thought," Quinn said from beside me.

"Enjoying the view," I told him. Part lie, part truth.

His head leaned on my shoulder as we looked out into the sheltering sky. "Whatever happens in the future, let's always be able to come back to this," he said.

"To what?" I asked.

"To us."

I nodded in agreement as the last few rays of light began to leave the sky, and a chill began to set in as night arrived. We sat there quietly but together as the stars started to show and the moon rose. As the night settled in, I whispered into his ear that I wanted him to stay. Part of me wanted to tell him that he was already home with me.

His answer was to snuggle closer into me.

CHAPTER 18

The days were getting longer, and I welcomed it. No longer did it feel like the day would get away from me, no darkness at five in the afternoon. It was seven now, and it only seemed like the sun was beginning to set. We were already running late to dinner. I blamed Quinn, mainly because he couldn't figure out what jacket to wear. I rolled my eyes when he went back to the one that he tried on in the first place. I reminded him it was just his parents, and that he had seen them yesterday. Nevertheless, he still took forever. I hadn't realized how much of a perfectionist he was until this.

I was just going to have to deal with him being stressed for the moment. I felt like this was the opposite of what should be happening. I should be one to be restless—granted, I was pacing back and forth while he changed. Hopefully, he would calm down once dinner started, and then I would. I hoped that they would serve wine—or any form of alcohol, for that matter. He was going to need it.

We arrived a little after seven. Quinn knocked quickly before entering. "Mom, we're here," he said, which echoed through the house.

The house was quiet, unlike the last time I was here, with people talking and music playing all around me. This time, I could tell it was a home—quiet, calming, and more family photos around. I must not have noticed them the last time.

"In the kitchen," his mother said.

We walked past a few works of art that I now recognized as Quinn's. There were many of them here, more than I thought there would be. I still couldn't believe his father had no idea that Elias Kerner was his own son. I found it strange still because for me, I feel like I would know deep down if it was my child's work. I would also support them no matter what, just because that was what my child would deserve from me—to be encouraged and loved, to be proud of them.

His mother was cooking over the stove in the kitchen, stirring a pot that released a fresh aroma into the air. The kitchen was very clean, even as she was cooking. It almost looked like one of those cooking shows on TV, yet here, I could smell it, making my stomach rumble, ready to eat whatever it was.

"Hi, Mom," Quinn said as she turned to him.

"Hello, dear," she said, wiping her hand on the blue apron she wore over her white, collared shirt before she hugged him. "How are you?"

"Good. You already know Kodak." He gestured to where I was awkwardly standing.

"Of course. How are you doing, Kodak? Enjoying Oregon?" his mother asked me.

"Doing good, and yes."

"Good. Wine?" she replied, gesturing to an already open bottle of pinot noir sitting on the counter. From the looks of it, she had already poured a glass for herself.

"Sure."

Quinn's mother proceeded to pour a glass for both her son and myself, then went back to cooking. "Should be ready in the next thirty minutes at so, then we can dig in."

"Where's Dad?" Quinn asked.

"In Chicago. Business trip," she said.

I could sense the tension in the air as Quinn just shook his head. "Should've guessed," he mumbled, just low enough that his mother couldn't hear it.

We moved to the living room while we waited for dinner to be ready. I guessed the furniture had been moved around for the gala, as now I could see how the space was decorated. It looked just like a picture from a Pottery Barn catalog, with natural driftwood elements and modern pieces to give it a coastal look. If it was daylight, I was sure it would blend effortlessly into the view of the Pacific that lay just outside the windows.

I shifted back to Quinn, who seemed to just be staring out the window into a black night

"You okay?" I asked.

He looked over at me. "Yeah, just can't say I'm surprised."

"It's okay. At least your mom is here."

"I know," he replied. "The food will be good." He perked up a bit after he mentioned that.

"So she cooks well then?" I asked.

"Masterfully," he replied with a smile. "Best food in town, guaranteed."

Quinn seemed to relax as the minutes passed, hopefully realizing that there was nothing he could really do about his father's absence. He just needed to enjoy the night with his mother. I, on the other hand, was in a weird place where I wasn't fully comfortable in this new environment, while I was also with someone who made me comfortable.

Quinn pulled one of the books from the coffee table. He flipped through it, revealing various Ralph Lauren styles. Occasionally, he glanced up at me, then either smiled or shook his head.

"What are you doing?" I finally asked.

"Just seeing how we're going to style you next," he poked.

"Oh, really?"

"Yes. I'm thinking of this look. What do you think?" He turned the book around to show a picture of a man dressed in a three-piece suit. It was a charcoal gray with a purple liner on the inside, very well constructed from what I could tell—of course, it was Ralph Lauren, so the expectation was good quality. The model was wearing a hat and glasses, holding an umbrella in his hands.

"The whole thing?" I asked.

"Glasses and all," he replied, laughing.

"I have good eyesight, thank you."

He turned the book back around and shifted through some more pages. He was having too much fun with this. He ended up showing me several other looks, all rather ridiculous and unaffordable for me. I swear I couldn't take him anywhere.

"Dinner is ready, you two," his mother announced from the kitchen.

We both shot up from our seats. The dinner table was set with a full spread, including a salad and vegetables, plus the main course of fresh Chinook salmon. The plates were pure white with little blue corals on the rim. It was a beautiful set that my mother would love.

"Have you ever had Chinook Salmon before, Kodak?" his mother asked me as we sat down.

"No, never."

"You're in for a treat then," she replied.

Quinn took a seat next to me and began to fix his plate, his mother doing the same across from us. We were at a small table right next to the kitchen, rather than the formal dining room, which was on the other side of the kitchen. This space was more intimate and probably used for more family moments—like this one.

The first bites of salmon were incredibly tender, almost melting in my mouth. The flavor was invigorating with a little sweetness to it, yet it didn't have that fishy taste that salmon sometimes had. This had to be some of the best food I'd ever had.

"This is really good, Mrs. Condor," I said.

"Please, call me Bridget," she replied with a smile. "You're basically a part of the family now." This time, her gaze was on Quinn. It was that subtle motherly moment, suggesting she already knew and approved. She just didn't have to say it out loud.

"I keep telling her she should open up a place," Quinn interrupted. "It would be a hot spot to eat in town."

"Yes, yes, I know, but I'm happy just being your mom." She smiled, then went back to eating her food.

The table was quiet as we ate. My father would have said that was the sign of a good meal—when everyone was too busy eating to converse. The wine that Mrs. Condor—I mean, Bridgett—picked out paired nicely with the food. We enjoyed every last bite. I waited patiently for someone to break the silence that had taken hold, not wishing to be the one to do it.

It was when there was no food left on the table that Quinn's mother broke the silence. "So tell me," she began, "what did you think of Olympic National Park? I heard you two went up to the cabin." Her gaze was fixed on me.

I thought about it for a moment. "It was beautiful. We don't really have places like that in the South," I replied.

"It's one of our favorite spots. I am sure Quinn told you that, though," she said, glancing at her son.

Quinn nodded his head in agreement.

"The meal was wonderful," I said, changing the subject but still remembering to be polite. I could practically hear my mother in the back of my head. She had conditioned me well, that was a sure thing.

"Thank you. It was one of my mother's recipes."

"Every recipe is from your mother," Quinn interrupted.

"Yes, and that's why I taught them to you, as well. It's a family secret," she said with a smile.

"Oh, so you can cook? This is news to me, Mr. Always-Going-Out-to-Eat," I replied.

166

"Thanks for ratting me out, Mom," Quinn joked.

"Hey, you did that yourself by not telling him." She laughed. "He's actually quite good at it."

"So when are you cooking for me?" I directed my gaze at Quinn, who stared back at me.

"Soon."

I shook my head as his mother erupted in laughter. "We'll see about that," I said.

He smiled—the smile that meant he was up to something. I didn't know what, but something was cooking in that brain of his.

"In other news, how is the writing going, Kodak? Hopefully, something good is coming?" Bridget changed the subject.

If she had asked a month or so ago, I wouldn't have known what to say, other than the struggle was real—like bad. Now, I could actually give an update, at least one that a writer would give. Not too much information, but just enough.

"Good. I've made some real progress lately. Hopefully, I should have something to share soon. I will say, I'm rather proud of what I've written so far," I reported. I was just happy I was no longer staring at a blank page.

"That's good. Can't wait to read it," she said.

"Me too," Quinn interrupted.

"Oh, like you haven't already tried to peek at it." I looked sternly at him.

"I plead the fifth."

He acted like I hadn't seen him trying to spy on my computer while I was writing. Quinn loved to act like he wasn't looking by casually moving his head in the opposite direction.

We finished our glasses of wine while we talked. I was happy to learn more embarrassing secrets from Quinn's childhood like the time he got on top of a table at a restaurant and started dancing mid-meal. His mother loved that story.

I stayed and helped with the dishes. It was the least I could do for the wonderful meal, plus my mother would have found a way to hurt me all the way from Memphis if I didn't. Bridget seemed to appreciate it, as Quinn watched while wiping the table down. I think he was secretly happy he was with someone who could roll up his sleeves and wash dishes. I couldn't see him volunteering to do them, unless he was ordered to—which could be arranged, if need be.

Shortly after that, we said our goodbyes and headed back home. The dinner had felt normal, like sitting at the table with my family back home. Everything was effortless, with no rules to have to follow or the feeling of stuffiness.

When we arrived home, I was eager to curl up with Quinn and fall asleep, thanks to the wine.

CHAPTER 19

I spent most of the next day writing. Quinn had a few things to do at the bookstore. "Month end," was what he said, and I assumed he was doing financial things. After further questioning, that seemed to be the one thing he did in the business, leaving Olivia with what he called the fun stuff. I guessed that included the marketing, sales, and ordering of books. The fun stuff was what I would call it too. I couldn't stomach staring at numbers all day and building reports.

Outside, the summer air was in full swing. Quinn reminded me it would still be chilly because of the Pacific, but we could go to the valley if I wanted temperatures closer to what I would be used to for summer. He has no idea, how hot it gets in the South.

Quinn returned in the early afternoon after I had written six pages. He looked tired as he walked through the doors, hanging up his coat in the closet next to the door, then placing his keys on the counter. "Hey you," Quinn said, coming up behind me and putting his arms around my torso.

I leaned back and enjoyed the warmth that his body radiated outwards. "How were the numbers?" I asked.

"Good, actually. It was a great month revenue-wise," he replied with a smile that I could see in the reflection in the window.

I turned around and pulled myself towards him as my lips touched his. It was strange to see just how domestic we had become over the month.

I felt a reverberation against my feet. Quinn held me tighter as if he felt it too.

His eyes grew wider as he looked down at me. "Come here!" he said.

Quinn grabbed my arms and shepherded me to a door seal. Along the way, I noticed the wall paintings and decor rattling, swaying back and forth against the wall. Some even fell down to the floor, shattering upon impact. I didn't understand what was happening, I'd heard earthquakes were possible in Oregon, but I'd never grasped how real that threat was until now.

We held each other as the world shook, trying to keep each other anchored to the ground as best as possible. It felt like hours as we stood there, just waiting for it to stop. Our grips were tight as we held on, wondering if it would ever end. Then suddenly, all at once, everything seemed to be still, and silence fell.

We stood there momentarily, taking stock of what had just happened. It seemed to have been a minor quake. The house didn't seem damaged—the windows were still intact, and the roof was solid.

"You okay?" I asked.

"Yes, you?" Quinn replied.

I nodded my head at him, and we moved away from the door. A few things from the wall had crashed to the floor, and little pieces of broken glass from a mirror were the only damage I could see. We stepped over them carefully as we ventured further into the room.

Quinn grabbed his backpack and some other items. "Grab a few things you need and leave everything else," he said.

"Uh, do I need anything particular?"

"Simple things you actually need, nothing else."

I headed to my room and grabbed the backpack that was sitting next to my bed, then added the first aid kit from below the bathroom sink and a few batteries. I remembered the emergency radio in the hallway closet, then I filled my water canister and placed it in one of the pockets. When I returned to the kitchen, Quinn had already grabbed a few protein bars from the pantry.

"You're scaring me," I said, noticing the seriousness on his face.

"Good. We both should be."

"Where are we going?" I asked.

"First to check on my mom, then to meet Olivia," he said. "From there, we head to higher ground.

I didn't like the sound of that. Higher ground. Why would we need to head to higher ground? Would the earthquake cause a flood? The more I thought about it, the more I remembered the blue lines on the street, and the signs all around town. A Tsunami. Now my heart raced as I recalled what I had seen happen in Japan in 2011 or Indonesia. I understood why Quinn was so serious—why we needed to move, and fast.

"Then we should get going," I said.

Quinn and I placed a few protein bars in our bags and headed out the door to his car. Once everything was packed, he began to drive toward his house. We noticed a few trees that had fallen over along the way, but nothing too serious. It seemed to have been a smaller earthquake. Then again, I would not call myself an expert on earthquakes.

My eyes were trained along the shore, waiting to see if I saw anything that meant a tsunami was coming, but there was nothing, just the regular waves crashing to the shore. Everything was holding its breath, waiting for whatever else was coming. I didn't think this was over just yet—I had a feeling that there was more.

As the car pulled up to the house, it looked like it had weathered the shaking well. There wasn't a crack to be seen on the concrete façade, nor were any windows shattered.

Quinn sprinted inside, yelling for his mother. I hustled behind him, and when I entered the house, it seemed like it had suffered no worse than mine. A few things had fallen from the walls, and a mirror lay shattered against the ground, but there was nothing major.

Quinn's mother stood in the living room. She looked over at me while she was talking with her son. Her hands shook as she looked around as if waiting for the earth to erupt again. This was starkly different from the more confident look I was used to seeing from Mrs. Condor.

"I'm glad you two are okay," she said as I approached, her voice still shaking.

"Mom, grab your stuff. We need to go," Quinn interrupted.

She stood there for a moment, just staring into space, almost as if she didn't hear him.

"Mom!"

"Oh, yes." She shook herself out of it, then headed to her room to gather what things she could.

"Everything okay?" I asked.

Quinn stared at me for a moment, his face stern and focused. "Yeah, I think she's just shaken."

"Aren't we all?"

"True."

Quinn bent down to pick up a photo that must have fallen during the quake. He dusted the broken glass to the floor as he looked at it. From what I could see, it was a family photo from when Quinn was younger, maybe thirteen or fourteen. In the background was a tall waterfall, with Quinn in the center and his parents at his side. His mother's arm was wrapped across his chest, and his father's arm was across his mother's shoulders. They seemed happy and together. Quinn carefully pulled the small picture from the frame and stuffed it into his pocket.

His mother reappeared from the bedroom with a small duffle. It seemed like they both had had this planned, a just-in-case measure. It made me wonder how long they had been expecting this.

"You ready?" Quinn asked.

His mother stood there for a moment, looking out at the sea. Then she nodded, and we slowly made our way out the door. The air seemed quiet as we walked towards the car. Quinn was trying to hurry, but still taking into consideration that his mother was shaken.

"Here, I'll get that for you," I said, taking her bag from her to put in the trunk.

"Thank you."

I let his mother take the front seat. I hadn't been in the backseat of a car since the wreck. My hands trembled, but I focused on breathing in and out as I tried to keep my face looking calm. I needed to overcome this. I couldn't spend the rest of my life scared of not driving or riding in the backseat just because of one accident, no matter how terrible it was. I just needed to breathe, and everything would be okay.

Quinn glanced back at me, then put the car into drive. I had no idea where we were going, but I knew we'd be safe from something that may or may not come. At first, I gripped the side of the car and the bag in my lap. I flinched at every bump, but I kept breathing. I kept my eyes forward as the trembling in my extremities started to slow. I was getting better at this.

Along the way, we passed a few houses. People were outside, some hugging each other, happy to be alive. Others inspected their homes to see if there was any damage after the shaking. Other than that, everything seemed quiet and normal. Even the breeze was soft. Inside the car, everyone was quiet, in our own minds.

My stomach turned as the pine trees blurred. Everything seemed off, just as much as it seemed like a normal day. It had to just be me, as I worried about the damn car when I should be thinking about anything else. It was haunting me, clouding my judgment and thoughts.

Breathe

A few cars drove past us, snapping me back to reality. We were venturing along the coast still, as the ocean came into view between the trees. Then it sank back behind them between the curves through the hills as we made our way to a higher elevation. I saw a lighthouse in the distance, its white paint shining in the sunlight. I remembered a little of where we were; I had explored this area one weekend I got bored. Up ahead was a greenish metal truss bridge that spanned a section of an inlet. On the other side, the road took you down to a beach. From there, you could hike a mile or so to the lighthouse.

Quinn drove through the tunnel, which gave way to the bridge on the other side. We were halfway across before we noticed the trees in the distance moving, shaking side to side, like the ground beneath them was shifting. Then the shaking began again as the bridge swayed, making it hard for Quinn to keep the car pointed straight.

"Quinn, get off the bridge!" His mother yelled as he tried to move the car forward.

My stomach dropped as I tried to keep calm while the vehicle lurched side to side. I clenched the handle above the door hard enough that pain shot up my arm. She was correct—we needed to get off the bridge. I feared this bridge would not hold up through another earthquake.

"I'm trying!" Quinn said as he worked to forward despite the shaking. The car shifted from side to side.

The last thing I saw were headlights as I closed my eyes. The impact was quick, lurching me from my seat as the seat belt caught me. I heard Quinn's mother scream, most likely from the shock of the car impacting us. I held on to what I could, and prayed. It felt the same as before, except I didn't fly out of the car this time. The window next to me shattered, and I felt pieces of glass hit me like small pellets bouncing off my skin.

The car spun around a few times before it stopped. My ears rang as I tried to get oriented again. I was alive—that was the first thing I could piece together. I saw Quinn move in his seat, looking over at me. He seemed fine, and his mother shifted in her seat. It seemed we all were at least moving after the wreck.

My hands shook as my heart raced, blurring my vision. The ringing in my ears spread to my head, making it hurt. I had to breathe, I had to breathe, I had to—

This can't be happening.

Not again.

"Everyone okay?" his mother asked.

Everything seemed to still shake, trees fell in the distance, and the movement of the bridge made it hard for me to get oriented, bringing me back to the world that was in front of me instead of the one in the past. We needed to get off this bridge and fast. I released my seat belt and opened the car door, placing the bag around my shoulder. I had to put my own fears to the side.

It took me a second to gain balance as the bridge convulsed around me. Trees fell as the side of the mountains collapsed, forming landslides down to the inlet below.

Quinn was getting out and heading to me when I noticed his mother's car door was smashed in. The other driver looked dead on impact, his body laying limp across the steering wheel. His mother shook at the door, trying to release it, yet even with all her effort, it wouldn't budge.

I could hear the metal of the bridge's support system buckling, and cracks spreading. Even as the shaking seemed to slow and finally come to a stop, I knew this bridge would not survive. It had only been seconds, yet it felt like several minutes had passed.

We both raced to the passenger door, trying to use our combined strength to open it. Even then, it wouldn't budge.

Quinn went to open driver's side door. "Mom, come out this way. We need to go," he said, reaching in to help her.

The look in her eyes said something else. She looked at me, pleading, then moved her eyes to her legs. Metal encased them, wedging her in, pinning her in place. Even as she tried to move them, there was no way she was wiggling out. We would have to cut the metal away, and I knew what wouldn't happen—even if I didn't want to believe it.

"Quinn," I said, putting my hand on his shoulder. We needed to hurry. The sounds of the buckling metal got worse, and parts of the roadway cracked beneath us.

"Honey, go," his mother said. Her look was steadfast, accepting her fate.

"No!" Quinn lurched forward, trying to grab his mother, pulling at her more.

"Quinn, I need you to go," she said again.

I leaned forward, trying to grab his arm.

She looked at me and nodded, begging me to pull him away, despite knowing how hard it would be. Knowing the pain it would cause.

"We need to go," I said, pulling at him.

"No!" he screamed as he pushed my hand away. He pulled harder and harder at her, but nothing would move.

The road began to give way as the towers of metal above us began collapsing. We were still 50 feet from the other end. It would be a sprint, but that was only if I could get Quinn out of there.

"Kodak, take care of him," she told me. "He's yours now. Love him."

It broke my heart to hear those words. I knew the feeling, but I had a job, so I grabbed his waist and pulled with every ounce of strength I could muster. I dragged him inch by inch away from the car, tears dripping from my own eyes, knowing what I was doing was unthinkable.

Quinn screamed, trying to fight my every move. "Let me go!" he resisted. "Dammit, let me go."

I pulled him, and it hurt with every step. I could feel his heart shatter as the tall metal beams of the bridge fell to the roadway, crushing it as the bridge collapsed.

Quinn's body went stiff as he resisted, pulling against me, screaming. His hand hit any part of me he could find, trying to be released. Yet I pressed on, pulling him away from the car as it slid further away from us. Wire and metal fell to the road as the asphalt cracked and splintered, the whole bridge failing. It would only be seconds more before it fell through the broken roadway.

As it did, Quinn's screams were deafening, his body was no longer stiff but limp. That was it. His heart was gone, and I felt the pain of it. I took advantage of the fact that he was no longer struggling against me to make it to the bridge's other end, moving us to land as the bridge we had just been standing on fell into the crashing waves of the Pacific against the rocky shore. Quinn might hate me for this, yet I knew I had fulfilled his mother's dying wish. He was safe, and that was all that mattered to her. If he had stayed to help her, he would have met the same fate.

"I'm so sorry," I said, holding him tight.

He sobbed as he stared at the cavern where the bridge once stood. The car was no longer in sight, the last remaining parts of the bridge sinking into the water, disappearing from view.

I looked at the sea because I couldn't see him like this. I couldn't see him broken. It was like looking in a mirror at the pain that I still felt and wished to escape.

I listened to his screams of pain between the heavy sobbing, each and everyone driving a stake through me. I didn't know what to say, or how to comfort him. How did you comfort someone who had just gone through something like that? How did you get up? I had only started to get to know her, yet now I never would. Quinn would probably never truly heal from this.

JAMES UNGURAIT

There were no words, only crying, as we sat there, mourning, while the earth was still.

CHAPTER 20

Quinn's crying stopped, replaced by a deafening stare out into the open water at where his mother once was. He was a hollow tree, empty and open, his soul bare and crushed. No one had driven on the road near us. We were alone, with no car or sense of where we were going. I would be shocked if I could get a word out of him, and that would only be if he didn't hate me.

"Quinn?" I said, seeing if I could get any sort of an answer.

All I got was the same stare.

I repeated his name.

This time, it took a second before he actually turned to face me. His eyes were swollen red, his face solemn. There was nothing in his eyes like his soul was gone.

"It's time to go."

"She's gone, isn't she?" he asked, his voice barely audible above the sounds of the roaring sea.

"I'm sorry, but yes."

He closed his eyes as more tears fell.

I pushed down my emotions. Quinn needed me, and he needed all of me, not the broken, shattered, lost boy part of me, the one that wanted to hide in a corner, shattering into little pieces, just like the metal and glass of the car upon impact. I still felt the force as I tried to shake it. I had to push it away, I had to. Quinn needed me, or at least needed someone who looked and seemed fine. Even if on the inside, I was shattered.

Quinn got up slowly, wiping the tears from his face. Then he walked past me, and I followed. But before I turned away, I did one final thing: I made a simple sign of the cross, then hurried after him.

The road twisted through the trees and slowly descended into a valley. It all seemed normal here, the smell of salt and pine in the air, like the quake hadn't even happened. We passed a campsite that was abandoned, with stuff scattered about. They must have left in a hurry.

Quinn didn't say a word the entire way. His whole body moved slowly, like all it wanted to do was stay in one spot. It had been ten minutes since the shaking stopped, and he hadn't even looked at me.

"Quinn?" I said. "Please look at me."

We were down in the coastal valley when he stopped. He turned to face me, his eyes still swollen, barely able to keep eye contact with me. "I don't hate you. I just don't have anything to say yet."

"Okay."

We walked some more. The trees here were low-lying and lopsided, probably from the fierce wind that blew in from the ocean. We were no longer underneath the tall pine trees that lined the hills of the coastal range. I could still hear the Pacific's roar as we walked on the road, but it soon fell silent. At first, he was ahead of me. I stayed back on purpose, letting him have space. As he slowed, I caught up to him. I reached my hand to his and was surprised he welcomed it. His hands were warm as I matched his pace of walking. He was still quiet, but I knew he was grieving in ways I couldn't understand.

I'd lost people, but not family, not my mother. I remembered how I felt when she was in the hospital. That had been heart-wrenching, yet I couldn't even fathom this pain—actually losing the person who had always been there for you from the moment you were born. Especially when there was nothing we could have done to save her.

"Kodak." Quinn broke the silence. "Thank you."

"For what?"

"Saving me."

I stopped and pulled him to an embrace. He clenched me hard as we stood on the road, near asphalt that was fractured from the shaking. He didn't hate me, and I had been sure he would after I pulled him away, keeping him from his mother as she died. Maybe he understood why, even if, at that moment, he hadn't wanted to hear or do it.

I let go and he grabbed my hand. We walked over the cracks and fallen trees in our way. It was still so silent, and even the wind was still. For once, it didn't feel like I would freeze from the breeze, but maybe it was just the adrenaline of getting off that bridge that kept me warm and numb. I watched the trees, just in case they began moving again. They didn't; however the birds didn't sing there sweet songs, and I still couldn't hear the ocean's waves. For a moment, I thought maybe the road was too far away to hear them, but a nearby sign that showed parking for the beach confirmed that we were still near the shore.

My hair stood on edge. Nothing seemed right, but how could it? I walked along an empty stretch of highway after experiencing an earthquake that was so violent it had taken a bridge down, and we'd lost one of our own. That was nothing ordinary about this. It was the second event to affect me in a traumatic way. I still didn't have the faintest idea where we were heading. I didn't even think Quinn knew. His mind was nowhere, lost in the fog of grief and pain.

The air was still cool, maybe in the upper sixties. I was glad I had my bag on my back and the jacket I was wearing, otherwise, I would be cold and shivering, even walking in the stagnant air. I felt my stomach rumble, and I was glad I'd packed some protein bars while trying to get out of the house. We stopped at a small stream with a bridge going across it. The bridge had broken in two down the middle, with a five-foot drop into the water.

From where we stood, I could see the ocean—or where it should be. Empty sand seemed to stretch for miles out to sea. There were no waves because there was no water.

Quinn looked in the same direction, and for the first time, I saw something else in him that wasn't sad—it was fear. "How long since the shaking stopped?" His voice was stern as he looked at me, his eyes were no longer dry but steadfast. Like his mind was finally returning to the world.

"I don't know, maybe twenty minutes or so," I replied.

I looked out to where the ocean should have been—that's when I saw it. I could barely see it at first, but I noticed the line getting bigger every second as we stood there. A giant wall of water was rushing to the shore at a speed I couldn't even comprehend. I could only stare as it petrified me.

It was here.

"Kodak, run!" Quinn yelled at me as we took off, running off the road and toward high ground. The further we ran across the flat surface, the more I knew we wouldn't make it. The roar got louder and louder with each step. I pushed my energy to outrun it, even if my brain told me I couldn't.

I grabbed Quinn. "Quinn," I said as he stared at me.

"I know."

We climbed up the highest rock in the vicinity and braced to hold on. He came close to me and held me, our arms around each other, our heads touching as we waited for the wave to greet us. It took only a few seconds before the mist hit our faces, and the wave crashed over the trees just beyond our view, taking them out in one motion, and pushing them forward as the trees snapped into pieces. The water was brown as it raced towards us, and there was nothing we could do to stop or get out of its way. We could only beg for its mercy.

"Hold on, and don't let go," Quinn said above the road of the water.

"I won't."

The water hit us like a truck, wiping us off our feet and submerging us in the cold. I held on to Quinn as tightly as possible while holding my breath, using all the strength that I possessed to press myself into him. We were lucky at first to only be hit by the water and nothing else. I could taste the sand and salt as we were pushed by the current.

I said a silent prayer, hoping we would make it through this.

I felt things hit my side, maybe trees or other items, as the water kept us moving. We finally surfaced to breathe air, and Quinn was still next to me, clenching on with every muscle he could.

"Kodak!" he screamed, and I nodded, letting him know I was still there.

The scene around us was chaotic. The water was fast-moving, and trees moved along with cars and parts of buildings caught in the wave. In the distance, all I could see was water. I couldn't even see the trees as I frantically tried to find something we could hold on to. The water must have been around 100 feet deep or so, as we were way above the trees from the looks of it.

We slammed into something sturdy and pain shot up my side, right where my scar was. I heard Quinn scream, and I looked up, noticing a large tree trunk floating in the waves.

"Grab it!" I yelled.

We pulled ourselves onto it, giving us a break from the cold water.

"I got it," he yelled back. He grabbed my shoulder as we took a moment to rest the best we could. Our clothes were soaked and we were still traveling fast, further into the valley. Every once in a while, the tree trunk hit something, sending us in a different direction. Despite the dire situation, I took a moment to be thankful that we were still alive.

The tree snagged onto something, stopping us in place as the water from the tsunami flowed around us. From what I could tell, it was another tree that seemed to be better anchored into the ground. I used the moment to inch closer to Quinn, to hold him tighter. Everything was fast-moving and loud, yet I could still hear his heart race.

I didn't know how long we held on, but I could feel every muscle in me burn as we did. I begged for the water to recede, yet it seemed to continue its onslaught, trying to beat us down. I wondered how the town of Alnwick was fairing. The damage must be unimaginable. All I saw was water, and it seemed to steadily rise, with more and more waves crashing over us.

In the distance, I saw something move toward us. It wasn't a tree, as it was too long and too big. As it got closer, it looked like a bathroom, like the ones at the beach, except this must have just been the shell. It barreled its way to us, and as it struck, it broke the tree in two, pushing us back into the rushing waves.

"Kodak!" Quinn yelled as his grip loosened.

I scrambled, trying to catch hold of him. "Quinn, grab on to me!" I tried to scream, but I felt his hand fall loose from mine. I cried again, trying to hold on, yet all I felt was water.

The crash of the building pushed me under once again. This time, I felt weightless as the waves tossed and tumbled me anyway it seemed fit.

When I surfaced, I tried to scream Quinn's name, hoping he was still nearby. I could hear him faintly the first couple of times, but the more time passed, I couldn't seem to hear him.

I must have submerged and resurfaced five more times, each time trying to hold my breath as long as possible, hoping not to drown. The sixth time, I was pushed against another large tree. As I felt the impact along my back, I quickly turned, trying to grab hold of it. The first time I missed and was pushed further along before I ran into another one. This time, I was able to maintain a grip. I held on and tried to pull myself up to the top of the tree. Several limbs stuck up close by, and I worked to get a hold of them.

It wasn't easy, as the tsunami still tried to pull me under again. I grabbed one final branch and hauled myself from the water's grasp. The tree was one of the tall fir trees that littered the hills. I was at the top crown—and now I knew how large the wave was.

Once I had a stable hold, I screamed out into the angry water for Quinn over and over again. I heard nothing back.

The angry brown water moved around me, rushing in from the ocean at a pace that seemed never to end. The air was cold as my soaked clothes clung to my skin, freezing me, but still I screamed 'til my voice hurt, hoping to see him or hear him. Tears covered my face, but all I could do was watch helplessly as everything around me suffered. Here I was, yet again, just watching, unable to help, just like I did all those years ago, staring at a burning car and watching my friends die. I was on my own island of misery, pain, and suffering. Surrounded by the waters of the Pacific.

I could see the coastal mountains from my perch, which seemed like small hills in the water, as more things passed—cars, trees, boats, anything the wave could find and push inland. How could this have happened? How could Mother Nature be this cruel? How could life be this harsh?

I held on as the water receded and then came back again. It happened four times in total. The whole time, all I could think about was one thing: Quinn. He was out there somewhere, and I hoped he'd found a spot like I did and survived. He had to. Today couldn't end like this.

There was no concept of time, or even place, for that matter, to know where I was or what time it was. I knew it was late afternoon thanks to the sun as it sauntered down toward the water level. It felt like hours as I held on to the tree, and I was so grateful that it had held steady in the wake of this wretched wave. For a moment, I let my eyes close to conserve what little energy I had left, trying to keep my core warm as I curled against the pine needles.

Another hour or so passed before I could see the ground again. The muddy brown ground seemed to have been stripped of everything. I stayed atop the tree until I could tell it was safe, the water no longer rushing to the shore. I began my climb down to the soggy ground.

Dear god.

When I arrived, nothing seemed to fit as I glanced at the landscape. It was broken and tattered. The trees ripped from the ground, mud, and sand flung over them. There were even dead fish and bodies of people piled in every which way, clear to the Pacific Ocean and to the mountains above. I didn't recognize the first bodies I came to, which made me feel better, sadly. They weren't Quinn, which gave me hope still. However, that didn't take away what my abdomen felt, what my brain screamed at me. We weren't meant to experience these things; I was sure of it. Nothing prepares you, even I wasn't prepared for this.

Numb—

Pain—

Death—

I looked up at the tree that had saved me. I could have been one of these poor people who lay dead on the ground, the ones that had been caught off guard like we were.

I set my sights forward as the sun lowered into the sky. My search began here, and I wouldn't stop until I found him.

CHAPTER 21

My feet sank deep into the mud as it spread across my shoes. The ground was still mushy and soft underneath them. The stench of rotten water and death filled the air. In front of me was a scarred, war-torn landscape—the trees stripped of everything or wholly uprooted, pushed away like twigs in a stream. Debris from structures and cars had been overturned, some stuck in the surviving trees twenty feet from the ground. I wondered if what I smelled was Quinn's body, but I had to keep my faith. He was still alive. I felt it. He had to be.

I traversed the scene in a daze, unable to think or feel. Every part of me felt on autopilot, searching—that's all I could do. Keep moving and search; search for Quinn. The more I searched, the more the bad thoughts wanted to creep in. The sound of glass shattering, the screams of my friends. It was all coming back, but I tried to push it out even as my hands shook.

Death—

Pain—

How could nature be so cruel, so destructive? Willing to damage itself like this, ready to cause pain. Why was it so willing to cause me pain? Why was I meant to have this much pain in my life? I didn't understand it. I didn't know if I ever would.

I walked past maybe a dozen or so more bodies as I tried to remember where it was that we had been separated. My focus still went back to the faces in my memories that seemed bloodied and stone cold, faces that now haunted me. it was like I kept seeing the same ones over and over again.

Nothing seemed familiar to me, even as I stepped over rocks and looked up at trees and the sky. All I could remember was the brown water that rushed against me, the salty taste of it as it filled my mouth. I thought back to the bridge. Quinn's mother had died, and then I'd lost him, all in one day. I didn't see why I was surprised that my life had been altered so much in one day. The same had happened on the day I lost my friends. Then it hit me—maybe I wasn't meant to have friends in this life.

Why me?

I heard a sound, just a slight shuffle. I stopped and looked around me, scanning the area for the source. Finding nothing, I began walking again when I heard it softly once more. Stopping, I called out. "Hello?" I said.

At first, it was just silence, then I heard a mumble.

"Hello?"

"Help!"

It was faint and raspy, but I could tell it was to the right of me. I turned in that direction and began to walk towards it, calling out, trying to locate the person. Secretly, I hoped it was Quinn.

"Hello? Where are you?" I called out again.

"Over here!" the voice said.

Now that I was closer, I could tell it wasn't a guy, so it wasn't Quinn. I felt a numbness again, but this person still needed my help.

I found her a few seconds later. She was pinned underneath a car that had flipped over, and the vehicle covered everything from her waist down. Her hand lifted towards me as I maneuvered around to look to see if there was anything I could do.

"I'm stuck!" the lady said as I stopped next to her. She was Hispanic; I could tell from her accent and skin color. She reminded me of one of my aunts on my mom's side. Her hair was dark like mine, yet long.

"I'm going to try and push the car up. Try to wiggle out," I said.

"Okay," she managed to say, but it was soft and labored.

I tried to position my feet to be stable against the ground. Once comfortable, I pushed my hands against the car's metal. I felt the muscles burn across my back and shoulders, but I didn't feel the vehicle budge an inch.

I stopped and tried to catch my breath. "I'm going to try again," I told her.

She nodded.

Once again, I pushed my feet into the soft ground to get deep through the mud to a more solid foundation. Then once satisfied, I used what momentum I could muster to push against the car. I pushed, using every ounce of strength that I possessed, but I couldn't find the force to move the car, even an inch. I looked down, but all I saw around her was blood. There was nothing I could do.

I looked back down at her and lied. "It's not moving; I'll try again here in a minute," I said.

The color was already draining from her skin, and her breath was slowing. She didn't know it yet, but she was bleeding out.

I sat down next to her to catch my breath and comfort her. Even if I wanted to leave and look for Quinn, I couldn't just leave her alone to die. She should at least have someone there to comfort her. "What's your name?" I asked.

"Isabelle."

"I have a cousin named Isabelle," I told her. "She lives in New Mexico."

"It's a good, strong name; at least, that's what my mother always told me." She tried to laugh, but barely could.

"It is." I smiled. I thought for a second if I should tell her, but I didn't think I had the strength to. How did you even tell someone that they were dying?

"You are looking for someone?" she asked, looking up at me.

"Yes, my boyfriend. We were separated in the wave," I replied.

She shook her head, just like my grandmother did to tell me she understood. "Have faith," she said as she patted her chest, where her rosary beads were lying.

I smiled and nodded. "I will try," I said.

"I do," she interrupted. "I have faith that you will find him." Her eyes were steadfast in her conviction. She didn't even know me, yet she was comforting me. "What is your name? I gave you mine."

"Kodak," I said.

"That is also a strong name," she replied. "You are Hispanic?"

I was surprised by the question. "Sort of. My mother is, but my father is white."

"The nose and hair give it away, at least for me." She tried again to laugh, and I smiled back. She must have noticed a look on my face as she stared up at me. "Be proud of it, hermano."

I nodded my head. It was something very sweet to say. "So what are you doing all the way out here?" I asked, trying to keep the conversation going.

"I was driving," said. "To see my daughter up in Newport. Then that damn wave."

"How old is your daughter?" I asked. I needed to keep her talking and focused on me.

"Eleven, and very proud." She smiled. "Her name is Marianne." She slowly moved her hand to her jacket pocket and pulled out a photo to show me. It was a school picture, rough around the edges, probably due to water damage, but I could still make it out. She looked a lot like her mother.

"She's very beautiful," I replied.

She handed me the picture. "Keep it."

I took it, then stared down at it.

"When you find her, tell her that her mother loved her," she said, her eyes watering. She knew.

"I will."

She moved her hand again, this time to her neck, and she pulled the rosary beads from her neck before handing them to me. They was simple and wooden, each bead carved with beautiful craftsmanship. "Give this to her, please."

I nodded, unsure of what else to do.

She smiled. "You are a kind soul, Kodak," she said. "Thank you. Thank you for being here with me."

Her breath came in shorter and shorter bursts, then nothing, and her body lay still. Her eyes stared up at the sky without any movement. At least she looked to be at peace. I looked down at the picture and rosary beads in my hand before putting them both in my pocket.

My eyes began to water, and then all I could do was cry. I mourned for a person I had just met, as she was dying. I'd promised to find her daughter and tell her that she loved her. To give her this rosary. Her daughter would grow up with no mother. She'd even called me brother, knowing I was only half. She had still called me brother.

Death—

Silence—

Pain—

I sat there and cried, looking up to the sky, wondering what the hell was going on around me. I wiped what tears I still had in my eyes and stood up. Have faith, she'd said. So that was what I would do for her. Then I would find her daughter.

I made one final gesture before I walked away, the same as I'd made for Mrs. Condor: a sign of the cross and a simple prayer. Once done, I turned and left her lifeless body as I wandered the landscape once more, looking for Quinn.

The sun was beginning to set on this awful day. The bare trees made strange shapes on the ground with their shadows as I walked past them. I had stopped counting the dead a while ago. It was heartbreaking to even think of the number of animals and people I had seen lifeless. Hell, I didn't think I could ever not see their bodies again. They were burned into my brain.

The one person I hadn't found was Quinn. That was a little relief, as it kept my hope alive that I would still find him—and among the dead.

I started to head for the sea, the one marker that helped me tell what direction I was moving. At least from there, I could try to figure out where to go next and get a plan together. Maybe he was there, just waiting for me. As I walked, the lower part of my back hurt, sending pulses of pain up my spine. It must have been all the walking, or maybe I had pulled something when getting us off the bridge. Either way, I had to push through it.

I came to a road, parts of it washed away, sand and mud-spattered across what was left of it. Trees lay sideways, blocking sections of it, making it impossible for a car to pass. When I looked west, I could see the Pacific's waves crashing against the shore, like nothing had ever happened. Continuing through the tangled trees, I walked up along the beach's sand. It stretched out before me as the wind hit me. It was empty, yet still peaceful, even through all of this.

While the vista in front of me was beautiful, behind me was only destruction. The sky had turned into a gorgeous pink, red, and orange collage. I guess that was nature's way of apologizing. I didn't think I could forgive it for this, no matter how beautiful the sunset. I placed my backpack down on the ground. It was soaked, but I opened it to see if anything had survived. My spare clothes were wet and would need to dry before I could wear them. My own clothes were soaked clothes, and the cold of the night would probably make me freeze.

I needed to find some dry wood and a place to set up a fire. Then I remembered the ridges that encompassed the coastal valley. It was probably a good bet that the wave hadn't reached there. I remembered seeing them still peeking through the water. There was no way I would find Quinn in the dark, so I set out for the ridge.

Back on the road, I saw a turned-over red truck. The driver was dead, blood pouring from his head as his body lay limp, curled against the top of the truck. Scattered around it were camping supplies that must have been stored in the bed of the truck. I noticed a bag that must have been a sleeping bag and a tent. I had never been a thief, but I wouldn't consider this stealing—mainly because the owner was dead, and I needed it to survive the night.

I took what I could carry; the sleeping bag was easy to place in my backpack as I carried the tent. It was still packed in a sealed, long, rectangular box like it had never been opened. I wondered what my mother would think of her son taking these things, but I kept telling myself it wasn't stealing. How could you steal something with no owner?

The walk up the hill burned my legs, but I passed the waterline about halfway up. It was literally a line of sand and sticks, kind of jarring to see, as it was a good forty to fifty feet up. Above it, the trees were thick and full as I tried to find a place just off the road to set up the tent. I found one next to a large rock that jutted out from the side of the hill. The tall evergreens encompassed it. I guess I would finally use those survival skills my uncle had taught me while I was growing up. After all these years, I just had to remember how to pitch the tent. The fire was easy; I found several sticks and pieces of wood lying about. The dead pine needles on the ground made an excellent starter for the fire. I was lucky that there was a lighter in the truck with the sleeping bag, and it hadn't been broken from the wave.

With the fire started, I could see a little better now that night had fallen. It made it easier to put the tent up. I ended up following the instruction manual that came with it. I was cold and ready to take these damp clothes off. While building the tent, I placed my clothes in my bag near the fire, hoping they would dry a little.

The fire was warm as I sat beside it, eating one of the Cliff Bars I had in my bag. I stared into the flames as they danced in front of me. Part of me wondered if Quinn was out there freezing, or if he'd been as lucky as I was. Then, of course, there was the thought that I tried not to think—what if he was dead, lying lifeless on the ground? I tried not to think about it, even as I felt a tear fall on my face. I had to keep hope.

I looked into the inner compartment of my bag, which was supposed to be waterproof, or at least resistant. Time to test the theory. Most of the items seemed to be dry. Shifting through, I saw the emergency radio and pulled it out. It didn't look waterlogged, so I tried to turn it on. The small screen turned green as it came to life.

"Emergency alert! Tsunami waves hitting the Oregon coast. Area deemed impassable. Head to higher ground. A tsunami warning has been issued for all coastal areas of Oregon."

A little too late, I thought. The waves were already here and gone. Maybe I should have turned this on sooner, and we wouldn't be in this mess. Maybe Quinn would even be alive with me right now.

The radio began to crackle again.

"A state of emergency has been declared in the states of California, Oregon, and Washington. All residents are to take shelter and wait for emergency services. The roads are deemed impassable."

I couldn't say I was surprised. If this didn't classify as a state of emergency, I didn't know what would. However, what scared me was that it said the roads were impassable, which meant no help was coming. I was on my own.

I'M THE SAME

I put the radio beside me and kept it on so that it could update me before I fell asleep. Looking into the fire again, I thought about what to do. If my sense of direction was correct, I was on the valley's southern end. Behind me was what was left of the bridge where Quinn's mother died. That meant Newport was to the north, about thirty-seven miles. It would be one hell of a hike, but I needed to find Quinn first. That would be my task once morning came.

CHAPTER 22

The sunlight began to sneak through the tent as I felt the coolness of the air hit me. For a moment, I thought I was on a simple camping trip, but then I remembered. It took me another moment to realize I should be up and moving by now. I had someone to find. Even if all I wanted to do was stay curled up into a ball, waiting for the world to pass me by, I needed to get going. As I opened the tent, I pulled myself from the ground and the sleeping bag's warmth, letting the sunlight pour in. The fire was still embers, and I'd piled wood next to the tent, just in case I needed it tonight. I would stay as long as I needed to find him.

I found another Cliff Bar in my bag and ate it for breakfast. I would need to find some better food today. These protein bars wouldn't last me long. I also needed to find fresh water; my bottle was running on empty despite trying to ration what I could. I wondered if the truck where I got the tent maybe had more there I could take. I hadn't had time to look last time as the sun had been setting. Now that I had more daylight, hopefully, it holds other surprises that could benefit me. I also remembered the campsite by the beach that we had seen together before the tsunami had hit. Maybe some supplies were there. Maybe Quinn was there waiting for me.

Like that's how it works. He is just out there waiting for me to find him. It was just my brain trying to comfort me. At least, that is what my shrink told me all those years ago. I stopped going about midway through my degree. It got repetitive, always the same thing. I needed to move on; I needed to pace myself. I needed to forgive. We never really got to the fun stuff, the whole outsider and bigotry stuff. Mainly because I never really talked about it. I didn't feel the need to.

What I needed was for Quinn to be alive. I couldn't do this again. I couldn't. I needed him more than I had even let him know. He made me feel more like a human again, not an empty shell that was just wandering the earth. He was alive, he had to be. I couldn't do it without him.

I placed some of the supplies into the tent, along with my bag, and then I did my best to blend it with the landscape by placing twigs and pine needles over it, camouflaging it so that no one would see it. Once I was content, I set off towards the road and then back into the valley, passing the waterline that told me I was in the tsunami area.

The ground was still moist, but the air felt warmer today as the sky was clear. It was like seeing everything for the first time again, shedding more light on the destruction of the coast. The trees were stripped and uprooted like toys being played with. Cars were smashed, wood scattered about, probably from a building destroyed by the wave and the Mud was everywhere. Coating everything in a greyish-brown goo. The one thing I didn't notice was life. I was the only thing alive down here. Everything else was dead.

I came back to the truck I had found last night. It was an old one, a Ford. The man was still lifeless in the driver's seat. The smell made me almost gag. I tried to sift through what had been thrown about. I bent down almost to my stomach to see what was underneath the turned-over truck bed. I spotted a box and reached for it, taking a few tries before I could wiggle it toward me. When I opened it, I found a metal pot.

"I could use this," I told myself.

I placed it and the box on the ground next to me then searched around me for more. To the right was a sealed bag. When I wiggled that out from under the truck, I found some food inside—a jar of peanut butter and bread—and plastic cutlery, all dry.

"Not bad, Kodak," I told myself.

I placed everything in the box and began heading back to my camp. It was then that I noticed someone following me. I could hear footsteps behind me, and panting.

"Who's there?" I asked, trying to project my voice a little.

The walking stopped, and then I heard a faint whimper. I turned around to find two very sad eyes looking up at me. It was a German shepherd, a girl. Her feet were muddy from walking through the wet ground.

"Well, hello there," I said, putting the box down and bending down to her level. I didn't want to scare her more than she already looked.

At first, she stayed still, but then she slowly walked toward me. I held out my hand for her, letting her make the first move. She took a moment but then moved her head to my hand.

"What are you doing out here?" I said, petting her as she got more comfortable with me. I looked at her collar. There was a tag for her rabies shot, and her name was Roxy.

"Roxy. That's a good name for a good girl," I said as her tail wagged harder and her tongue found its way to my face. I smiled for the first time since the tsunami happened as I got up and grabbed the box.

"Why don't you come with me?" I told her.

She wagged her tail again, seeming to agree, and began to follow after me. I would give her some bread and peanut butter for a snack once I returned to camp. Maybe she could even help me find Quinn.

I'M THE SAME

Roxy followed close to me, her tail wagging away with her tongue hanging out of her mouth. I wondered what had happened to her owners. I had a hunch. If I was right, the poor thing was all alone, probably hungry.

I'd had a dog when I was little, a yellow lab named Bosco. Bosco had died when I was in junior high at almost seventeen years old. It made me happy to think about him again. Now, I had this German shepherd following me, so might as well make the most of it. Plus, I could use the company. We were both alone out here, so we might as well team up.

We returned to the ridge, and I veered off the road to the campsite. It was still there, thank goodness. I placed the box down by the tent and pulled out the pot. When I opened it, I noticed a smaller bowl in it—a dog bowl. I looked over at Roxy; I guess I'd found her owner. Poor thing. No wonder she was by the truck.

I pulled the bowl out and poured a little water from my bottle. When I placed it on the ground, she instantly began to drink as I petted her head. She stopped once it was gone and licked her lips as she looked up at me.

"Sorry, girl, that's all I've got right now. We'll have to go find some more," I said.

Her head tilted, and I smiled again, scratching her ear.

"Why don't we go look for some more, and maybe you can help me find someone," I said.

Again her head tilted and her tail wagged away.

"Come on."

We walked away from the campsite and back into the valley. I brought my bag and bottle this time, along with an empty plastic one that must have been there the last time I used it. Roxy was very obedient, staying by my side the whole way. I could tell she was very well trained.

We passed the truck and continued on down the road toward the stream, the same one we had come to right before the wave hit.

When I arrived, I found the bridge thoroughly washed away, with the remainder of the small stream flowing down towards the sea. I put a small amount in the bottle cap to taste and ensure it wasn't salty. It wasn't, so I filled the bottle so I could take it back and boil it later.

Roxy took her chance with the stream to get more water. I shook my head. I wouldn't take my chances, but I was also human and not a dog.

Once she was satisfied, her head drifted back towards me, little drops of water falling from her mouth, and I knew we were ready to move on. The wave had pushed us back pretty far, so I knew I needed to head more inland into the valley. That's probably where Quinn would be.

"Quinn!" I shouted as we walked.

Roxy's ears perked up as she looked up at me, then stared at the damage around us.

I stood there, silent, trying to see if I heard anything, but there was nothing, just the Roxy's pants and the sound of the waves behind me. I said his name one more time just to see, but still, nothing.

"Come on, girl," I said. "Let's go find him."

We searched for hours. Roxy was a good sport about it, right by my side at every step. Twice, we stopped for a break. She was good at finding somewhere I could sit, and she laid down next to me. Despite the hours that had gone by, I hadn't seen Quinn. We were almost to the valley's edge before it rose back up in elevation. Part of me still had hope. I should have found his body lying on the ground if he had been dead, stone cold and silent. He had to be alive and moving.

I'M THE SAME

The late afternoon sun was starting to wane in the distance. I had worked up a sweat with all the walking, even in the cool air. It had been warmer again today, and I assumed tomorrow would continue that trend. The ground was even starting to dry slowly. Water was still hiding in areas that hadn't drained. I'd even seen a few people floating in them, and I'd checked them all to make sure they weren't Quinn. There were a few that almost made me sick to look at. Even they didn't compare to the horrors that still haunted me some nights, though.

"We should start heading back," I told Roxy.

She lifted her head, and her tail wagged with endless energy. I would be surprised if she thought it was about time.

I was frustrated then, trying not to take it out on the dog. We had walked most of the day and come up empty, finding not even a single person alive. I felt like I was walking in hell, where nothing was living. The only thing keeping me in reality was the German shepherd walking next to me. I didn't mind the company at all.

We walked in a diagonal path towards the road, trying to cover more ground, still holding out hope. Even if my mind was starting to tell me that there was no way he could survive out here this long, I had to hold on to hope. I wondered if there was going to be a moment when I would have to make a decision—one would involve me deciding to move on towards Newport and admitting that I had lost him.

I didn't want to think about it, so I tried to think about anything else. That was when I realized my parents were probably having a complete panic attack on the other side of the country. I was sure they'd heard about the disaster on the news by now and had probably tried to call me. It wouldn't have gone through, of course, mainly because my phone was soaked and dead in my bag somewhere. The phone lines were probably jammed, or worse, the cell towers down. They would just have to wait and pray that I was alive.

I tried to think of something else, something cheerier, and naturally, I came to my writing. I wondered how I could turn this experience into a book, and along the walk, I started to form some good ideas that I could use.

We reached the road as the sun was setting. The sky turned to the same beautiful array of colors that it had the night before. I still found it weird that the Pacific was so peaceful, even after all of this, knowing that it had been killed and destroyed in seconds. Roxy sat beside me as we watched the sunset momentarily. I reached down to pet her as she snuggled her nose into me.

After a moment, we began walking down the empty road back towards the campsite. We arrived just as the night began falling and the last ray of sunlight began to leave. I quickly built a fire, and Roxy comfortably sat beside it. The air had started to cool again, and the fire warmed the area. I made a peanut butter sandwich for Roxy, and she ate it with little mercy. Poor thing was hungry, and all I could give her was that. I made a second one and offered it to her too. I couldn't resist her eyes.

After she ate, she came and laid down beside me, placing her head on my lap. I stroked her head, letting my hand run through her soft fur. We sat like that for an hour or so, just taking it in, letting the past two days wash over us, and trying to let the wounds begin to heal.

Roxy's head shot up from my lap as she stared out into the night. Her eyes perked up, and her gaze held steadfast.

"What is it?" I whispered to her as she let out a slow, rolling growl.

She got up on all fours and walked to the other side of the fire. Her tail was down, and her eyes were trained into the night. Roxy let out another growl before she barked.

Someone or something was there.

I'M THE SAME

I got up from where I was sitting but had nothing to defend myself with except a piece of firewood. I would have to take my chances. If it was a bear or a wolf, I was toast.

Roxy barked again.

This time, I heard footsteps. These were human, but that didn't make me feel any better. What if they were here to take what I had, to kill me? I just had to do whatever it took to survive.

"Who's there?" I shouted. "Show yourself."

Roxy barked, echoing my statements.

There was nothing for a moment. Maybe we had scared whoever it was off?

Then Roxy let out another bark, and then another, each with more intensity.

"Who's there?" I shouted again, a thick piece of firewood in hand. I was ready to use it, even as Roxy looked ready to attack.

A shape slowly began to step forward, the fire showing their silhouette against the background, but there wasn't enough light to make out their features.

Roxy let out another bark as they came forward slowly, their hands up.

"I saw the fire. Please help," a low voice spoke.

With a gasp, I dropped the piece of firewood and ran toward them.

CHAPTER 23

I ran straight into him, placing my arms around his waist. At first, he seemed stunned, but I could recognize that voice anywhere.

"Kodak?" Quinn said as I turned his face towards mine. The fire now showed the features of his face.

Tears filled my eyes as the emptiness that I had been feeling faded, replaced by the warmth of his body. "Yes, you goof," I replied.

Now it was his turn to squeeze me, and I just let myself melt into him. "I thought I lost you," he said. His eyes were watering.

"Me too."

We broke apart, and he smiled at me. From what I could see, his clothes were tattered, and there were a few scrapes and bruises visible. Other than that, he was alive. I'd found him—or rather, he'd seen me.

I looked back at Roxy, who looked confused as she approached us. She slowly brought her noise between us, and she sniffed Quinn, probably making sure he wasn't a threat.

"I leave you, and you find a dog," Quinn said, looking down at her.

"She found me as I was trying to find supplies," I said, bending down to pet her. "Her name is Roxy."

Quinn bent down to her and slowly placed his hand on her head. I think it helped that I was there; she was uncomfortable with him.

"Hey, Roxy, have you been taking care of Kodak?" he said.

Her tail began to move again, then she began to rub her head against him. Once Roxy had declared him a friend, I took Quinn back towards the tent and we sat beside the fire. Roxy lay next to me while Quinn's eyes stared into the fire as he told me everything that had happened

"How did you do it?" I asked.

Quinn looked over at me. "I kept walking. I searched for you once the water receded. I saw the fire last night, but didn't dare to come this way."

"Why not?"

"I thought it was just some stranger, and with my luck, they would shoot me."

I laughed. "It's a good thing I wasn't a stranger then."

Quinn smiled and leaned his head against mine. "I'm glad it was you. I don't think I could lose you too."

I glanced down and noticed some blood trailing down his leg. I leaned over and pulled his pant leg up. There was a pretty nasty gash going up his leg. "Quinn, you're hurt," I said.

"It was just a cut. I must have hit something in the water."

"Well here, let me clean it up a little," I told him as I reached for my bag, pulling out the first aid kit I had brought from the house. I found the alcohol wipes and then tried to see if there was peroxide, but we weren't that lucky. I thought it best not to tell him and instead just place it on the wound. He screamed for a second as his body tensed from the pain, startling Roxy.

"Sorry, but I need to clean it," I told him.

His eyes watered, and I knew it hurt, but he nodded his head, his teeth still clenched. Once I wiped it, I found some gauze and wrapped the wound tight. He flinched a few times, but soon, I was done.

"There. It should start to heal, but I need to watch it to ensure you don't get an infection."

"Thanks. Where did you learn that?"

"First aid?" I replied. "It's not that hard, plus my aunt is a nurse."

"That makes sense," he said, looking at the work that I had done.

"Have you eaten?" I asked.

"Just the few Clif Bars we had," he said, pulling a wrapper from his pocket.

I laughed. "Well, I have peanut butter and bread if you'd like a change in food," I said. That, of course, perked the dog's interest.

"Please," he laughed.

I made him a sandwich, which he devoured in a second.

Roxy tilted her head at me.

"You already had two," I told her.

She huffed and then laid her head back down. I didn't think she was happy with that answer, but we also needed to save food. I did, however, put some water in her bowl, which she drank before resting her head again.

Quinn's gaze was still locked on the fire. I watched, trying to see if I should say something. I knew he was still suffering. He'd lost his mom. That wasn't something you easily walked away from.

"How are you doing?" I asked.

"Fine, now that I'm here."

"No. Seriously, Quinn, your mom?" I poked hard.

His eyes watered, but he just shook his head as he tried so hard not to completely break. My heart ached, seeing it. God knew how I would have been. I might not have even been able to fight my way through the wave.

"It's okay. I got you." I said, bringing him to me so I could hold him as he tried to pull it together.

"It hurts," he managed to say. "It feels like I have this void in me."

"I know, but it will get better."

I'M THE SAME

"Does it? Kodak, I see how it has you. The dreams, the fear in your eyes, and I don't want to even imagine how the car wreck affected you." It brought it into focus a little, how perceptive he had been. He noticed the pain, even though I was hiding it. What do I say to him now?

"We will get through it together, one step at a time."

I just rubbed his back as he sat there, letting him grieve, letting him know that I was right there next to him, where I would always be. We were still for maybe an hour or so.

"We should head north tomorrow," I said.

Quinn shifted his head a little, sniffling. "Yeah, I don't think we can go south back to Alnwick. Not with the bridge out."

"Also, I need to find someone," I told him as I pulled out the picture in my pocket.

Quinn looked at me strangely for a second, but I told him about the woman I had met and her dying wish. It was weird to tell him that story, that moment. It was the one time these past few days that I hadn't been thinking about or trying to find him. I just comforted a dying mother.

"Then we head to Newport," he said. "It would be our best shot anyway. Most of the town is above the tsunami zone, so we could get a ride to Alnwick."

"We should rest, then, since we'll be walking tomorrow."

"Hey, no separating this time." He smiled.

"Absolutely not."

We retired into the tent, and Roxy laid with us. I curled up and held Quinn, letting the warmth of his body warm me as I laid awake, thinking about how lucky I was to have him alive, for us both to be alive. The breathing of Quinn and the dog comforted me, and with their sounds, I drifted into my first sleep in days.

We woke early as the sun was only beginning to peek above the mountains behind us. I quickly took down the tent and packed it tight in the bag. Quinn split the supplies between us to carry to make it easy on our backs, as it was going to be a long walk. Roxy was ready to go, seeing that we were up and moving. Once, she did her business in the woods, of course.

Roxy came back and shook her collar as it jingled. That was our cue that we were ready to head out, to march north. I held Quinn's hand, and we walked towards the road through the trees and ferns that lined the path. We made our way down to the valley, this time, determined to make it across together.

The sun was up by the time the road leveled off. Quinn pointed to the place he had stayed the night before. It was near the beach, a small shelter where he could keep warm. We passed the overturned truck, and Roxy whined a little as we passed. I told Quinn what I'd found there, believing the man to be Roxy's owner. He was still dead in the driver's seat, curled against the roof. Quinn couldn't even look at the body as we walked past.

It took us maybe an hour before we reached the point where we had been as the wave was coming ashore. Crossing the small stream took us a minute, and Roxy got a quick drink in.

Our feet had to be placed perfectly to avoid falling, which would have only been a few feet, but still. I had no desire to be wet anymore. I'd gotten more than my quota this week.

"Here," I said to Quinn as I held my hand to him. I helped stabilize him as we stretched across the creek and made it to the other side. Roxy had no care in the world about walking straight through the water and emerging on the other side. Her tail wagged away, enjoying the walkway too much.

"Thanks," Quinn replied as we walked down the road, which turned through the landscape and toward the coast. The waves roared ashore and the smell of salt filled the air. It was better than a few hundred feet inland, where it smelled like death.

We passed a line of twigs, sand, and leaves, a marker of where the water's height was. We were entering the tsunami zone yet again. I couldn't say I was excited about that; I would be spending the entire journey looking over my shoulder, wondering if there was another wave coming. I had been trying to keep it together the whole morning. My chest felt tight like everything inside me was shaking, the earthquake within me now.

I had Quinn with me now, and I didn't want to lose him again. I scanned around us, making sure there was nothing that could take him away.

"Can we stop for a few minutes?" Quinn asked. We were on the road, near a nice clear area where we could sit and look out into the ocean.

"Sure thing," I replied. We had made good progress that morning, and I didn't see why we couldn't stop and rest. My legs hurt, so I couldn't imagine how Quinn was holding up. "Let me look at your leg."

Quinn found a rock to sit on as he raised his pant leg. It was still tattered and dirty. As he did, I could see the bandage was still holding up, but it had a soft, reddish-brown spot in the middle. I had expected that, as it was still bleeding when I patched it up last night. With his leg resting on my knee, I pulled more badges from my bag. I was glad I had picked up the first aid kit on our way out of town.

"It's going to hurt again, isn't it?" he said, looking down at me.

"Well, it's either that or I cut it off."

"I'll take the pain."

"I thought so," I said as he grinned at me.

I pulled the bandage off. The wound still looked rough and ugly, but it wasn't actively bleeding, which made me feel better. As I placed another alcohol wipe on the wound, he flinched. I wrapped it again, tight, with a new bandage. I maybe had enough for one more wrap after this one, so this would need to hold for a while, or at least until I could find more.

"All set." I placed the excess materials back in my bag as Quinn looked down at me. Roxy had joined him on the rock, her head on his lap while he rubbed it.

"Who knew that Kodak was a doctor," he joked.

I smiled and narrowed my eyes. "There's a lot of things you still don't know about me, Quinn."

He looked at me with his eyebrow raised. "Oh, I intend to find out everything."

"I bet you do," I said, removing his leg from my knee. "Come on, rest time is over."

Quinn slid down from the rock with Roxy following after him. It was nice to see the two bonding. As we traversed down the road, the sun rose in the sky as the temps rose. It was still pleasant to me. Quinn, on the other hand, was starting to sweat a little. I swear he wouldn't be able to handle the sauna of summer in the South. I barely did.

Looking up at mountains rising in the distance, it was jarring to see the line of damage from the tsunami as it had pushed and uprooted trees in its path. We saw a few houses that had been in its path, and they had been knocked clear off of their foundations. All that was left was the slab of concrete left bare in the sunlight.

"It's so sad to see it this way," Quinn said.

"Funny how nature can be so giving, and then take it away in seconds."

"Very true, but it can also give us a new beginning."

I tried to seem happy at that, but all I saw was the destruction, I did my best to at least seem like it made sense with a faint smile.

Quinn interlocked his hand with mine, and we continued onward. We finally came to a structure that was still standing. It looked like an old inn, with a worn, blue paint job that must have been brushed away by the wind and rain all these years. Quinn went to the door and knocked on it, but no one came. He knocked again and then pulled at the door. It was locked. It seemed abandoned like they had evacuated after the quake.

"I'm going to break it open," Quinn said.

"What? Why in the hell would you do that?" I said. Just because it was abandoned didn't mean we should break into it.

"We can see if there are any supplies," he said, searching the ground for something.

"Quinn, that's looting." I was shocked he was even considering this.

"It's either that or we starve. That peanut butter won't hold us over much longer."

I didn't like the idea, even if he had a point. He found a rock that he could break the glass with, then turned towards the door and paused briefly before throwing the rock at it. The glass shattered. Quinn used his uninjured foot to push the rest of the glass through so he could unlock the door.

I took a deep breath; we had just committed a crime. Even if it was for survival, this whole area was closed off to the outside world because of a major disaster. It was still a crime, but Quinn was right. We needed to survive.

The inside looked like a mess, with furniture that had fallen over and moved about. A large crack went up the wall and across the ceiling, the whole structure creaking and moaning as the wind blew against it.

"Quinn, let's hurry," I said, not like the state of the building.

"Okay, but look over here." Quinn was on the other end of the room now, next to two large, fallen pieces of furniture. As I got closer, I noticed they were vending machines, their glass shattered and products exposed. "More food and water," he replied, grabbing items and placing them in his pack.

I ventured behind the counter and found nothing useful besides scattered papers and overturned chairs, along with a few pieces of the ceiling that had fallen. I returned to Quinn, convinced nothing here was worthwhile. My hands sweated as I fidgeted, waiting for Quinn to finish.

I moved to where Roxy guarded the door. Inside felt claustrophobic, and the fresh air helped calm my nerves. I knelt beside her. She glanced at me momentarily, then trained her eyes back on the horizon. I scratched her ear and told her she was a good girl. Even then, she kept her guard, but I did notice her tail wag just a little.

"You ready?" I heard Quinn come behind me.

"Yeah," I said.

Roxy took the cue to get up from where she stood to watch. We set out on the road once again. The sun was still high in the sky, lowering ever so slowly as the day progressed.

We'd needed the food. Then again, was the world ever black and white instead of an ever-expanding area of gray?

CHAPTER 24

B y that afternoon over three hours later, Quinn was sweating more than he should be, even with as much exertion as we'd had. It was maybe a balmy upper sixties, maybe even seventy, in the sunlight outside. His face was turning red, and he was beginning to slow down. He glistened in the sunlight as he hunched over, trying to catch his breath. The real giveaway was Roxy; she wouldn't leave his side, constantly placing herself next to him, tail low. I knew something was up, but I couldn't put my finger on it.

"You sure you're okay?" I asked again.

His glare told me he was getting tired of me asking. "Yes. It's just hot out," he replied, this time with a little more force and agitation.

"Quinn, it's not that hot." Even the cracked asphalt we walked on was cool.

"You're from the South, Kodak. The version of hot you know is hell."

Fair point, but still. He could at least keep the attitude at bay. This made me worry more, as I knew how I could be when sick. My parents hated to be around me when I was; it was probably the only time my mother had ever called me a bitch. I did deserve it.

I kept walking, but often looked his way to ensure that he was keeping pace, my eyes peeled for any sign he was faltering. It had been maybe an hour or two since we left the inn, and the sun was lowering as we slowed our pace to nowhere near the brisk walk we'd had this morning. Maybe it was the lack of food getting to him, or water. Once we stopped, I could boil some more and perhaps it would help. However, that didn't explain the sweating.

We moved up and down in elevation, passing lines of pure devastation and then back into dense conifer forest. It felt like a rollercoaster, only in slow motion. Despite the tranquil environment—when we weren't surrounded by destruction, at least—my mind was still preoccupied. I needed to get to Newport, yet the closer we got, the farther it seemed away. I would see evidence of structure only to find it to be a small area of civilization on these desolate shores that was left.

Whether we were in the woods or on the coast, the only constant was the sound of the waves crashing. For most of my life, I had found that sound relaxing. Now, it mocked me, telling me to quit and lay next to it so it could sweep me away. It whispered in the air like a siren's song. Maybe that was where the myth had come from, this very experience. If we actually made it, I might have to use that line. How could I even think about writing right now?

I didn't even know if my work was still at the house. Was the house even there, or had it been washed away with everything else? Was the town of Alnwick still standing, or had it been destroyed, wiped from the map in one single wave of Mother Nature's destruction? We didn't even know if Olivia had made it. Quinn had said she would meet us, yet we hadn't made it—the bridge had made sure of that.

My mind snapped back to reality. I looked back to ensure Quinn followed me. He was, but he was lagging further behind. I slowed my pace to match his and Roxy's. Her eyes looked up at me, and this time, there was something in them that I hadn't seen before: worry.

"Do you want to stop and rest?" I asked. Quinn had been quiet for a while.

"No, we need to keep moving," he replied. He seemed even more tired than he had been just a few minutes ago.

Then his knees buckled.

Roxy let out a yelp, sniffing him and licking his face.

"Quinn!" I yelled, reaching him just before his head hit the ground. I placed my hand on his forehead. It was searing hot, and his body was soaked in sweat. I shook him, not knowing what else to do. He didn't move, and his breath was shallow. I shook him again and yelled his name.

His eyes fluttered open. "What – – "

I grabbed him under his knee and shoulders and slowly picked him up. I could feel the strain in my back, but this was the only way. I held him in my arms and began to walk as fast as I could under the circumstances. Roxy followed after me, whining every so often. She was scared, and frankly, so was I. I carried him along the road at the best pace I could manage. Quinn laid in my arms, barely lucid, and he was heavy. I couldn't do this for long before my muscles would give out. We rounded a curve and came to a parking area off the side of the road, a lookout to the ocean. There was even a section of beach down below, but that wouldn't help him.

Up ahead was a sign that pointed to a visitor center of some sort. I prayed that it had some medical supplies or an emergency kit. Maybe even an actual, live person could help.

Step by step, I carried him until I could see the gray wooden structure.

"Is anybody here?" I yelled. "Anyone? We need help!"

I was met with silence. It seemed dark and quiet on the other side of the glass doors. I placed Quinn down on the ground as I banged on the door and pulled, but no luck. It stayed locked and shut. I searched, desperate to find anything that I could use to get the door open. All I saw was a bike, and without thinking, I picked it up and threw it at the door. I did it again and again until cracks started to stretch across the glass.

"Break, you stupid door!"

As I threw the bike again, the glass cracked like a spiderweb.

Screw it.

I backed up into the parking lot, then I ran toward the door, my eyes set on my target. I generated as much speed as I could muster, and as I approached the door, I pushed my shoulder out, smashing into the door through force. The glass shattered, giving way as it fell to the floor inside the visitor center. Along with myself as I screamed in pain. However, that didn't matter so I quickly unlocked the door, then headed to Quinn, picked him up again, and brought him inside. Roxy slowly walked after us, careful to step on as few shards of glass as possible.

Near the door was a counter that seemed to be the main reception desk, filled with documents and maps of the area. The walls were light brown wood with darker beams to make them stand out. I laid Quinn up on the counter as his eyes fluttered again.

"Quinn, wake up," I said. "Quinn!"

I pulled his pant leg up and took the bandage off his wound. My heart sank; it was red and swollen. Streaks of red spread from it, and now there was yellowish-green puss oozing from it. It was getting worse.

I searched the counter and drawers for any medical supplies, but all I found was a turned-over and cracked computer screen, and papers and brochures everywhere. I tensed as I felt the heat of my body rising, and blood rushed to my head. I lashed out, grabbing the computer and throwing it to the other end of the room, where it shattered.

Roxy jumped at the sound.

"I'm sorry, girl," I said to ease her. I couldn't let my anger get the better of me. I should have seen this coming. He had been out there all day and night before finding our campsite, and I should have known the wound would get infected. What he needed was medicine, which we didn't have. The nearest hospital was in Newport, and Quinn was in no shape to make it there. Not now.

I looked elsewhere for a first aid kit. There had to be one here somewhere. I moved toward the open door at the far end of the room. Inside the office were falling ceiling tiles, a few desks, and filing cabinets, and I tore through them all. Just as I was about to lose hope, my eyes landed on a tall cabinet in the back corner of the room, next to a Smokey Bear sign about wildfires. I wrenched open the metal latch and opened the cabinet.

On the inside, it was filled with more paper and boxes. Some old maps were rolled up, along with other things that seemed irrelevant. At the top, however, was a bright orange bag. Bingo. I pulled it out and placed it on one of the desks, unzipping it to reveal its contents. Sure enough, it was a first aid kit. My skin no longer felt like it would burn from the inside out. I searched through the kit to find bandages, cloth wraps, alcohol wipes, and Advil. It would at least help keep his fever down, but he would need more than just that. He needed strong antibiotics—something only a hospital would have.

I quickly filled a small cup of water from a nearby jug, then raced to Quinn's side.

"Here, take this," I told him as he moved his hand slowly towards it, taking the small tablet, and throwing it in his mouth. He took a swing of the water, and swallowed it. He stared for a moment; I don't think anything was registering with him. However, that was all the lucidness I needed from him until the fever died.

I slumped down next to him as he lay quiet. His eyes closed again.

What was I going to do?

Silence—

Pain—

Helpless—

I rested my head against him, trying to think as Quinn's breathing slowed, his chest moved up and down slightly with each breath. I closed my eyes and wondered why the world hated me so much. Why was I doomed to always feel this pain of losing someone? We would never make it to Newport, not in this state.

I would stay with him until it ended. Even if that meant this was my end, I would be there with him through it all. My soul would be crushed and then shattered, but I would stay, just like I had for her. My mother had once told me that this was the price of love, the cost of caring. I looked at it as more like a loan, which eventually, would come due. I guessed mine were all short-term loans, then. It didn't matter because I didn't know how long I could keep doing this—caring, then losing.

I tried to manage the knot that kept forming in my abdomen, a numbness spreading over me. Even with the tears that threatened to develop and fall down my face, I held it all back and just laid there, staring into the empty space of the visitor center. He was dying, and I could only offer him something to soothe the fever. My worst fear was coming true, and I could do nothing. Even Roxy seemed depressed, her head just lying across his lap. The only sound was an occasional soft whimper from her.

We sat there as the sun began to set and the air grew cooler. I got up at one point to try and put some peroxide on the wound since the medical kit had some. Quinn didn't flinch or wake when I rubbed it on his leg, and I knew it had to hurt; peroxide always did. The only sign that he was alive was his shallow breathing, and when I wrapped clean bandages around his leg, I could feel his heart race. By the time I was done, darkness had begun to fall and the last remaining sunlight began to escape the sky, to be replaced with stars.

I covered Quinn in one of the blankets from the gift shop area. It was a thick, wool blanket with a Southwest geometric pattern on it. I had seen several of these in shops, even in Alnwick, and it must have been a local Oregon brand. Outside, I built a fire a little way from the building, boiled some more water, and ate what food I could, even if I wasn't hungry.

Roxy refused to leave Quinn's side. I brought her a bowl of water and food. She picked up her head and ate some before lying back down on his lap.

"Good girl," I said as I scratched her head.

"Kodak," I heard Quinn mumble.

"Hey, you," I said, coming next to him. "Here, take some water." I gave him the bottle I had just filled up. It was still a little warm, but he needed the fluids.

He took it and drank it slowly. "What happened?" he asked.

I felt his head, which was cooler, not as hot as a few hours ago. The medicine must have been helping a little.

"You passed out," I told him. "Your leg, Quinn, it's getting worse."

He looked up at me, his eyes meeting mine. "It's bad, isn't it?"

I nodded as he closed his eyes and tried to sit back again. He saw the medical kit beside him, its contents spread out and looked out into the building.

"Where are we? Did you—" He squinted at the shattered glass by the door.

"It's a visitor center, and yes, I did," I answered before he could finish his sentence. I knew what he would have said, and I wasn't giving him that satisfaction, even if he was sick.

"Must be Cape Perpetua. I didn't take you for the criminal type," he replied.

"Shut up." I knew he was poking at me for my earlier comments this morning. At least he still had his sense of humor, even if it was to my detriment.

He tried to smile, but it wasn't very successful.

It had been a few hours since he'd last taken some Advil. I made him take two more. He took them willingly and tried to make a joke about me being his nurse. I chose to ignore it.

I laid next to him and curled up under the blanket with him. His head rested against my shoulder, our combined body heat warming us as the chilled air settled across the floor.

"You're going to be okay," Quinn said, his voice low and raspy. "I'll always be here." His hand moved over my heart, which ached at his touch, filling me with what felt like hard stones that couldn't break.

Not again—

"With you next to me. Always." I struggled to get the words out.

"I need you to go," Quinn told me.

"What? No," I replied. "I'm staying right here." He must have been getting delirious. Why would I leave him? He was crazy to even consider it.

"Kodak, you need to leave," he said as his eyes gazed into mine in the moonlight. "That's the only way. I'm not going to make it to Newport."

"I'm staying. That's the end of it," I replied, trying to hold back the tears that pressed against me.

"Kodak—"

"No," I interrupted him. "I'll search for medicine in the morning. I'm not losing you, not like I lost everyone else."

I couldn't. Not again. I wouldn't; I would fight to the end of the earth if I had to. I would not lose someone else that I loved. The world had done nothing but suffocate my will, my life. Today, I would not let it.

"It wasn't your fault," Quinn mumbled. "Not this, and not then."

"Yes, it was. I told them." I trembled at the memory. "Just as Jordan made that turn. He lost control because I told them to turn, just as Becca had pushed me to do."

Silence—

They were dead because of me. Everyone who blamed me was right.

"Jordan hit the tree, and they all died. They still haunt me. I see that damn scar every day, reminding me of what I did."

"You didn't kill them," he told me as he stared out into the night. "Jordan missed the turn because he just missed the turn. Jordan was probably speeding, and it was just an accident. It would have probably happened whether or not you told them. At least they got to see the real you. All of you, like I do."

I wanted to believe him, yet I couldn't. Jordan had been speeding; he was right about that. I remember the officer telling me the same thing, that it wasn't my fault, and I hadn't believed him then either. This was my curse to bear. So I let him think he'd won and just snuggled next to him. I still heard my own words echoing in my head, just as everyone screamed and everything burned. All because I'd told them how I felt, who I was, and why I was different.

"Kodak, it's ok to forgive yourself. You don't have to hold on to it, to remember them." Quinn shifted as best he could towards me as he placed his hand over my heart again. "They will always be here."

I held his hand, maybe it was time. As much as it all hurts.

"Quinn," I said. "I need you to live." I at least needed to tell him because this might be my last chance. Who knew what I would find in the morning, and in what state he might be in? I might only have a day or two left with him.

He shifted closer to me. "I know."

That was what really did it—what brought me to tears was hearing him say it. After everything, I had found it in Oregon with someone I never would have imagined. He had come out of nowhere and snuck up on me, even while I tried to run away. He'd pulled me back in; he'd fought for me. He'd held me through the nightmares, pulled me from a frozen river, and found me through rubble and destruction. What had I done for him, other than try to escape?

We held on to each other through the night. The wind swayed the pines, and silence haunted the land. I could make out stars in the sky as the moon rose high, lighting the sky to dark blue instead of pitch black. My arms wrapped across Quinn as he fell asleep.

I remained awake, plotting my next move. It was my turn to fight. He had been there for me this entire time, but now it was my turn—my turn to hold on, to love, to care. My turn to not rest, to march until I succeeded, until we survived.

It was either that or perish.

CHAPTER 25

Quinn's fever returned overnight, and he began to cough. The moon was beginning its descent as I gave him another Advil dose to help with it. It was safe to say that Roxy and I hadn't slept well. Not with Quinn like this. He was suffering, and I couldn't help him as much as I wanted. If I could have, I would've carried him to Newport, but we wouldn't even make it a mile before my back would give out.

Throughout the night, there was only a little moment where I could rest my eyes before they were open again, as I wiped sweat from Quinn's forehead or listened to the sound of him coughing up his lungs. I tried to pour some more peroxide over his wound again; this time, he winced before settling back down and sleeping once more. Rest would help his body fight off the infection.

As the sky lightened, I gathered a few things in my backpack, trying to keep the sound to a minimum so Quinn could rest. Roxy looked my way, but still laid beside him. I packed the flares I'd found, the knife, a bottle of water, and one of the last Cliff Bars we had. I even took a map of the area. Up north was the small town of Yachats, and I prayed that there was a clinic somewhere that had the medicine Quinn needed to hold on. All I asked was for him to be able to survive this.

Yachats was just past Devil's Churn, a point of interest next to the coast which had a small outpost. A few others were to the south, but I wasn't there to see the sights. There was one problem, however—a small bridge led into Yachats. I hoped that it had withstood the earthquakes, otherwise, getting to the other side would be a chore, if not impossible in the timeframe I had.

I folded the map, placed it into my pocket, and put on a zip-up hoodie from the gift shop with Oregon Coast written across it. I knew I wouldn't need it as the day warmed, but it was cold and valuable for now. To make myself feel better, I put some cash on the counter to pay for it.

I walked back to Roxy and Quinn. Quinn's eyes were closed as his chest moved up and down slowly. Roxy looked up at me, her eyes steadfast.

"Watch him, girl," I told her. "Protect him for me; I'll be back."

She tilted her head and laid it back against him. She knew what to do. She was going to protect him because she knew that was her job. Funny how dogs were, how unconditional their love was, even if you'd just met them. She was a keeper, that was for sure. I placed some water in her bowl and left a bottle for Quinn, then I set out into the dark morning. The sun wasn't even awake yet.

I traversed back to the highway. Everything was still; even the ocean was calm, the tide still out. I could see the sun begin to peek above the mountains to the east, painting the sky in pink and light purple that slowly faded to a bright yellow. The air was still cold as the salt of the ocean carried in the wind that was just beginning to pick up. To the west, I saw a small sandy beach between rocky shores.

I came to the viewpoint of Devil's Churn, with two gray, wooden buildings; one was a public bathroom. It wasn't the nicest, but it worked. When I was done, I walked into the inlet to the small stone lookout area. The waves came crashing in as the water sprayed over the rocks, shooting up into the air. It was pretty impressive, and I shook my head in amazement. I could watch this for hours if I didn't have other things to do – like save Quinn.

I walked across the empty parking lot and back to the road, which snaked up the hill some more, making my thighs burn with every step. I stopped at the top to sip my water before pressing on, passing more viewing areas of the Pacific. I tried not to look at it; part of me was angry at what it had done. I hated it. I blamed it too. I wanted to scream at it. How dare you do this! How dare you take everything away from me!

I kept walking through the twists and turns of the road underneath the tall pines. Just as the road rose, I slowly started to walk downhill, making me watch my every step over the large cracks and upheavals in the pavement from the earthquake. The damage didn't make me feel better about the bridge ahead, but I had to continue. I had to at least try. Not long later, I passed a sign that showed the town was only two miles ahead. I hadn't realized how close it was.

As I descended into Yachats, the devastation was heart-wrenching. Trees were scattered and littered across the ground, structures wiped from their foundations. Even the road was almost impassable as I had to climb over debris and trees. It wasn't green like I had become used to seeing along the coast; it was now an ugly brown, life seemly drawn out of the landscape. It smelled of death.

I was careful not to step on any power lines that could still be live, or any other hazards that could be around. I wandered through the streets of the quiet town. The town itself was tiny, probably 1,000 people. I had heard that it was primarily a tourist town, other than the small fishing industry located there. However, now I would be surprised if there was even one person left. Which made it so much harder to find what I really needed, what Quinn needed.

I made it to where the bridge stood. It wasn't completely gone, but it wasn't sturdy either. It seemed to be barely hanging on to life. If another aftershock or even a truck crossed over it, it might fail, making it harder for me to get to the other side. It wouldn't be impossible, just more challenging. Sections of it had already fallen, making the road a patchwork of cement held together by rebar.

I paused, debating whether I should cross or take the hard way and try to climb down and then back up. The latter would take forever, and Quinn didn't have that time. My decision was made.

I cautiously walked across the bridge. It shifted slightly with every step, but for the most part, it held. My nerves nearly paralyzed me any time the bridge made a sound. It took me longer than I expected to get across it, mainly because every time I took a step, I froze in fear, hoping that it would not fall out from beneath me.

When I finally made it to the other side, it was much the same as before. Destruction was everywhere I turned. I searched for at least one standing building or a pharmacy that might be intact enough to hold medicine. I passed gift shops, houses, and a few restaurants— all had been utterly wiped away.

On this side, bodies littered the street, some crushed under structural damage. It was like no one had survived; the only ones who had survived were those who'd fled.

I approached one mostly intact building, a simple wooden structure. The door had been pushed in, making entering easy as I tried to see what was left of it. All I saw was a store ravaged by water, the debris line near the ceiling. There was really nothing here. I struck a nearby rack, throwing it to the other side of the room. I didn't need trash. There was nothing in this damn place that I needed. Every small step felt like I was just falling further behind.

I stepped out back into the sun. It was higher in the sky now, finally warming me. I looked around to see if any other places were still standing. There was nothing, not a single building still standing enough for me to even enter it.

I didn't even know why I'd picked this town to stop in, other than it was close. I could have easily pressed on more to see if there was another in better shape. It was tiny, barely a blip on the map. Why would it have the medicine Quinn needed? Why would the world even let me have it? It had been trying to tear me down and kill me from the moment I'd entered it, like I was some bug that needed to be squashed.

That was the story of my life, and it was still being written in the same clichéd way, just pounding me into the ground and being cruel enough to let me taste something good before going and destroying it. It was this that fueled the ever-burning rage inside me. I didn't want to feel it, yet it was there—the pure anger of a world that hated me. I knew what I was really feeling—the sadness and grief had started to hold me like an old friend I hadn't seen in a while. I couldn't say I was glad to see them.

I knelt down in the middle of the street and screamed, letting out all the emotions I had been holding in, pushing every ounce of the pain away as tears streamed from my eyes. My face burned as the screams turned to a never-ending sob. Soon, it was replaced with cold, as I had no emotions left to feel. My mother had once described this stage as a statue. After the wreck, for months, she'd said it looked like I had no feelings. She'd hated seeing me like that when all I gave her back was a blank stare. I couldn't say that was one of my proudest moments. Of course, she didn't know the full extent of the trauma I had experienced. She still believed that I had been unconscious through it all. I hadn't had the heart to tell her everything—how I'd seen and heard them all die. Those last moments with Becca.

Why was I different? Even after all I did to fit in, it had never been enough. Why did I feel pain? Why couldn't I just love and be able to keep them? I wanted to stay here and let the pain take me, let the world wield its final blow. Maybe that was when I'd find peace.

I wiped what tears were left on my face with my shirt, then took a breath and stood up. I still had a job to do. I needed to save Quinn and find Isabelle's daughter in Newport. I had to; I couldn't let my inner demons eat me again. If I did, it would just be better if I died. I had made promises, and I needed to keep them, even if I hadn't been able to keep the one I gave Becca—the promise that everything was going to be okay, even though I knew she was dying.

I could keep these ones.

I walked along the road as it rose, and I found a few buildings that seemed to be above the waterline. Maybe there was hope there. I would take anything at this point. The first was a home. Even as desperate as I was, I felt like breaking into a home wouldn't help Quinn. Why would they have what he needed anyway? That would be a stretch, even now.

However, the second building had an Rx sign hanging from it. It seemed to be precisely what I had been looking for—a pharmacy. It looked small and family-owned, but hopefully, it would still have what I needed.

It had green siding and a roof that looked worn. There were some cracks along the side wall, probably from the earthquake. At least it was high enough in elevation that it seemed to have avoided the waves. Hopefully, its contents were intact. The door was old, the glass shattered and locked. Figured I wouldn't be that lucky. Part of me still questioned if I should break into a pharmacy. I didn't even know what I was looking for or what would help Quinn with the infection spreading through his body.

I reached through the broken glass, careful not to let the exposed shards cut me, and reached for the handle. I carefully flipped the lock, then pulled at the door. I stopped as I felt something touch the center of my back.

"Stop right there!" a low voice commanded behind me.

CHAPTER 26

The object pressed harder against my back, the pressure making my nerves flare.

"What do you think you're doing?" the voice said again. From the sound of it, it was an older man.

I turned slowly to face him, making sure not to give him a reason to shoot me, at least not yet. That would ruin everything—not to mention the fact that I didn't want to die.

"I need medicine for my friend; he's hurt."

The man stared at me, his gun still facing me, now aimed straight at my chest. The man was older, and rough-looking, wearing overalls and a shirt. His hair was gray with age, his skin wrinkled, and he looked frail, but I didn't want to be the one to underestimate him. His boots were wet with mud; he must have been walking around the area. I would be surprised if he hadn't heard my screaming. Maybe that was what brought him over here.

"You could easily be lying, boy," he spat. "Lots of prized merchandise in there you could sell or distribute, just like the rest of them hooligans that try and steal our livelihoods."

He must have thought I was some junkie or dealer looking for a quick score. That couldn't be further from the truth.

"I swear, my friend has a wound that's infected. He's dying," I pleaded with him.

"Sounds like he needs a hospital, boy, not drugs." The man pointed the gun closer to me as he stepped forward.

I instantly took a step back as my heart jumped into my throat.

"Nice try to appeal to my humanity. I lost my daughter to those damn things."

"I'm not trying to appeal to anything. I'm serious, but I am sorry about your daughter," I said, trying to get him to realize that I was being serious. By the looks of his face and the fact that the gun still hadn't moved, I didn't think it'd worked.

His eyesight was steadfast. "Get in!" he ordered, stepping towards me as I backed into the store.

"Why?" I replied. "I can just leave. Just let me walk away, please, sir."

"Oh, no, you don't; you'll stay here," he said. "Otherwise, you could just come back when I'm not around. I'm not going to let hooligans like you strip my town bare. You'll stay here until the authorities finally get here."

"My friend is dying. He can't wait for the authorities. Besides, if they haven't come yet, I don't think they will." I hadn't seen one this entire time, not one. It was like they had abandoned us here to rot. They were probably busy in the bigger cities after the earthquake. Resources had to be spread thin, leaving remote areas alone.

The man pulled his gun back, and then struck my head with a blow that made me see stars. I fell to the floor, shocked and bruised. Pain spread throughout my body. I reached up a hand to feel my head, where blood was beginning to ooze. I just stared at him as he stood over me.

"Watch your mouth, boy!" he yelled. Then he was upon me, pulling a rope from behind him.

I backed up, sliding across the floor, trying to escape him. He must be insane. I pulled at a rack, letting it fall to the floor, blocking the man trying to get me. That gave me just enough time to get to my feet. He yelled as the rack crashed to the floor in front of me. In his rage, he aimed the gun, and I quickly ducked behind a counter as the first shot rang out, striking the wall next to me. The sound rang in my ears.

"Come out, boy, you can't run."

I moved, rolling behind another counter just as another shot went off, this time, striking the floor. His aim was getting better, and I looked around to find something I could use. Behind me on the shelf were some bottles of cough medicine and other liquids. I looked through them, finding nothing for Quinn, but I could use them to get out of the way. I grabbed a few bottles, one filled with an orange liquid and one with purple. I raised my head just enough to see where the man was, then ducked back behind the counter as he fired another shot.

I threw both bottles at him, each striking him quickly, one even bursting, covering him in the purple liquid.

"I kill you for that!" the man screamed. I must have really angered him now, and I believed him.

"Then you're no better than the criminal you mistake me for. I told you I need medicine for my friend who's dying."

"Stop lying!" he yelled, shooting again in my direction.

I flinched at the sound of impact next to me. If only I could get that gun away from him, it might give me a chance to get out of there. At least then, I would be alive, which was better than the alternative.

I heard his footsteps move, getting louder as the seconds passed. The wood creaked underneath them as my heart raced. I looked in every direction, trying to come up with something, anything.

"Come out, you creature," he spat, the last word washing over me. "There will be no trade for your kind here."

At his words, an anger rose up in one, one that had always lurked below. He considered me less than a human—a creature, other, different. His intent was to purge such creatures from existence. That was all I was to him—less than human. I had always that to people, never enough. Today, that wouldn't stand. I was just like everyone else—not inferior, not different. Today, I was the same.

"Who you calling 'creature'?" I said, walking out from behind the rack I was hiding behind. I threw caution out the window, ready for him to face me.

This time, it was he who stepped back. The gun was still pointing toward me, but he was hesitant.

"If you're going to kill me, you will at least recognize me as a human, not some creature."

I intended for him to look me in the eyes as he killed me. I wanted him to feel something, to realize the gravity of what he had reduced me to. I was no creature to slaughter.

"Get on your knees," he said.

"I don't kneel to men like you," I replied, holding my ground.

He puffed up his chest to seem significant as I challenged his superiority. "I said kneel," he yelled, but I still stood.

I inched my way toward him, ready to strike, waiting for the opening I needed.

"Kneel," he said. His hands shook on his gun. "Kneel," he repeated. His voice had risen and was shaking now too. He was trying to hold his composure. "Kneel."

"No."

As he stepped further back, he stared into my eyes. He took one more step backward, this time, tripping on the downed rack that had been thrown earlier. He fell to the floor, his finger firing the gun as he fell. The bullet hit the ceiling above him. He screamed, and I used the moment to race out of the building. I needed to find cover.

In the sun, I lurched toward the nearby house, knowing full well that he would soon be mobile and on the hunt for me again.

I hid next to the house with blue siding, trying to catch my breath from the sprint I'd just made. The sun was still high in the sky as I worked to slow my breathing, waiting for the man to emerge. It felt like time was moving slowly as I stood there, bracing for what was going to come, wondering how this would all end.

As I stood there, I realized it wasn't time moving slowly; there was just no movement coming from the shop, not even a sound. It was silent, just like it had been before.

I stayed where I was, ensuring he wasn't just waiting for me to give myself away. Then I wondered if maybe I had just imagined the whole thing.

I slowly peeked my head out from the side of the building. There was nothing by the road or other structures. Nothing in the pharmacy moved. It was quiet and deserted, just as it had been before the man came after me.

I slowly walked my way back over to it, my eyes alert and focused. I approached the door, but nothing stirred or made a sound. As I crossed the threshold, I flinched, thinking the old man would swing at me. But he didn't move.

The man was right where I had left him—on the ground, where he'd tripped over the rack. The gun was still in his hand. I kicked the firearm over to the side of the room, away from him. Even then, he didn't move, and my stomach sank. I moved closer to find his eyes wide open, yet there was no life in them. I placed my hand on his skin, feeling no pulse or energy. It was then that I noticed a piece of metal poking out of his stomach. Blood pooled on the floor.

I fell to the floor as my vision blurred, unable to think or do anything as I felt my breathing intensify. I tried to grab onto anything I could, yet I could only stare at him as I inched backward on the floor. He was dead, and I had killed him. God, I killed him.

Silence—

Cold—

Death—

The last thing he'd seen was me telling him no. He'd been scared as I approached him.

My lungs were on fire, like my skin was peeling from my body. My chest felt tight as I fought for air. I killed him. How? How did I—? How did—? What could I even do? How could I do such a thing?

Silence—

Cold—

Death—

I closed my eyes and tried to gain control over myself. It felt like every nerve was shouting at me. My body rejected what I had just done, hating me. It felt like it was trying to separate from my soul, leaving my body here with the dead man on the floor. It, too, would die, suffering from what it had done.

Breathe—

Breathe—

Kodak—Breathe.

I tried to calm down, to think, to stop sitting there. It took a moment before I started feeling better, feeling less like I was splitting in two. When I could focus clearly, my face was wet, and my body burned. I sat against the wall, just staring at where the man lay, still bleeding out. What would they think when someone found him? With all the damage, there would be a possibility they would just assume he died in the earthquake, or would they know? Would they know that I was here?

I couldn't think like that. There was nothing to figure out, nothing to do—there wasn't anything I could do. He was dead because of me, and there was no fixing that other than letting him rest in peace. What did his family think, if he even had any?

I sat there as the sun lowered, unable to really move until I realized Quinn and Roxy were waiting for me back at the visitor center. I remembered why I was there in the first place.

I picked myself up and began to look for anything that could help. I walked to the back, where the over-the-counter section was. The sad part was that I had no idea what he needed.

I searched around, my eyes landing on a book on the counter. Maybe it would lead me in the right direction.

I flipped through the table of contents, trying to find a section about infections. I found something under infected cuts/wounds. It recommended antibiotics, along with a slew of other things. I didn't have access to intravenous antibiotics, which it recommended for severe cases, so antibiotics would have to do.

I searched the nearby racks for amoxicillin, finding two options— an oral pill and a liquid solution. I grabbed the oral tablets and went back to the book, hoping it would tell me how to mix the solution. I was lucky that it did, and I followed the instructions on how to mix it. When I was done, I took both bottles with me, along with a few other supplies that I found around.

Then I left and headed back to the bridge. I quickly but carefully walked back to the other side. When clear, I ran as fast as possible, stopping only a few times to catch my breath. The world was a blur of colors as I raced back to Quinn. I hoped I wasn't too late, hoped he was still holding on. He had to, and I needed him to. I needed him to stay alive just a little longer so I could save him. The part of the road that increased in elevation burned my calves and thighs with every step, but I didn't let it stop me. I didn't even look at the ocean, keeping pace as I worked to move forward.

The road descended as I passed by Devil's Churn. I knew I was close as I followed the road until I saw the sign pointing to the visitor center. I ran up the path, pushing myself to continue on, to push forward, past all the pain. I let it all fade into the background. Nothing mattered, only this.

As I reached the door, Roxy barked and ran to me. Quinn was still sitting beside the counter, but he didn't move.

"Quinn?" I said, but he didn't answer. "Quinn!"

I kneeled next to him. He was still warm, but his heartbeat was faint.

"Quinn!" I yelled, desperate to wake him up. "Quinn!"

He still didn't move. I shook him. I couldn't lose him; he couldn't leave me.

I took out the liquid medicine, quickly poured some into a measuring cup, pulled his mouth open, and poured it in.

There was nothing. I reminded myself that it would take time for the medicine to take effect—time I don't know if he had. My eyes filled with tears as I leaned my head against his. I prayed for him to make it, for him to live. I stayed there, and Roxy whimpered while I cried. I held him, waiting for him to come back. I hadn't been fast enough. I hadn't been enough—again.

"Dammit, Quinn, wake up!" I screamed with a force that made Roxy flinch.

Silence—

Cold—

I sobbed, desperately pleading with anything that would listen. Please bring him back to me. I can't live like this, always losing people I love. I can't stand it anymore. I screamed as pain spread through my veins, controlling my every thought.

"Please, wake up, please, please!" I cried.

Silence—

Pain—

"Kod – " I heard a mumble. "Kodak?"

I saw his hand move, twitch.

"Quinn?" I gasped as his eyes fluttered open.

"What the hell did you just give me?" he said. "It tastes awful."

I let out a laugh. Out of everything he could say, that was what he'd decided to tell me?

"Medicine," I said, wiping the tears from my eyes. "I thought I lost you."

He smiled at me. "Not yet. You can't kill me that easy."

"I love you," I said.

Quinn glanced up at me. It took me a moment before I realized what I had said. I meant it too. I'd loved him for a while now, I just hadn't dared say it aloud. His mother had seen it, even as she was dying.

"I love you too," he replied as I kissed him.

Relieved, I snuggled in next to him, thankful he was still alive. Now I just needed us to get to Newport in one piece because that medicine wouldn't fix him.

"We still need to get you to a hospital," I told him.

He nodded, knowing we wouldn't be able to stay there. "Can we rest tonight, at least?" he asked. He looked pale still, probably exhausted, as his body was fighting the infection running through him.

"Yes, of course."

"I'm going to have to take more of that stuff, aren't I?" he asked.

"Yes, every three to four hours. According to the book."

He shook his head. "I don't even want to know." He laughed.

We sat there, and I looked above me and muttered, "Thank you." Maybe someone was looking out for us after all. I hoped so.

At first, all I heard was the same silence that I now found comfort in, only the faint sound of pine needles swaying, the roar of the waves as the tide came ashore. But there was something else as I listened. It thundering, like a faint machine. No—helicopter blades.

I jumped up as Quinn flinched. I ran towards the door to see if I could spot it through the trees.

"What is it?" he asked, trying to pick himself up.

"Can you hear it?" I asked.

He tried to listen. It was getting louder. He looked over at me—he heard it too.

"That's a helicopter. Maybe it's the National Guard finally making it here," he said, his smile from cheek to cheek.

I moved to the emergency kit on the floor, rummaging through it to find the flares. There were two stick flares and one flare gun. This was our chance—maybe our only chance to make it out of here.

I ran outside to the parking lot, keeping my eyes trained on the sky. I could still hear the helicopter, the sound getting louder. Where was it?

Quinn moved to stand at the door, while Roxy stopped next to me. Minutes later, I saw it as it was headed up the coast, coming from the south. Knowing this was my moment, I fired the flare gun.

The flame shot up into the air and exploded a couple hundred feet above us. I shot another one, lighting the sky in a red haze. I hoped that would get their attention as I lit one of the flares and threw it onto the ground, letting it light the parking lot. They had to see it. They just had to.

"Kodak!" Quinn called me.

I walked over to him, putting my arm around him to support him, and we waited as the flare burned on the ground, Roxy by our sides. The sound seemed to stop for a moment, and I worried that they had passed us without seeing the flares. It was just us, the red flare in the parking lot, and the pine trees surrounding us.

We were on our own yet again.

"They must have passed us," I said.

"Have faith, Kodak," Quinn replied.

"I'm trying, Quinn."

But it was hard not to think. They'd just passed us like nothing, like we didn't matter. We weren't being saved today. Tomorrow, we would walk—and that was if Quinn physically could.

"They're gone," I said. My head hung low as I was defeated and broken, wishing for something that would never come. This was just more proof the world hated me.

Then the silence was broken by the same sound. The thundering got louder until the wind picked up, moving the trees viscously around us.

"Look!" Quinn yelled, pointing to the sky. The sound was loud and furious now.

The helicopter was coming in for a landing in the parking lot.

We'd done it. We'd survived.

After everything we had been through, we would get Quinn the help he needed.

I started to cry again—this time, with joy. "Quinn, we survived," I said.

He grinned. Roxy barked as the helicopter landed on the parking lot's pavement. A small American flag was painted beside the cockpit—it was indeed the National Guard. The blades above it began to slow as three uniformed soldiers approached us.

"Is everyone alright?" the first soldier said. He was taller than both Quinn and me.

"He's hurt, and the wound is infected. He needs a hospital," I told him.

The soldier looked at Quinn, noting the bandage on his leg. He turned to the woman next to him. "Narvasa, get the gurney and tell the medic we have one incoming," he ordered.

My heart almost flipped. He was getting the help he needed.

The woman ran back to the helicopter and, with the help of another member of the guard, brought back a gurney and a medical kit.

"I'm Ella. We'll take good care of you," she told Quinn as they laid the stretcher on the ground before him. I walked over and helped them get him on the stretcher so that they could take him back.

"I'm Orin. I'm glad to see you two have survived." He reached out and shook my hand.

"I can't tell you how happy I am to see you guys," I said.

"Good job on the flares. It made us jump in our seats. Let's get you guys out of here."

"Thank you!"

I gathered our two bags and got Roxy calm enough to get her into the helicopter. Luckily, Orin seemed to be good with dogs and was able to get us both aboard. Quinn was lying in the center on the stretch. Ella and the medic were tending to him, the wound. Orin got me strapped in, and the rudders above began to hum and turn as the sounds again grew. I held on to Roxy. She snuck in a kiss or two as we rose into the air.

Soon, we were above the landscape, the visitor center getting further and further from view. Everything looked so small as we flew overhead. We could see the extent of the damage, the vast swath of land that had been obliterated by the tsunami. I was thankful it was over. The coast seemed so different now. Even the ocean seemed to stretch endlessly into the horizon as it shrank in the distance.

"Where are we headed?" I yelled to Orin so he could hear me over the engine noise.

"To a field hospital in Eugene. It's a forward-operating base for the response," he yelled back.

It wasn't Newport, but Eugene was probably better suited to help Quinn and, hopefully, had less damage than Newport. As we flew over the mountains below us, I thought of the woman who had died underneath that car. I felt around in my pocket to make sure I still had the photo of her daughter. When I had the chance, I would head to Newport to fulfill my promise.

For now, it was time to heal, for Quinn to heal. I could finally try to get a hold of my parents. They were probably tearing their hair out, wondering what had happened.

Quinn's hand reached for mine, and I took it, holding it tight.

Ella grinned as she watched us. I still had him, but what would they think if they knew what I'd done?

CHAPTER 27

The helicopter landed as more soldiers came to us. They took Quinn away into a giant green tent with a small cross on it. It was like his own army taking him taken care of. It was warmer in Eugene as Orin and Ella ushered me off the helicopter. From the looks of it, the camp was pretty large, with several soldiers setting up more tents. Rows and rows of green tents stretched for what seemed like miles, with people moving about, supplies being carried off trucks and pushed into more tents, or being sent out of the camp to the places that needed it.

Once we were away from the helicopter and could hear better, I turned to Orin and Ella. "How bad was it?" I asked. "What we witnessed was pretty bad."

"The whole fault ruptured. The earthquake was felt as far away as Las Vegas and Salt Lake City. The worst of the damage is from Seattle to Northern California, not including the damage from the tsunami," Orin told me. "We haven't been able to survey much of the coast yet."

"So bad?" I said.

"Really bad," Ella cut in. "You guys are lucky."

I took in her words as we entered the hospital tent. Roxy was right by my side on a leash that Ella found nearby. We stopped in a waiting area with chairs and a massive curtain blocking the view of the other side.

"Do you have a phone somewhere?" I asked.

Orin reached down to his waist and pulled out what seemed to be a satellite phone. "Here. Let them know you're safe," he said, handing it over to me like he knew exactly what I needed it for.

I took it and walked over to the side of the tent as I dialed the number my parents had long ago made me memorize. It rang a few times before my mother's voice answered. At first, I was silent taking in her voice. Something for a while I didn't think I would hear again. Then after she called my name, I answered.

I talked to her for a while and told her I was okay. She was so happy, she cried. Hell, I cried, despite trying so hard to keep it together. After the last few days, it was hard. I mentioned Quinn and let her know that it might be a second before I could call back. I wasn't sure when I'd be able to get a phone or for the cell towers to work again. I gave her as much detail as I could about his condition, and she told me she'd say a prayer for him. She was happy that we were okay and alive.

Once I hung up with her, I gave Mr. Condor a call. I also had his number memorized, as he was the contact person for the fellowship. I called twice before he answered. He was glad to hear from me, and I let him know that Quinn was here in Eugene at a field hospital. He was still in Salt Lake City, trying to get a flight in.

I didn't have the heart to tell him about his wife. That was best to do in person. Honestly, if anyone but me could say to him, I would be thankful. Seeing her die had been enough, but I knew there was a distinct possibility I'd have to be the one to tell him when he arrived.

I gave the phone back to Orin once I was finished just as two doctors came up to me. "Are you Kodak?" one asked.

"Yes," I replied.

"Quinn is stable. We had to give him a sedative and intravenous antibiotics, along with anti-inflammatories to get the swelling down. The wound was very infected, which is common in disasters like this. He mentioned that you gave him medicine. What was it?"

I took one of the pill bottles out of my pocket and handed it to him.

He looked at it and smiled. "You saved his life with this. This was a good find." The doctor handed it back to me. "We can take you to him if you'd like."

I nodded. "Thank you for saving us," I said to Ella and Orin before I left.

"You're welcome. Go be with him," Ella said.

The hospital was full of people on beds and doctors working. The level of pain that was being felt through this place was immense. You could hear screams as doctors worked to cure and fix the people. I was ushered back to a wing with areas sectioned off like rooms with privacy curtains. The little room where Quinn rested was big enough for a bed, the medical equipment he was hooked up to, and a chair.

"Here you go. He'll be out for a while. I'm going to have a nurse come take a look at your head." The doctor pointed to the gash from being pistol-whipped. I had almost forgotten about it.

When he left, I sat in the chair and waited for the nurse as Quinn slept. He looked so peaceful as his chest rose and fell. His leg was severely bandaged up again in fresh wrappings, the IV dripping medicine into him. Now all I could do was wait. Roxy sat next to me as we waited. The doctors had brought a water bowl and some food in for her, which she happily ate.

The nurse came in a few minutes later to clean the gash on my head.

"How did you get this?" She asked.

"I fell." I lied as she wiped it down and washed it. It stung as she did, but it quickly faded. Unlike the old man's face, I kept seeing in my head.

"Some fall, but it's not too deep. It should heal nicely." She replied finishing up and bandaging it.

She also checked on Quinn to ensure everything was where it should be. "I bet you two have a good story after this," she said, trying to make conversation.

I laughed at the comment. "I guess we do," I said.

She bent down and petted Roxy, who appreciated the effort with a tail wag.

The nurse left, and I settled more comfortably into the chair. As I sat there, everything caught up to me. I was exhausted. I had barely slept since the first earthquake, pushing myself harder than ever. I let my eyes close now, knowing that there was nothing that could harm us and that we were safe. With Roxy at my feet and Quinn in the bed, I slept for the first time. No dreams, just pure sleep.

I woke to find Roxy asleep on my feet. From the looks of it, it was morning. Quinn was still sleeping in the bed as I stretched my arms. The movement stirred the dog, who lifted her head up at me.

"Good morning, girl," I said as I rubbed her head.

"Good morning," Quinn said as his eyes opened. He tried to sit up, so I leaned over to help him. Roxy came up to him and sniffed his hand before licking it. "Good morning to you too."

"Glad to see you up. How are you feeling?" I said.

"A lot better, thank you," he replied. "How about you?"

"I'm good. The nurse said we must have a good story to tell," I told him with a laugh.

He smiled. "Did she know you were a writer?"

"Probably not, but hey, she's not wrong," I replied.

He shook his head, then looked down at his leg. "You know, I'll probably have a pretty cool scar. It won't just be you anymore," he said, pointing to it. There was humor in his voice.

I just shook my head at him. "You couldn't just let me have that, could you?" I joked.

"No, not at all. I needed one too." He laughed.

"So that was your excuse to get hurt?" He just smiled. It was the first time I had seen his smile since the bridge.

What was I going to do with him? He was over here making jokes after all of this, but then again, it wouldn't be Quinn if he wasn't. I told him that I had gotten ahold of my parents and his dad.

His face darkened at the mention of his father. He asked if I had told him what happened.

I shook my head. "I think that would be best coming from you," I told him.

"How do even do that?" He asked. "We've always had our moments, but he did love her."

"You start with that; you both loved her, and you will both remember her. So, it's okay to grieve together."

He nodded in agreement, his smile gone and defeat painted across his face. He was probably thinking of his mom.

"Oh good, you're up, Mr. Condor," the nurse said as she walked into the room. "How are we doing?"

Quinn shot a funny pun back at her and put on his happy face again.

She just shook her head.

"He's fine," I interrupted before Quinn could embarrass himself.

The nurse let out a laugh. "Well, good, because you have a visitor," she said.

Quinn looked at me funny.

I shook my head, also unsure. The only person I could think of was maybe his dad, who could have gotten a quick flight.

The nurse checked his vitals before turning to leave the room. "I'll go bring her back."

"Her?"

A few minutes later, she returned, this time with Olivia in tow, who rushed over to us as the nurse disappeared again.

"I'm so glad you two are safe," she said, hugging me.

"How did you find us?" Quinn asked. "Please tell me you didn't track me again."

I looked up, very confused.

"That was one time in high school, you goof," she shot back to him.

"Um, I need to know more about that," I said.

"A story for another day," Quinn laughed.

"I've been searching all the shelters and hospitals since you never showed up at the meeting place. This morning, I came here, and they said they had you." She looked down at Roxy. "And who are you?" Olivia said, petting her on the head.

"This is Roxy. Her owner died in the tsunami, so she decided to join the family," I said.

Roxy's tail wagged in approval.

"Speaking of family, where is your mom?" she asked Quinn.

The mood changed. Quinn's face darkened, and I thought of the bridge again. Tears welled in his eyes, and he was barely able to keep it together.

Olivia placed her hand over her mouth, sensing the change and coming to a conclusion. "I'm so sorry, Quinn," she said. Then she looked to me for more answers.

I didn't even know what to say. How could I explain something like that? All I could do was look away.

"Yeah, I wouldn't be here if it wasn't for him," Quinn said, looking over at me.

Olivia smiled.

"Can we change the subject?" I asked.

Olivia agreed and began to tell us about Alnwick, which parts of town were severely damaged. The bookstore would need a lot of work to open again. Quinn said that wouldn't be a problem. The good news was that the house I had been staying in was completely fine, besides minor damage from the earthquake. Olivia said it was high enough to avoid the water as it rushed ashore.

I took a moment to be grateful that we were all together. We were all safe, and tomorrow, we would still be there, living life.

Quinn glanced over at me as he told Olivia about the whole "I love you" thing, which made me turn red, mainly because it was still so new. She was happy and offered to plan our wedding. I laughed and told her to slow it down. It was three words, not a proposal. Everyone laughed again as we sat there telling our stories.

Olivia and Roxy left for a bit to grab some food for us all, which left Quinn and me alone again.

"So what now?" Quinn asked as he sat up in bed, looking over at me.

"We live life," I said. "Of course, once they release you."

"I know that you fool," he replied. "I meant about us."

"Well, I guess I should get back to writing, as I'll need a job. Plus I have to finish something for the fellowship. That is, if I'm going to stay out here."

He smiled. "I'm sure we could find something for you to do if you want to work."

"Stop throwing money around," I ordered.

He just snickered at me. "I know, I know."

"You better be glad you're cute," I told him. "Also, you'll have to deal with my mother, who will not be happy that I'm staying out here."

"Okay, I will. They can move out here too," he said. "You know, since we're a family now."

"Yeah, I guess we are," I said with a smile. We even had a dog, friends, memories, and stories. I couldn't believe how much life had changed since I first came to Oregon.

Olivia came back with real food—not the Cliff Bars or peanut butter that we had survived on for the past few days. I had never been so happy to eat chips and enjoyed all their salty goodness. The burgers that Olivia brought us were just as good. Roxy eyed them, drooling all over. I gave in and gave her a small piece when nobody was looking. I couldn't stand her eyes anymore; they were too cute and adorable. This girl had me wrapped around her paws like nobody's business.

The doctors later told us that Quinn would be ready to be released in a day or two. Of course, Quinn had to stay on antibiotics for two to three weeks to ensure the infection was gone. He would also probably have a scar, which he was excited about. Olivia couldn't figure out why; frankly, that was a story for a different day. They also told us they had a tent for us to stay in until we could return home.

Later that afternoon, Mr. Condor finally arrived. He rushed in past Olivia and me and bear-hugged Quinn in bed. I honestly had never seen him that openly emotional. Even Olivia seemed surprised. However, he then noticed the person who was missing. Olivia and I stepped out as Quinn told him about his mother. The scream pierced through me as I winched. Olivia just stared out endlessly. Even with all the good, we had still lost a loved one and still had scars that would always remind us of our pasts.

We gave them a moment.

"Kodak?" Olivia said. "How are you doing?"

"Right now, thankful. I pulled him away, and it hurt. I can't stand here and say that everything is going to be ok, but each day I know it will get easier. Because there will be a day that we will smile again at their memory."

"I look forward to that day, and I hope that it will come for you." She never said it but I think she might know. Know that I am still grieving from all these years, but for the first time even in all of this. I can say it doesn't hurt, not as much. "Kodak, you are one of the kindest souls, never let anyone define you. You are perfect just the way you are."

"Thanks, I'm glad I get to call you a friend," I replied.

"Oh, you are stuck with me now. Quinn is a package deal, if you have not figured that out yet."

Mr. Condor stepped out for a minute. His eyes were red. We returned to find Quinn no longer smiling, but he seemed lighter.

"You were right, we both loved her, and she would want us to work it out. Doesn't make it hurt less." He broke at the last part.

It was about an hour before Mr. Condor returned. I assumed her took a moment to mourn privately and collect himself. When he did, he sat next to his son and for the first time, I saw them talk. Not avoid each other.

Quinn took the time to tell his father about the paintings. The surprising part was his laugh at the end of it as Quinn braced for an impact.

"I've known they were yours for years. Why do you think I bought so many?"

"You've known?" Quinn was shocked.

"Yes, you're my son. You don't think I would recognize them? I've seen your artwork since you were in kindergarten." He laughed.

"Hey, those were masterpieces. They were on the fridge," Quinn shot back jokingly.

I just shook my head.

"I was just waiting for you to tell me."

"I'm sorry, I just thought you would be proud of them or me since it wasn't real estate or something prestigious." Quinn looked down at his sheets. Mr. Condor frowned.

"Quinn, I'm always proud of you and proud of the work you have done. I'm sorry if me pushing you on everything else made you feel that way." Quinn teared up again, and I would lie if I said Olivia and I didn't.

"Thanks, Dad."

"I'm glad you guys are safe, even if this one got himself hurt," Mr. Condor joked with Quinn.

"Dad, there was a tsunami. I couldn't exactly help it."

"I know."

It was good to see them have a relationship because they would need that now that Quinn's mother was gone.

The only thing left to do was wait for what tomorrow would bring.

CHAPTER 28

Months later, the Pacific Northwest was still rebuilding from the worst natural disaster in the nation's history. Thousands were dead, and many more were still missing. Billions of dollars in damage had been done, and the world rushed to aid the area. It was the first time that the country had had to deal with a disaster on this scale, with this much destruction and death.

In those few months, I saw how people picked themselves up and went right back to life, rebuilding their homes and businesses, caring for their neighbors, and helping those who mourned their lost loved ones.

Mrs. Condor's funeral was a simple service, and we buried an empty casket since there was no way we could find her body. My parents even flew out to be there, and to see both Quinn and me. Quinn delivered a beautiful eulogy, and their family donated large sums of money to help rebuild the town, including the bookstore. Now, it seemed that most of Alnwick was on its feet again. Novel had just reopened about a week ago, celebrating with a week-long event of authors coming to town. Olivia had me speak in a forum-like setting. I was slowly getting used to speaking in front of audiences, which I was going to need to do more now that I had a finished draft under my belt.

Quinn and his father had rebuilt their relationship and were getting along great. Not saying it was easy, they had a lot to get through. At least they tried and I think they knew what Quinn's mother would have wanted. It helped to know that his father approved and was even proud of the artwork Quinn had been producing. I wondered if Quinn was really holding a lot of his pain and insecurities in. All the pain he felt about his mother.

Mr. Condor even let us keep the house, which my mother was impressed by when she came to stay. I kept telling her I wished she had seen it before the wave, as there were still scars in the landscape that would take decades to heal.

Despite everything, Oregon still seemed to find ways to impress me. The mountains were still majestic, and the summer months were full of bright, warm, sunny days that seemed like they would never end. We had become accustomed to sitting out on the beach and watching the sunset for the last few months.

I never mentioned the man in the pharmacy to anyone. I had never heard anything about him, either, so I assumed rescuers had just written it off as another death attributed to the earthquake. Some nights, he still haunted me, the memory of him lying there glued into my brain. I guess that was my scar from all this, the thing that would always be there. It was a secret I intended to keep, at least until I was ready to share. In time, I thought I would tell Quinn, but only him.

Speaking of scars, Quinn did have one long one on his leg. He wore it with pride, and for the first few weeks after the bandage came off, he couldn't stop looking at or talking about it. It was unbearable; who knew having a scar was such a cool thing? Even as we were finally driving to Newport, it came up.

"Will you give it a rest over that damn thing?" I said.

Quinn laughed. He enjoyed annoying me. If only he knew how much grief that scar had given me while it was open and bleeding.

"You ready?" he asked.

I had waited months to finally escape everything and come to Newport to fulfill the promise I had made. Quinn had done some research and it took a long time to track them down, let alone get in contact with them. It helped when we worked with emergency services to identify the body. I remembered where the body was, which made it easy for them to find her. From there we were able to get in contact with her next of kin. This was after the notification was given. At least they didn't have to wonder. Part of me didn't really know what I was going to say when we met her and her father. However, I'd promised to do so, and I kept my promises.

We arrived in Newport, which was still rebuilding. Luckily for them, much of the main part of the town was above the tsunami zone and just had damage from the earthquake. Quinn drove to a community center near the center of town. It was the meeting place we had decided on when we contacted them. It was busy as supplies were still being handed out near the cork boards full of the names of people who were missing. People looked them over, hoping to find their loved ones.

When we pulled up, we got out of the car and searched for the father and daughter. I checked my pockets to make sure the picture and rosary were still there.

"Over there," Quinn said, pointing to a less crowded area where a man and girl stood.

I took the picture out and compared it. She was a perfect match for Marianna. We walked over to greet them.

Quinn shook the father's hand and thanked him for meeting with us. I kneeled down to the girl, who was holding her father's hand. She looked exactly like a mix of both her father—who was white— and her mother—who was Hispanic. As I looked at the girl, she reminded me a little of myself. She, too, was caught between two different worlds.

"Hello, I'm Kodak," I said.

"Hello," the girl said shyly.

"Your mother gave this to me," I told her, showing her the picture and pulling out the rosary beads. "She wanted me to make sure you got it, and to tell you that she loved you very much."

As she held them, I could see a tear form in her eyes, and then the girl reached out to me and embraced me. "Thank you," she said, then moved back next to her father.

"You're very welcome."

"This means everything to us," her father said. "Thank you for being there with her."

"Of course. I hope this helps," I replied, not knowing what else to say. I'd never handled these conversations well, but I knew that what I had done really did mean everything to them. It gave them some closure to know that she had died with someone there.

After a moment, we parted ways, and Quinn and I headed back to the car.

"You did a good thing, Kodak," Quinn said as we got in.

"Thanks," I said. "It felt good." I stared at her for a moment. "What is it?"

"She just like me, split in two. I hope that she will love herself and her identity. So that she never know that pain that I do."

"She will, and so will you. Be proud of it."

"I'm not there yet, but I think I will be." I smiled.

Quinn grabbed my hand. "Now, let's get some food. I'm hungry.

"You're always hungry," I joked.

He smiled. "I know a good place that should still be standing."

"Should still be standing" was heard all the time in our post-disaster world. Anytime we find something standing it's a cause for celebration. It gives us that little sense of normalcy, however, we know that we will never be the same.

We drove a bit before coming to a place that, despite everything, was still standing—and, frankly, was very busy.

"I'll go get us a table," he said, getting out of the car.

I looked down the street to the Pacific Ocean, which glimmered between the buildings and down the slope.

A moment later, he came back with one of those buzzer things. "It's going to be about a thirty-minute wait."

"Okay. I think I'm going to walk down the street for a minute. Call me when the table's ready," I said.

"Be safe," he said. I think he knew I wanted a minute, and despite everything, Quinn was good at giving me space when I needed it.

I walked past more cafés and shops, just like the ones in Alnwick, then houses. As I began to descend toward the ocean, toward where the damage started, I discovered houses and buildings already being rebuilt, new trees being planted, and the ground beginning to heal. I even passed one of those blue lines that marked a tsunami zone. I just hoped we didn't have to do that again for a long time. I'd survived, not just this horrible disaster, but my grief. I'd survived everything the world threw at me, the racism, the bigotry, and it made me stronger each and every day.

I came to the beach as the sun began to set. The colors mixed in the sky as I took my seat upon a lonely piece of wood that had washed ashore the night before. I looked out into the roaring waves of the Pacific as the evening breeze flowed across me. No longer angry and full of fury. It was empty on the beach, with no one in sight. I had started this journey alone, trying to find my way, running from all the pain that had haunted me. I had even run from myself, never able to truly feel like I belonged.

I was torn, and those scars will always be there. However, I realize that those scares are what make me the person that I am. The person that Quinn loved that my parents are proud of, the person that Olivia said was a kind soul. Maybe it was time that I stopped hating myself for what I thought was a hindrance, a blemish. So that I could truly be myself and no longer torn in two, but one person who had the blessing of being a bridge between the two worlds I belonged to.

JAMES UNGURAIT

Now, as I sat and watched the sunset, I dreamed of my future, one full of joy and love. One where I loved myself and didn't try to mold myself into a society that seemed to only want one thing. I longed for the day I would be looked at and not seen as different or other. It would take work, patience, and humility. It would not be solved by one idea from one person but with the ideas of many. It would be an effort from us—a country, a world, a species.

One day, we would all be truly equal.

This is my crusade.

EPILOGUE

"**K**odak, grab that, please," Olivia ordered as she pointed to books sitting on the table that needed to move to the other end. It was already pretty much full, the gray tablecloth ready to be abused for the next few hours.

"Got it," I replied. "You do realize you're making me move my own books?"

"Yes, now move them to your table so you can sign them," she ordered again.

She was being very bossy, despite it being my release party. Granted, it was being held in her bookstore, which had been rebuilt. It had been over a year since the earthquake and tsunami came rushing ashore, killing thousands of people and causing billions of dollars in damage along the coast. Many scars still hadn't healed, but it was getting better each day. Like everyone else, we took it one day at a time.

I took the pile of books and added them to the table next to the cash register so I could sign them later after reading parts of it to the audience. Olivia was controlling every aspect of this event to the point where my publicist was in the corner on her phone. She'd learned quickly not to get in Olivia's way—much like Roxy, who was hiding at home, waiting to snuggle with us later once this was over.

"Where is Quinn?" Olivia asked as we got the final touches ready.

"I don't know," I said, throwing my hands up.

"You don't know where your fiancé is?" she shot back with a rather stern eye.

"Look, I don't track him, plus it's only been two weeks" I replied blushing.

"You should. Now you know why I did it back in high school. He has a habit of disappearing when I need him."

There was a reason for him disappearing when she needed him. I low-key wanted to do the same right now, but this was my book launch event, so I had to deal. I just hoped she wasn't going to plan the wedding. I would prefer my mother to do that, because, sadly, that would be saner than this.

It took us a few minutes before we were fully set up. Drinks were ready, and the piles and piles of books. I wondered if they'd ordered too many. Would I even sell this many copies? My publisher hoped I would; that was what they had forecasted. Yet part of me still wondered if anyone would want to read a story of surviving an earthquake and tsunami. Yes, I had written about the trauma of the West Coast's own natural disaster. I'd changed quite a few things to give it a good conflict and such, of course, and there had been things the editor and my agent wanted to change—welcome to publishing.

Someone stepped behind me and covered my eyes. I stood there, not impressed. It was a bit clichéd, and I knew who it was. "Quinn, really? You're doing this?"

"Um, yes? What did you expect, flowers?" he replied as I turned around to face him. "Happy pub day! Future bestseller inbound."

I smiled at his optimism. "Thanks. You better hide before Olivia sees you. She's on a rampage."

He looked around for a place to hide, but before he could go anywhere, she emerged from out of nowhere. "There you are. I need you to make sure all the electronics are working. Stop staring endlessly into his eyes. You have the rest of your life for that," she ordered.

"That was rather poetic, Olivia. Well done," I said.

Quinn smiled before heading off to complete his task.

"Stop sucking up. You better sell all these books tonight," she shot back as she ran to the next fire that needed to be put out.

Soon, guests began arriving and filling the seats. My parents came up and hugged me. My mother was already carrying the copy that I had mailed to her. She had gotten one of the advanced copies, and of course, I had signed it. I greeted people as they approached me. Mr. Condor came by and shook my hand before heading off to talk with my parents. Somehow, he and my father had found a common interest in soccer.

As time passed, it was my turn to be on stage. I was introduced, along with another guest speaker of the night—a local Oregon author I didn't really know well. She had reached out a few times since we were published by the same imprint. She would be doing the question-and-answer segment of the night.

She introduced me, and we talked a little about my book and the reviews it had gotten so far. "So let's get right to it then," she said. "What inspired you to write a story of survival and belonging?" she asked.

I looked into the audience, where Quinn, Olivia, my parents, and Mr. Condor stood. It had all come together in a sense—not in any way I would have foreseen, but it had. Life always had a way.

"Well, that's a rather long story."

ACKNOWLEDGMENTS

This book has been a journey, one that has taken the form of thousands of miles and too many all-nighters to remember. It had been a labor of love and sometimes anguish. It started with me sitting on a piece of driftwood looking into the Pacific Ocean. (hmm that sounds familiar) I was debating on what my next book would be and at the time was living in Oregon. Safe to say I figured out rather fast where I wanted it to be set, however coming up with the story was another matter. Luckily it came and here we are. Like with any book, it takes an army of people to bring it to life and get it ready for you the reader to enjoy.

First, I have to thank Ben, and Ella for making me feel welcome in Oregon when I moved. They were the ones who showed me all the state had to offer from its beautiful landscapes and wonderful people. Next, would be my parents who support me no matter what, even when I have crazy ideas to move across the country and a year later back again. (They were much happier on the return move.) Even my brother JT helps, but again don't let it go to his head, please. Along with my extended family of Aunts, Uncles, and cousins who shout from the rooftops about my book to their friends.

I also need to shout out to my work family, who even in the thick of it support my writing and champion it out into the world. I could not have stayed the course without Ashley, Rollins, Dani, Mariah,

Maddie, Fink, and Krystal. I need to thank all the people who survived all my endless questions when researching the different topics in this book. Along with my editor Jessica who whipped this thing into shape.

With any of my writing adventures my dedicated friends of writers who critique and call out my stupidly when needed need a special thanks. Emma, Blair, Calley, and Addison have provided valuable feedback and moral support throughout this journey. I can't forget you for reading and hopefully enjoying this work, you are the reason this is all done. Lastly, thank you to Oregon for being welcoming even in the thick of the pandemic and offering some much-needed fresh air.

ABOUT JAMES UNGURAIT

James Ungurait is an American novelist and publisher whose work explores survival, memory, and the mythic weight of place. He is the author of I'm The Same (Ungurait House, 2024), a lyrical debut novel set in Oregon and Mississippi that examines trauma, queer identity, and the long echo of grief, and Phoenix Knight: The Lost Son (Ironwake, 2025), the opening volume of a mythic fantasy cycle that fuses Southern gothic textures with epic, emotionally charged storytelling.

Born and raised in Mississippi, Ungurait's fiction is shaped by the South's haunted landscapes—its silences, its inheritances, and its fractured legacies. His prose is at once intimate and expansive, weaving personal vulnerability with broader cultural and mythic resonance. Critics have praised his work for its emotional honesty, lyrical depth, and refusal to chase trends, positioning him among a new generation of writers who balance literary craft with urgent, lived truth.

When not writing or editing, he can often be found along the Gulf Coast, the mountains or Pacific shoreline—spaces that inspire his work's recurring dialogue between place, loss, and renewal.

www.jamesungurait.com

ABOUT
UNGURAIT HOUSE

Ungurait House is an independent publisher dedicated to literary fiction, fantasy, and lasting storytelling. We believe great books don't chase trends—they challenge them. Every title we release is crafted with intention: from the words on the page to the weight in your hands.

We are not a traditional press, and we are not self-published. We're something else entirely—fiercely independent, vertically integrated, and reader-focused.

Our imprints include:

Ungurait House, for fiction that reckons with identity, survival, and the human condition; and IRONWAKE, for bold, mythic fantasy with a literary edge. Each book is designed and typeset in-house, printed to last, and available through bookstores and our direct shop.

To explore our catalog or unlock exclusive editions, visit:
https://www.unguraithouse.com

Follow along @unguraithouse